SPECIAL MESSAGE TO READERS

THE JOCKEY

A man calling himself the Jockey begins a campaign against those who he believes have besmirched the good name of horse racing, escaping conviction through lack of evidence. In a message to the press, he vows that those who have amassed crooked fortunes will have the money taken from them, whilst those who have caused loss of life will find their own lives forfeit . . . When the murders begin, Superintendent Budd of Scotland Yard is charged to find and stop the mysterious avenger. But is the Jockey the actual murderer?

GERALD VERNER

THE JOCKEY

Complete and Unabridged

LINFORD
Leicester

First published in Great Britain

First Linford Edition
published 2015

A catalogue record for this book is available
from the British Library.

ISBN 978–1–4448–2521–3

Published by
F. A. Thorpe (Publishing)
Anstey, Leicestershire

Set by Words & Graphics Ltd.
Anstey, Leicestershire
Printed and bound in Great Britain by
T. J. International Ltd., Padstow, Cornwall

This book is printed on acid-free paper

To
HANS ANSBACHER
BECAUSE HE'S LEARNED
TO LAUGH AT TROUBLE

1

The Inquiry

Lord Mortlake, senior steward of the Jockey Club, that august body which rules vigilantly over all matters appertaining to the Turf, came into the long room behind the Stands at Newmarket with a troubled face. A stout, genial man, whose grey eyes habitually twinkled, his solemnity was unusual.

'Good morning, Latimer,' he grunted as he laid his hat and gloves on a side table. 'This is a nasty business — an unpleasant business!'

The junior steward, who was warming himself by the fire, for in spite of it being July the day was cold, nodded gloomily.

'It seems to be,' he agreed. 'It's the sort of thing that gives racing a bad name.'

'Can't understand what induced him to do it,' muttered Mortlake, wrinkling his brows irritably. 'Wharton is the last fellow

1

you'd expect capable of such a thing!'

Sir Godfrey Latimer shrugged his shoulders. He had less faith in his fellow men than the good-humoured, easy-going Mortlake. Thin, grey-haired, with a tight-lipped mouth that had a cynical twist to it, he possessed few illusions and none that concerned the foibles of humanity.

'There's no accounting for what people will do in a crisis,' he answered.

'But Wharton!' Mortlake shook his head incredulously. 'I can't believe it!'

'Well, we'll see what he has to say,' remarked his colleague.

'I'd have staked my life on his honesty!' Mortlake went on, as though he hadn't spoken. 'His father and I were at school together — '

Latimer's narrow shoulders twitched again.

'Does that really make any difference?' he inquired. 'He's lost a lot of money lately, I've heard rumours. There may have been a strong temptation, but of course we're not concerned with that.'

'No, no,' agreed the senior steward

hastily. 'All that concerns us is the facts. It's going to be pretty rotten for him though. His engagement to Westmore's girl was only announced last month. Hello, Bastion!' He broke off to greet the man who had just come bustling in.

'Mornin', Mortlake. Mornin', Latimer!' said Colonel Bastion, the third of the stewards, in his habitual husky voice. 'Nice start for the meetin', what? Begad, it's given me a sleepless night thinkin' about it!'

'I don't suppose Wharton feels too good,' said Latimer.

'Silly young ass,' growled the colonel. 'Stupid to do a thing like that, what? Is he here?'

'I expect so.' The junior steward looked at his watch. 'The inquiry was called for twelve, and it's nearly five past.'

'Well, let's get it over.' Mortlake sat down at the table, wrinkling his round face distastefully. 'We haven't got long before racing begins.'

He pressed a bell and a thin man with stooping shoulders and pince-nez entered. 'Is Mr. Wharton here, Pyecroft?' asked the

3

senior steward, and the secretary nodded.

'He's been here for twenty minutes,' he said, laying the folder he was carrying on the table in front of Mortlake. 'Wills and Corbett have just come in. Cowan hasn't arrived yet.'

'Cowan's the man who wrote to us, isn't he?' interposed Bastion.

Mortlake nodded.

'Yes,' he answered, and extracted a letter from the folder and held it out. 'Here's his letter.'

'I wish we hadn't got to go through with this,' grumbled Bastion.

'So do I, but it's what we're here for,' Latimer reminded him.

'Yes, I suppose so.' The colonel was frowning gloomily at the fire. 'But it's unpleasant all the same.'

'Let's have him in and finish with him,' said Mortlake impatiently, sorting through his papers. 'Ring, will you, Pyecroft?'

The secretary took his seat at the table and touched a bell.

'Ask Mr. Norman Wharton to come in, will you,' he said to the attendant who answered the summons.

The man withdrew and there was an uncomfortable silence. Mechanically Bastion and Latimer pulled up chairs to the table and sat down.

The man who was presently ushered into the room was pale but outwardly calm. His crisp, brown hair and youthful features gave an impression of boyishness that was belied by the lines about nose and mouth, although Norman Wharton was still on the right side of thirty.

'Good morning, Wharton,' said Mortlake. 'Sit down, will you, please.'

He indicated a chair, and the young man took it with a faint smile of greeting. The senior steward gave a preliminary cough.

'Now,' he said, 'there's no need for me to explain why you've been called here. The stewards at Ascot were dissatisfied with the running of your horse, King's Holiday, in the Coronation Stakes, and the matter has been reported to us. The suggestion is that you were not trying.'

'That is quite untrue,' said Wharton. 'Anyone who saw the race — '

'Yes, yes!' interrupted Mortlake. 'There's

no question about the horse being 'pulled'. The Ascot stewards are quite satisfied about that. But that doesn't exonerate you. The jockey and the trainer state that you issued instructions on the morning of the race that the horse was to be given an easy run, that if possible he was to finish fourth or fifth.'

'I issued no such instructions,' said Wharton, eyeing him steadily. 'It was my intention to win the Coronation Stakes with King's Holiday. The horse was only beaten by a short head by Gay Lady, surely that's sufficient proof that I was trying?'

Mortlake shrugged his shoulders.

'It only shows that the jockey was trying,' he said curtly. 'Both he and Corbett state that they disobeyed your instructions.'

'I don't know why they should tell these lies!' said Wharton, 'But surely the fact that I was trying is testified to by the amount of money I put on the horse. I should scarcely have backed it if it had not been my intention to try and win the race.'

'You backed the horse heavily?' asked Bastion.

Wharton nodded.

'To the extent of two thousand pounds,' he replied.

'With whom did you place the bets?' inquired Latimer.

'With Paddocks, my usual bookmakers,' answered the other.

Latimer glanced at Mortlake and the senior steward frowned.

'The Ascot stewards wrote to Benjamin Cowan, of Paddocks,' he said, slowly and distinctly, 'and Cowan denies that you backed the horse at all. He states in a letter which I have here that you cancelled all bets on King's Holiday during the morning of the race.'

'That is absolutely untrue!' declared Wharton, but his face was a little paler.

'You're suggesting,' said Latimer sharply, 'that Cowan is lying?'

'I'm more than suggesting,' retorted the other. 'If he says that I cancelled my bets on King's Holiday he *is* lying.'

'Why should he do such a thing?' grunted Mortlake. 'What object could he have?'

'That I don't know,' said Wharton, 'any more than I can tell you why Joe Wills and Corbett should have lied concerning these alleged instructions I am supposed to have given them. The fact remains that it is all lies! I assure you that the horse was trying.'

The stewards looked at each other.

'Since the horse came in second,' said Mortlake, after a pause, 'you would naturally lose your money?'

'Yes, I did,' said Wharton.

'Then there must be some record of the transaction in Cowan's books,' continued the senior steward.

The other's face clouded.

'There should be,' he said hesitantly, 'but — but I doubt if there is.'

'How do you mean?' said Bastion. 'If you've paid him this two thousand pounds it must appear in Paddocks' books.'

'Not necessarily,' said Wharton, and there was a dryness about his throat that made speech difficult. 'The transaction took place at my house at Ascot, I didn't settle by cheque. At Cowan's request I paid him in notes.'

'But the numbers can be traced,' said Latimer.

'Can they?' Wharton smiled ruefully. 'I won a lot of money that day, betting on the course. I have no idea of the numbers of the notes I gave Cowan.'

There was a silence, broken at last by Mortlake.

'So there is actually no proof that you backed King's Holiday at all?' he said.

'Only my word,' said Wharton.

'Which is not substantiated by Cowan's,' said Latimer. 'You can give us no convincing proof that you ever backed King's Holiday?'

'Unless you accept my statement, I'm afraid not,' said Wharton, a little hoarsely.

'I'm afraid we can't do that,' said Mortlake. 'We must go by the evidence, Mr. Wharton.'

Wharton knew this only too well. For the first time he was beginning to realise the gravity of the situation. The palms of his hands grew damp.

'You say,' continued Mortlake, 'that you issued no instructions to your jockey and trainer that King's Holiday was to be held back, and that in proof of this you backed the horse to the extent of two thousand pounds with Paddocks? Is that right?'

Wharton nodded.

Mortlake leaned over and held a whispered consultation with Bastion and Latimer.

'Let's have Corbett in,' he said presently.

2

'Warned Off'

The trainer sidled into the room nervously, a red-faced, sandy-haired man, with pale, rather furtive eyes. He studiously avoided meeting Wharton's gaze as he stood deferentially in front of the table.

'Good morning, Mr. Corbett,' said Mortlake coldly. 'We are inquiring into the running of King's Holiday in the Coronation Stakes at Ascot. What do you know about it?'

The trainer licked his lips nervously.

'I gave my evidence before the stewards at Ascot,' he said huskily. 'Mr. Wharton gave instructions to Joe Wills and me that the horse was to be pulled.'

'It was you, I think,' said Latimer, 'who first brought the matter to the notice of the Ascot stewards?'

'That's right, sir,' said Corbett. 'I

11

thought it was my duty. I've always had a good reputation — '

'You've been twice nearly warned off,' said Mortlake curtly, 'and only escaped by the skin of your teeth. However, that's nothing to do with this inquiry. You assert definitely that Mr. Wharton gave specific instructions both to you and Joe Wills that the horse was to be 'pulled'. Is that right?'

'That's right, sir,' said Corbett.

'Where did he issue these instructions?' asked Mortlake.

'At his 'ouse at Ascot, on the mornin' of the race!' declared Corbett.

'He issued them to both of you in each other's presence?' inquired Latimer.

The trainer nodded.

'Yes, sir,' he answered. 'Wills will tell you the same.'

'You realise, I suppose,' grunted Bastion, 'the seriousness of this charge you are making against Mr. Wharton?'

Corbett licked his lips.

'Yes, sir,' he muttered. 'I shouldn't 'ave done it only I thought it was my duty — '

'Yes, yes! We know all about that!' said

12

Mortlake. 'The question is do you still adhere to what you said?'

'Yes, sir,' said the trainer.

'Do you wish to ask any questions, Mr. Wharton?' asked the senior steward.

Wharton shrugged his shoulders, and he was pale now to the lips.

'What's the good!' he said. 'All I can say is that there is not a word of truth in this man's story.'

'I'll take my oath it's the truth!' protested Corbett, and Mortlake interrupted him.

'This is not a court, Mr. Corbett,' he said coldly. 'You can go.'

The trainer gave a little gasp of relief and stumbled to the door.

'Send for the jockey, Joe Wills,' said Mortlake, and the secretary obeyed.

Joe Wills, undersized and wizened, came in jauntily. In answer to Mortlake's questions he told the same story as Corbett and stuck to it. He had called with the trainer at Wharton's house at Ascot on the morning of the race. Wharton had said that he was 'saving' the horse for the Hardwicke Stakes, and that he was not to

13

'try' with him for the Coronation Stakes. Both he and Corbett had argued, but Wharton had been firm. At a conference later they had decided to disobey instructions and let the horse have his head.

Nothing could shake Wills' story. He stuck to it in spite of all questions, and was eventually dismissed.

The stewards exchanged glances when he had gone. There seemed no doubt the charge was well founded. There was no reason whatever why Corbett and the jockey should enter into a conspiracy against Wharton unless what they said was true.

'You still deny having issued these instructions, Mr. Wharton?' asked Mortlake, and Wharton nodded dumbly.

'See if Cowan's arrived yet,' said Latimer, and while the secretary was attending to this: 'Of course if Cowan substantiates your statement that you backed the horse to the extent of two thousand pounds it puts a different complexion on the matter.'

'He's already denied it,' said Mortlake. 'In writing.'

Bastion shrugged his shoulders.

'Let's see what he has to say, anyway,' he muttered.

Benjamin Cowan came in, smooth, suave and immaculately dressed. He nodded to Wharton, receiving a stony glare in return, and took the chair which Mortlake indicated.

'Now, Mr. Cowan,' said the senior steward, 'you are, I believe, the head of a bookmaking firm known as Paddocks?'

'That is quite correct,' replied Cowan smoothly.

'Mr. Wharton states,' went on Mortlake, 'that he backed King's Holiday with your firm to win to the extent of two thousand pounds. Is that right?'

'No, my lord, it is not right,' answered Cowan. 'I regret having to say this, Wharton' — he looked apologetically at the white-faced man — 'but in the circumstances I can't do anything else. Mr. Wharton *had* backed King's Holiday for the amount you mention, but he cancelled all bets on the horse on the morning of the race.'

'That's a damned lie,' muttered Wharton hoarsely.

15

'That'll do, Mr. Wharton,' said Latimer sharply. 'You are certain you are making no mistake, Mr. Cowan? The bets were cancelled?'

'They were,' said the bookmaker.

'And did Mr. Wharton offer any reason?'

'Yes!' Benjamin Cowan took a long breath and looked from face to face. 'He said that his horse was not trying for the Coronation Stakes and he had decided to keep it for the Hardwicke Stakes. That if it came in fourth or fifth the price would lengthen and he could make more money.'

Norman Wharton listened — stunned, and his heart was cold. Why this man who sat so calmly uttering a tissue of lies should conspire against him he had no idea, but the fact remained. The weight of evidence against him was overpowering, and nothing he could say would make any difference.

Cowan was questioned closely, but steadfastly, and it appeared reluctantly, he reiterated his previous statement, leaving the room eventually with a sorrowful look at Wharton, and a nod to the stewards.

They consulted in low tones and Wharton was asked to leave for a few moments. He retired to the secretary's room where he waited, guessing the result and hoping against hope.

At the expiration of a quarter of an hour he was sent for.

'Mr. Wharton,' said Mortlake, 'we have come to a decision, on which we are all agreed. You have committed a very serious offence against the rules of racing and we feel that there is only one course open to us.' He raised his voice slightly. 'You are warned off Newmarket Heath and all courses under the jurisdiction of the Jockey Club.'

Norman Wharton heard the dread sentence, white-faced and tight-lipped. There was no appeal and he made none. With a bow to the men who had passed judgment on him he turned and left the room, hurrying through the crowd already assembled in the paddock for the day's racing with lowered head . . .

The racing editions of the morning papers on the following day carried the usual curt notice:

'The stewards of the Jockey Club held an inquiry into the running of King's Holiday at Ascot and, having heard the evidence, warned Mr. Norman Wharton off Newmarket Heath and the courses under the jurisdiction of the Jockey Club.'

But Norman Wharton never saw it. Unable to face the disgrace resultant on the finding of the inquiry he had shot himself at his flat in Berkeley Street on the previous evening.

3

The Head of Paddocks Ltd.

The offices of Paddocks Ltd., turf commission agents, occupy the whole of the second floor of a large building in Piccadilly. It is a place of many clerks, rich carpets and polished rosewood, for Paddocks conduct a profitable business and are one of the largest firms of bookmakers in the country. There is an attendant in a sombre uniform to conduct such clients as wish to make a personal call on the firm up in a special lift provided for that purpose, and a waiting-room with comfortable chairs and the latest editions of all the racing periodicals for their convenience if an interview cannot be arranged immediately.

An air of prosperity pervades the entire establishment, and nowhere is this more in evidence than in the private office of the managing director. Here the carpet is a little thicker than elsewhere and the feet sink gratefully into the soft pile. The woodwork, instead of being rosewood is walnut, polished until it gleams mirror-like and catches every stray ray of light. The curtains draping the big windows overlooking the street are of velvet, a special shade blended of old rose and cerise and chosen specifically to satisfy the aesthetic eye of Mr. Benjamin Cowan.

The light fittings and the electric fire are of silver; the shades of a silk which matches exactly the curtains and the close fitting carpet.

The room is large and airy and because of its size, the huge walnut desk, bare, save for blotting pad, silver inkstand, calendar and the four telephones which are so essential to Mr. Cowan's business, looks small by comparison. It is more like a boudoir than an office, but it suits the artistic taste of its owner, for Mr. Cowan can never forget that he started life in the Whitechapel Road and he likes to surround himself with concrete evidence of the distance he has travelled from that unsalubrious neighbourhood during the fifty-three years of his eventful life.

He came into his office on a sunny morning towards the end of May, the May following that summer during which poor Norman Wharton had found such a tragic solution to his problems, and having removed his hat and overcoat, stripped his lemon gloves and sat down heavily in the padded chair behind his desk.

For a moment or two he stared thoughtfully at its neat, polished surface, and there was a worried look in his brownish-green eyes. A certain matter had been troubling Mr. Cowan for many months past, was likely, unless he could see a way out, to trouble him a great deal more in the future, and the way which suggested itself did not appeal to his fastidious nature. There was an element of risk attached to it which had prevented him carrying it out when the idea had first come to him, and risk was one of the things which all his life he had done his best to avoid.

Much as he loathed the risk, however, he hated parting with money more, and the steady drain on his resources was becoming unendurable. Perhaps the risk could be eliminated?

He opened a drawer in his desk, helped himself to a cigar, carefully removed the band, and piercing the end with a little gold attachment which he carried on his watch-chain, lighted it.

Neglecting the letters which his secretary had placed in a neat pile at the side of his blotting pad he stared gloomily in front of him, his smooth, fat face wreathed in the fragrant smoke.

The soft-toned buzzer of the telephone which connected him with his secretary's office disturbed his musing, and he picked up the instrument.

'All right, show her in,' he said, frowning, and dropping the telephone back on its rack leaned back in his chair and removed the cigar from between his thick lips. His brows were still knit when his secretary ushered in the visitor.

'What do you want?' he growled ungraciously. 'I thought you were in the country.'

The girl who had come in walked

languidly across the thick carpet and sank into a chair.

'I came up this morning,' she said. 'I was bored stiff! I thought a day's shopping might cheer me up.'

'I see. You've come for the wherewithal, I suppose?' he grunted.

'That's very clever of you,' said his daughter. 'How did you guess?'

Cowan shrugged his shoulders.

'Do you ever come here for anything else?' he asked. 'How much do you want?'

Iris Cowan looked at him from under drooping lids. She was pretty in a flamboyant way, rather over made-up and over-dressed, but attractive, with a veneer of breeding that was apt to wear thin at the slightest provocation.

'Twenty pounds will do at the moment,' she murmured.

'Why do you want all that?' he demanded. 'You've already had fifty pounds above your allowance this month. D'you think I'm made of money?'

She lifted one shoulder and glanced round the expensive appointments of the room.

'You're not exactly poor, are you?' she answered.

'I should be if you had your way,' he retorted. 'Can't you do with less?'

'Well, I might manage on fifteen.' She pouted. 'You're a mean old skinflint, aren't you?'

'I have to be where you're concerned,' snapped Cowan, and she smiled.

'You can't say I'm very extravagant,' she protested, 'and I don't worry you much.'

'Only when you want something,' he replied, and putting his hand into his breast pocket he withdrew a wallet, skinned three notes from a roll and threw them across the desk. 'There you are,' he said. 'It's no use coming to me for any more, that'll have to last until your next allowance is due.'

She smiled sweetly.

'You always say that,' she said picking up the notes and stowing them away in her handbag.

'I mean it this time,' he grunted, 'so don't forget, Iris. I may be making money, but I've got a lot of calls on my resources. You don't seem to understand that.'

'If you'd make me a decent allowance,' she said, 'I shouldn't have to worry you.'

'Nonsense!' he answered. 'If your allowance was as big as the National Debt you'd spend more. I don't know what you do with your money. Are you staying in the flat to-night?'

She nodded.

'Yes, I've had enough of the country,' she said.

'Well, run along,' grunted her father. 'If you feel like going out to-night you'd better go, I shan't be in to dinner.'

'I should go anyway,' she answered coolly. 'Dining with you at home is not my idea of a cheerful evening.' She rose and walked to the door. 'Bye-bye,' she said. 'I expect I'll see you sometime.'

He muttered something, and when she had gone resumed his interrupted thoughts.

His wife, a thin, complaining woman, had died a year after the baby's birth, a happy release for both of them, for they had lived in an atmosphere of constant

25

bickering. But it was neither of his dead wife nor of his daughter that the man was thinking just then. He had dismissed the girl from his mind almost before she was out of his sight, and concentrated his thoughts on the problem that troubled him.

If only he could see a safe way —

Once again he was interrupted by the buzzing of the house 'phone, and picked up the receiver with a muttered imprecation.

'I can't see anyone,' he snarled. 'Who is it?' He listened while his secretary explained. 'Oh! All right, ask him to come in.'

His expression was hard as he replaced the receiver. Was it a coincidence that the man who had occupied his thoughts should have chosen this moment to make a call? He turned towards the door as it opened and Mr. Corbett swaggered in.

4

The Advent of the Jockey

The trainer was dressed in a loud check suit, in his dazzling tie a diamond glittered and another flashed from a ring on one of his red and not over-clean hands.

'Mornin', Cowan,' he greeted huskily. 'What's the idea of keepin' me waitin', eh?'

'You haven't been waiting long,' growled Cowan.

'Any time's long to me,' retorted Mr. Corbett, his bloated, puffy face hardening. 'Remember that, Cowan! When I come up to see yer I want to see yer, and not be shoved in a waitin' room to suit your convenience!'

The bookmaker glared at him angrily.

'What have you come for, anyway?' he demanded. 'Haven't I told you over and over again to keep away from here?'

'What right have you to tell me anythin'?' said the trainer contemptuously. 'If anyone's goin' to do the tellin' I'm the one to do it! You want to know what I've come for? Well, that's what I've come for.' He thrust a big hand into his pocket, and slammed a crumpled envelope on the desk in front of Cowan.

'What's this?' asked the bookmaker suspiciously.

'Read it and see,' snarled Corbett. 'What d'yer think I give it yer for?'

Cowan picked up the envelope with a frown, turned, it over in his fingers, and finally extracted the single sheet of paper it contained. Unfolding this he read the typewritten lines that ran across it.

'By swindling and blackmail you have amassed a small fortune. Your balance at the Lewes branch of the Southern Bank is approximately twelve thousand pounds. Two-thirds of this I am taking from you. On receipt of this letter you will immediately withdraw eight thousand in treasury notes, and to-morrow night at twelve you will

place them on the desk in your study. I shall come for them. Fail to carry out these instructions and you will die.

'The Jockey.'

'What's all this nonsense?' grunted Benjamin Cowan.

'That's what I want to know,' said Mr. Corbett unpleasantly. 'Know anythin' about it, Cowan?'

'Me?' snarled the bookmaker. 'How should I know anything about it?'

'I was wondering whether it wasn't a little joke on your part,' said the trainer suspiciously. 'A little scheme to try and get some of yer money back.'

'Don't be a fool!' growled Cowan. 'D'you think I'd go in for this childish stuff?'

Mr. Corbett still appeared unconvinced.

'Whoever wrote it seems to know a lot about me,' he grunted.

'D'you think I'm the only person who knows anything about you?' snapped Cowan. 'I'd no idea you were worth as much as twelve thousand. Why have you been squeezing me if you had all that money?'

'Why shouldn't I squeeze you?' retorted Corbett. 'I've had to do yer dirty work, haven't I? That business over Wharton was risky.'

'You were well paid for it,' said Cowan.

'Well paid!' sneered the trainer. 'A measly thousand and I 'ad to split that with Wills.'

'D'you know how much you've had out of me since?' said Cowan. 'The greater part of that twelve thousand is my money.'

'It *was* your money,' corrected Corbett, 'it's mine now, or part of it, some of it belongs to Wills, and I'm keepin' it for 'im. So you don't know nothin' about this letter?'

Cowan shook his head.

'No,' he answered. 'What are you going to do?'

'What d'yer think I'm goin' ter do?' asked Corbett. 'If this Jockey feller, whoever he is, thinks 'e's goin' ter frighten me into partin' with eight thousand 'e's got another think comin'. If 'e turns up to-morrow night at twelve 'e'll wish 'e 'adn't, see?'

Benjamin Cowan's brain was working rapidly. The glimmer of an idea had come to him, an idea so simple and yet so stupendous that it almost took his breath away. Here was the complete solution to the problem which had been bothering him for the past four months; a solution that removed that element of risk which had kept him from putting into practice the scheme he had evolved for ridding himself for ever of this man who had so systematically blackmailed him.

'Don't be too hasty, Corbett,' he said. 'This thing wants thinking over. I don't like the sound of that threat in the last line at all.'

'Bunk!' sneered Corbett, snapping his thick fingers. 'I'm not so easily scared as that!'

'All the same, you ought to take precautions,' said Cowan seriously. 'Why not pretend to comply with this fellow's demands? Draw out eight thousand pounds in treasury notes, as he says.'

Mr. Corbett stared at him.

'What d'yer take me for?' he said. 'A mug? That money's safe in my bank and there it's goin' ter stick!'

'Don't be silly,' said the bookmaker, keeping his temper with difficulty. 'This letter may be all bluff, on the other hand it may be dangerous. It's the 'pay and live' racket which has been so popular in America under a different form. If there's a possible chance we ought to 'scotch' this jockey man before he tries the same game on anyone else.'

The trainer looked dubious.

'I don't see why I should take the risk of losin' my money — ' he began, but Cowan interrupted him.

'You won't be taking any risks,' he said curtly. 'You won't lose the money. My suggestion is that you follow the instructions in this letter. Get the money, put it on your desk, and you and I will wait for this chap. When he comes we'll collar him and wait for the police.'

The trainer considered this.

'Not a bad idea,' he said after a pause. 'I'll get some of the fellers as well.'

'You'll do nothing of the sort!' snapped Cowan. 'Don't you see, you fool, that it's more than probable some of your staff are in this? Where did this fellow get his information from concerning your balance? If we're to do anything about this you've got to keep your mouth shut. Otherwise I wash my hands of the whole concern. You'll say nothing! Not even that I'm coming down. We'll handle this on our own, and if this fellow turns up he's going to wish he hadn't.'

Corbett nodded slowly.

'I get you,' he said. 'We just say nothin' and set a trap?'

'That's the idea,' agreed Cowan approvingly. 'What time do your staff go to bed?'

'Round about ten,' answered the trainer. 'They 'as to be up early for the mornin' gallops.'

'Well, say nothing to anyone,' continued the bookmaker quickly. 'I'll come down to your place soon after eleven. You can admit me, and we can await the arrival of this jockey gentleman together.'

Corbett agreed to the suggestion, and shortly afterwards took his leave.

For a long time after he had gone, his other business neglected, Benjamin Cowan sat at his desk smoking thoughtfully and perfecting the plan which had formed itself in his mind. Here was his chance, the chance he had been hoping and scheming for for so long without result. This letter from the unknown, signing himself 'The Jockey', presented him with an opportunity, not only of ridding himself of Corbett for ever, but of getting back the greater part of the money which that unscrupulous man had extracted from him under the threat of making public the truth concerning the conspiracy which had driven Norman Wharton to a suicide's grave.

5

Murder!

Superintendent Budd, that stout and lethargic man, came ponderously into his cheerless office a little breathless, as he usually was, from the exertion of ascending the many stairs that led to his room. The lanky form of Sergeant Leek rose from the desk at which he had been seated and hastily put away the paper he had been reading.

'Don' move,' said Mr. Budd sarcastically. 'Make yourself comfortable. What were you doin'? Pickin' winners?'

The melancholy sergeant cleared his throat.

'I did think of 'aving a bob each way on Laughing Water,' he admitted. 'I don't know nothin' about 'orses but the name took me fancy.'

'It would,' said Mr. Budd, eyeing the thin, lugubrious face before him. 'You bein' naturally of a cheerful disposition.'

'That's right,' said Leek. 'I don't believe in lookin' on the black side of things. Keep a cheerful 'eart's my motter.'

Mr. Budd grunted. Anything less cheerful than the outward appearance and general behaviour of Sergeant Leek it would have been difficult to find.

'You remind me of that feller what's 'is name — in the *Arcadians,*' he said, as he went over to his desk and squeezed his huge bulk into the padded chair.

'What's the *Arcadians*?' asked the sergeant, puzzled. 'A public 'ouse?'

His superior gave him a withering glance.

'No, a musical comedy,' he answered. 'Haven't you got a mind above beer and 'orses?'

Leek's face assumed an injured expression.

'I don't drink,' he replied mournfully, 'and it ain't orfen I 'ave a bet. 'Ow was I to know you was talkin' about a musical comedy?'

'I admit,' said Mr. Budd, producing one of his thin, black cigars from his waistcoat pocket and sniffing it appreciatively, 'that it was stupid of me to expect you to know anythin'. Who are you goin' to put this money on with, that street bookmaker round the corner?'

The sergeant looked confused.

'Well, I was thinkin' — ' he began.

'For the first time in your life, I'll bet!' grunted the superintendent, searching for his matches. 'A nice thing, I must say, aidin' and abettin' the breakin' of the law.'

'I wasn't goin' to give it 'im meself,' protested Leek.

'The Chief Commissioner was goin' to take it for you, I suppose,' said Mr. Budd. 'What race is this 'orse of yours runnin' in?'

'The three-thirty, at Gatwick,' answered the sergeant. 'Smike's ridin' it, and it ought to be a good price.'

Mr. Budd leaned back in his chair and stared thoughtfully at the ceiling through the smoke of his newly-lighted cigar.

'I'll 'ave five bob each way with you,' he remarked, to Leek's surprise, 'and if it isn't in the first three there'll be a black mark against your name on your sheet!'

The sergeant's face lengthened.

'I ain't sayin' it's a certainty,' he said. 'It's only just a fancy of me own.'

'I didn't suppose you had any inside information,' said Mr. Budd, glancing through the letters and reports on his blotting pad. 'See who that is,' he added, as the telephone rang.

The sergeant stretched out a long arm and picked up the instrument. It was the house telephone and he listened to the staccato voice of the assistant-commissioner.

'Blair wants to speak to you,' he said, covering the mouthpiece with his hand.

'Colonel Blair!' corrected Mr. Budd. 'Always speak respectfully of your superiors.' He took the telephone from Leek's hand and put it to his ear. 'All right, sir,' he said, and dropped the instrument back on its rack. 'I'm goin' along to see him,' he announced, hoisting himself with difficulty to his feet.

'What's 'e want?' asked the sergeant.

'I dunno,' said Mr. Budd. 'Maybe he's heard about that horse of yours and wants to have a bob each way too!'

He left the office and made his way to the assistant-commissioner's room. Colonel Blair, grey-haired and dapper, looked up over his big littered desk as the superintendent came in.

'Good morning, Budd,' he said. 'Sit down, will you?' He waved towards a chair near the desk and Mr. Budd seated himself. 'I've had a request,' went on the assistant-commissioner, glancing at the papers in front of him, 'for assistance from the Chief Constable of the Sussex Constabulary. There's been a murder near Lewes and they want us to give them a hand. You're not on anything particular at the moment so you'd better take the inquiry.'

'When was the crime committed, sir?' asked Mr. Budd, his sleepy-looking eyes half closed.

'Some time during the night,' answered the colonel, consulting his notes. 'According to the doctor's statement between eleven and twelve. The body was discovered in the early hours of the morning, and I must say the Chief Constable acted with commendable promptness in getting in touch with us. I wish all these country people would do it, instead of waiting until all the clues have been messed up and then expecting us to do miracles. The dead man is a well-known trainer, called Simon Corbett. His training establishment is at the foot of the Sussex Downs, about ten miles from Lewes. He was killed in his office by being stabbed with a thick-bladed knife, and there was a letter or something found among his papers demanding money with threats, signed by a person calling himself 'The Jockey'.'

Colonel Blair rubbed his neat moustache irritably.

'It all sounds like something out of a novel, but there it is. This fellow, Corbett, according to the Chief Constable, didn't have too good a reputation. That's all I can give you. Superintendent Tidmarsh, of the Lewes Police, is in charge. You'll report to him and he'll probably be able to give you further details.'

Mr. Budd suppressed a yawn and rose wearily.

'I'll get along at once, sir,' he said. 'I'll

take Sergeant Leek with me.'

'All right,' said the assistant-commissioner, his mind already beginning to grapple with another matter that was of equal importance to the murder of the trainer. 'All right. Let me have a report as soon as possible.'

The stout superintendent left him and returned to his own office.

'We're goin' to Lewes,' he said. 'You'd better find out the next train.'

The sergeant's eyes opened.

'What are we goin' for?' he asked.

'Somebody's killed a man called Corbett,' answered Mr. Budd. 'A trainer of race horses. 'E didn't train that horse of yours, by any chance, did he?' he added, as the thought struck him.

Leek shook his head.

'No, Laughing Water's trained by Winters,' he replied, and picked up the telephone.

A brief inquiry elicited the fact that there was a train from Victoria in half an hour.

'We'll catch that,' said Mr. Budd, and fumbling in his pocket produced ten shillings. 'You'd better go and get that money on,' he remarked, holding it out to Leek. 'If by a miracle that horse of yours wins and I forgot to back it I'd never forgive myself!'

6

The Black Cap

They reached Lewes shortly after midday and were met by Superintendent Tidmarsh, who had been notified by wire of their coming.

Tidmarsh was a stocky, red-faced man, clean-shaven and the possessor of an extraordinary good set of teeth which gleamed whitely every time he smiled, which he did very readily. He escorted Mr. Budd and the lugubrious Leek to a police car, and when they had squeezed themselves in, directed the driver to take them to Corbett's training stables.

During the journey Mr. Budd endeavoured to extract some further information concerning the murder, but Tidmarsh could tell him very little more than he already knew. Corbett had been a bachelor, and had lived alone, with the exception of a man and his wife. The woman cooked, and cleaned the house, and the man helped in the stables. It was Mrs. Glossop who had made the discovery. Her husband suffered from rheumatism and had wakened in the night in such pain that she had come down for a bottle of embrocation, which had been left in the kitchen.

Seeing a light in Corbett's office and the door half open she had peeped in. At first she had believed that her employer had gone to bed leaving the light burning, and she had raised her hand to switch it off when she saw a foot protruding from behind the desk. Going further into the room she had discovered Corbett lying on his back, the front of his clothes smothered in blood, and the handle of a knife sticking out of his chest.

Her scream brought down her husband, and they immediately telephoned the police. This was a little after four in the morning, and the doctor, when he had made his examination, testified that Corbett had been dead for over four hours.

'The french windows were open,' said

Tidmarsh, 'and there is no doubt the murderer came and went by way of the garden. The stables are on the other side, and he could have done so easily without being seen. Even if there had been anybody awake,' he added, 'which there wasn't.'

'Nobody heard anythin' durin' the night?' asked Mr. Budd sleepily.

The superintendent shook his head.

'You know how these fellows sleep,' he replied. 'They're up with the dawn and they have a hard day. When they go to bed they're like logs. No, nobody heard anything.'

'No finger-prints on the knife?' queried Mr. Budd, and again Tidmarsh shook his head.

'No, that's the first thing we looked for,' he answered. 'It's a queer business altogether. I've just had a talk with the manager of the bank where Corbett had an account and he tells me that the day before yesterday the dead man made arrangements to draw out eight thousand pounds in treasury notes. They hadn't got so much in that particular currency on the premises and had to send to their head office to get it. Corbett called and collected it yesterday afternoon, just before closing time.'

'And there's no trace of it, I suppose,' said Mr. Budd. 'Well, I've known less than eight thousand pounds form the motive for a murder. Wasn't there somethin' about a letter among Corbett's effects?'

The local superintendent nodded.

'Yes,' he replied. 'Signed by someone calling himself 'The Jockey'. There's no doubt he's the fellow we want. The letter mentions an appointment with Corbett round about the time he met his death, and also contains a threat against his life.'

''The Jockey,'' muttered Mr. Budd, his eyes completely closed. 'He's a new one on me. I know all sorts of criminals with peculiar names, but I've never come across that before.'

He was silent for some time, and Tidmarsh, who had never met him before and was unaware of his peculiar characteristic, was under the impression that he had fallen asleep. This impression was dispelled however, when Mr. Budd suddenly opened his eyes.

'What about the dogs?' he inquired.

The local man looked at him, his homely face was astonished.

'Now how in the world did you know anything about that?' he inquired. 'We didn't discover it until after we'd telephoned the Yard.'

Mr. Budd yawned.

'Nothin' very surprisin' about it,' he remarked. 'They always keep dogs at racin' stables, and I was wonderin', since nobody heard anythin' durin' the night, why this particular dog or dogs hadn't given an alarm.'

'Well, it's rather funny,' said Tidmarsh, frowning. 'As a matter of fact they keep two dogs, big brutes, but yesterday afternoon Corbett gave instructions to one of the stable-boys to take them over to the vet at Ditchling.'

'What was the matter with them?' asked Mr. Budd.

'Nothing,' said the superintendent. 'That's the surprising part of it. I interviewed the head lad and he said the

47

dogs were as fit as fiddles. He told
Corbett so, but the man insisted that they
should be taken to the vet and arrangements made for them to stay the night
there.'

'H'm!' muttered Mr. Budd and his eyes
were very wide open. 'Peculiar! Almost
looks as though he was expectin'
someone and didn't want the dogs to kick
up a row.'

'That's what I thought,' agreed Tidmarsh. 'But it seems queer. This 'Jockey'
fellow said in his letter he was coming,
and you'd think, knowing that, Corbett
would have liked to have had the dogs
around.'

'Maybe,' murmured Mr. Budd, and
once again he was his habitual sleepy-
eyed self.

The car had turned off the main road
and was running along a lane, the surface
of which was churned by the countless
hooves of many horses. It widened
suddenly, and they came to the white
gates of a house. Further on Mr. Budd
saw the high closed gates of a stable yard.

'This is the place,' said Tidmarsh, and a

constable, who was standing by the gate, sprang to attention and opened it, saluting as they passed.

The house that came into view round the bend of the short drive was old and straggling. It stood in an acre and a half of neglected garden, the back facing the rolling downs. To one side, running parallel with the lane along which they had come, were the stables and boys' quarters, forming two sides of a large courtyard. As Mr. Budd got ponderously out of the car he heard a horse whinnying somewhere and the kicking of hooves in the loose boxes.

The front door was opened by a thin, sour-looking woman, whom the superintendent introduced as Mrs. Glossop. Behind her hovered a man in open-necked shirt and riding breeches, a coarse-featured, unshaven man with a patch of baldness showing through the greying hair on the top of his head. Mr. Budd concluded that this was the rheumaticky Mr. Glossop, and received confirmation from Tidmarsh.

'The body's been removed, I suppose,'

he said, and to his surprise Tidmarsh shook his head.

'No,' he said. 'The Chief Constable gave orders that nothing was to be touched until you'd seen it. The room has been sealed up, and it is just as it was when we made the discovery.'

He had crossed the square, sparsely-furnished hall while speaking and paused by a door on the left.

'This is the room,' he said, and breaking the seal took a key from his pocket and twisted it in the lock. Holding open the door, he motioned Mr. Budd to enter.

The stout man did so, Leek and the local superintendent remaining on the threshold.

The room was a small one and there was little furniture. A desk with a roll-top occupied the centre, a filing cabinet stood in one corner and a threadbare carpet covered the floor. One arm-chair and a desk chair, together with a small book-case, completed the contents of the room.

For a moment or two Mr. Budd stood just within the doorway and allowed his eyes to travel slowly round the office. From here he could see nothing of the dead man except a booted foot that protruded from the back of the desk. After a moment of taking stock he moved forward, rounded the desk, and stood looking down at the body.

It lay midway between the desk and the french windows. Corbett had been fully dressed when he met his death, in an old suit of tweed; his coat and waistcoat were soaked with blood and there was a look on his face which showed that death had come to him swiftly and unexpectedly.

'You removed the knife?' said Mr. Budd, without taking his eyes off the dead man.

'The doctor removed it to make his examination,' said Tidmarsh. 'It's at the station, where it was taken to test it for prints. You can see it presently.'

'There's no hurry,' murmured the stout man. 'The thing I'd like to see is this letter.'

'That's here,' said the superintendent.

He went over to the desk and picked up a crumpled sheet of paper and an envelope. Mr. Budd searched in his pockets and deliberately drew on a pair of cotton gloves.

'I suppose you've raked this for prints?' he inquired as he took it from the superintendent's hand.

'Yes,' said Tidmarsh. 'There were two sets, the dead man's and somebody else's.'

'It 'ud be interestin',' murmured Mr. Budd, 'to know who that second set belongs to.'

With an expressionless face he read the type-written epistle.

'It's like somethin' out of a detective story,' he commented, gently rubbing the lowest of his many chins. 'It don't belong to real life, this sort of thing. Did you — ' He broke off at the sound of a commotion in the hall.

As he swung towards the door a white-faced stable-boy appeared on the threshold.

'There's another of 'em,' he cried. 'Miss Westmore found 'im over by the 'edge!'

'What are you talking about?' demanded

Tidmarsh sharply. 'Found who?'

'A dead man, sir,' stammered the boy. 'Over by the 'edge!' He pointed vaguely in the direction of the window.

'A dead man,' began Tidmarsh. 'Who — '

'Do you mean over there?' interrupted Mr. Budd, and jerked his head towards a belt of trees that bordered the garden.

The agitated boy nodded.

'Yes, sir. There's a hedge and a little gate that opens on to the downs just there!' He was breathing heavily and hoarsely.

'Show us the way,' said Mr. Budd, and, breaking the seal on the windows, opened them.

The boy led them across the rank lawn, through a patch of shrubbery to a narrow path that ended at a small gate. Opening this he passed out into a meadow enclosed by a wire fence, and beyond which was the undulating expanse of the downs.

'There!' he said huskily, and pointed to where a few yards along, by a straggling hedge, stood the figure of a girl.

They went towards her.

'Good morning, Miss Westmore,' greeted Tidmarsh deferentially. 'This lad's just told us an extraordinary story — '

The girl interrupted him. Her face was white and there was a hint of terror in her eyes, but her voice when she spoke was calm and collected.

'Just down there,' she said, and motioned with her hand. 'By — by the hedge!'

Tidmarsh glanced in the direction she indicated, but Mr. Budd had already seen. Lying a yard from the hedge and almost hidden by the long grass, was a man, a little, undersized, wizened man, whose dreadful face stared up into the smiling sky. He had been strangled, and in consequence was not pleasant to look upon.

Mr. Budd and Tidmarsh bent over the body and then the stout man looked over his shoulder at the scared stable-boy.

'You know this feller?' he inquired.

The lad nodded.

'Yes, sir,' he answered. 'He's a tout. The Guv'nor had trouble with him a few days ago. We caught him watching the trials. I dunno 'is name — ' He stopped, for Mr. Budd was obviously no longer listening.

His attention had been attracted to something gripped in one of the dead man's hands, a soft, black something. As he gently unclasped the stiff fingers and detached the object there was wonder and surprise on his face.

It was a cap of black silk with a wide peak.

'A jockey cap!' breathed Tidmarsh, and Mr. Budd nodded.

7

Leek Becomes Sentimental

A sound escaped the girl, a little suppressed intake of the breath, and Mr. Budd looked towards her quickly. She was staring at the black cap in his hand, her eyes wide, and something that was a mixture between surprise and fear on her face.

'Yes, Miss?' he murmured questioningly. 'What were you goin' to say?'

Whatever had been the cause of her sudden agitation she controlled herself instantly.

'I wasn't going to say anything,' she replied, and in that moment Mr. Budd became aware of her in the sense that she emerged from the background and became an object of interest.

His sleepy eyes rapidly catalogued her visible qualities. Tall, slim, neatly dressed in a tweed coat and skirt; more than averagely pretty, with a determination expressed in the set of her chin that was unusual in women. The wide-set grey eyes returned his look without flinching.

'You were the first to find this man, weren't you, Miss?' he asked.

She nodded.

'Yes,' she said. 'I was coming over to see Mr. Corbett. I'd opened the gate when I happened to glance along the hedge. I thought the man was a tramp sleeping at first, and then, when Pinder and I looked closer we found he was — dead.'

'That's right,' put in the stable-boy. The colour had come back to his face with the passing of the first shock of the discovery, and he was beginning to realise the importance of his position.

'You were coming over to see Mr. Corbett,' murmured Mr. Budd slowly, checking Tidmarsh, who was on the point of opening his mouth. 'What were you comin' to see him about?'

The girl looked at him a trifle haughtily.

'I don't know what right you have to

ask me that — ' she began, and the stout man turned wearily to the local superintendent.

'Tell her, will you?' he said.

'This is Superintendent Budd, of Scotland Yard, Miss Westmore,' exclaimed Tidmarsh hurriedly. 'He's come down at the request of the Chief Constable to help us to investigate the murder of Mr. Corbett, which took place last night — '

'Murder — Mr. Corbett!' The girl gasped the interruption, and her face went ghastly white beneath the thin film of make-up.

'Yes,' said Mr. Budd, watching her from under his drooping eyelids. 'You didn't know, of course? You didn't know that Corbett was dead.'

'No, I didn't know,' she breathed the words uneasily. 'How did it happen — who — '

'He was stabbed in his office,' said the stout man, 'by a feller calling himself 'The Jockey'.'

She made a supreme effort and pulled herself together.

'How — how dreadful!' She was

58

outwardly calm again. Only her eyes betrayed the terror that possessed her, and for the second time that morning, Mr. Budd found himself inwardly admiring her self-control.

The news had been a tremendous shock, a bigger shock than the sight of the black silk cap which still dangled from his fingers.

'Naturally you know nothing about it,' he said, 'otherwise you wouldn't have come over this mornin' expectin' to see him.'

'No!' She uttered the negative mechanically.

'Why did you come, Miss Westmore?' asked Mr. Budd softly.

'I came — ' She hesitated, and then went on rapidly: 'I came because Mr. Corbett had two horses for sale and we were thinking of buying them.'

'Which would those be, Miss?' Pinder put the question, his eyes surprised.

'Two — two bay mares,' said the girl quickly. 'Mr. Corbett met — met my father in the village and mentioned the matter to him.'

The stable-boy frowned.

'That's funny, Miss,' he said. 'We ain't got any bay mares — leastways, not for sale.'

'Perhaps Mr. Corbett was going to buy them if we were interested,' continued the girl hurriedly. 'Most likely that's what it was. Anyway, that's what I was coming to see him about.'

And that's a lie, thought Mr. Budd. You offered that explanation on the spur of the moment. Aloud he said:

'You live near here?'

She nodded, but before she could answer Tidmarsh interposed.

'Colonel Westmore lives at Downlands,' he said, 'about a couple of miles away.'

'I see,' murmured Mr. Budd. 'And you walked over?'

'Yes,' she answered.

The stout man nodded several times, but he said nothing, and it was the girl who broke the awkward pause.

'When — was — was Mr. Corbett killed?' she asked.

'Sometime between eleven and twelve last night,' volunteered Tidmarsh.

60

'And you say,' went on the girl, 'it was somebody called The Jockey?'

'So we believe.' Mr. Budd spoke slowly, his eyes fixed dreamily on a solitary tree that grew in the middle of the meadow. 'There was a threatenin' letter signed by The Jockey written two days before his death — who's this?' he ended abruptly.

They looked in the direction he was staring, and saw the big chestnut and its rider cantering towards them.

'It's my father,' said the girl, and there was a tinge of uneasiness in her voice.

The horseman came nearer, passed through the open gate of the meadow and came to a standstill beside the little group near the hedge. The lean, grey-haired man in the saddle looked down at them; the faded eyes, surrounded by innumerable wrinkles, were worried and anxious.

'I guessed you'd come here, Pamela,' greeted the newcomer. 'I hoped I'd be in time to stop you. 'Morning, Tidmarsh.'

'Good morning, sir,' said Tidmarsh respectfully. 'This is an unpleasant business.'

'What? What's unpleasant?' The question came sharply, and the watchful Mr. Budd saw the anxiety deepen in the old man's eyes.

'Mr. Corbett has been murdered, Father,' put in Pamela quickly. 'Mr. Corbett and another man.' She nodded towards the place where the body of the little tout lay.

'Corbett murdered? Good heavens!' The colonel shot a quick glance in the direction the girl had indicated, but it was obvious his interest was centred on the death of the trainer. The anxiety, too, Mr. Budd noticed had been replaced by a look of relief.

'Tell me about it, Tidmarsh.' He swung himself out of the saddle and joined them, tossing the rein to Pinder, who soothed the impatient horse.

The superintendent gave a sketchy outline of what had happened.

'Extraordinary!' commented Westmore. 'You've no clue to this 'Jockey' person?'

'Only the letter and the black silk cap,' said Mr. Budd.

'Black jacket, black sleeves, black cap,'

said Pamela, and there was a strange note in her voice.

'Eh, what's that?' Colonel Westmore swung round towards his daughter. 'What do you mean, my dear?'

'Norman's racing colours,' she answered, almost inaudibly.

'Good God!' The old man's expression was startled. 'You don't mean — you're not suggesting — '

'I don't mean anything,' said the girl. 'It just occurred to me. It was stupid — '

'To whom were you referrin', Miss?' asked Mr. Budd, but it was her father who answered him.

'She was talking about Mr. Wharton,' he said. 'My daughter and he were engaged. There was some trouble — a year ago — '

'Oh, yes,' said Mr. Budd. 'I remember. Mr. Wharton was 'warned off' by the stewards for instructin' his trainer and jockey that one of his 'orses was to be 'pulled' — '

'It wasn't true!' broke in Pamela fiercely. 'It wasn't true! Norman was incapable of doing such a thing!'

The colonel laid a restraining hand on her arm.

'Don't upset yourself, my dear,' he said gently. 'There can be no connection — '

'Wasn't it Corbett who gave evidence against Mr. Wharton?' interposed the stout man gently. 'He and a man called Cowan, a bookmaker, and a jockey, they were the principal witnesses, weren't they?'

Westmore's face was troubled as he nodded.

'H'm!' remarked Mr. Budd. 'I thought so, I've a good memory. What was on your mind, Miss, when you mentioned these racin' colours?'

'Nothing!' said the girl. 'The coincidence just occurred to me, that's all. I was foolish to say anything.'

'Maybe you were, maybe you weren't.' The superintendent stifled a yawn. 'Well, we'd better be gettin' on with things. I don't think I need trouble you any further, sir. If there's any further information you can give later we know where to find you.'

He turned away and ambled slowly

towards Leek, who had been standing rather disconsolately beside the body of the unknown little tout. Westmore hesitated for a moment and then took the bridle from the stable-boy's hand.

'Come on, Pamela,' he said. 'Morning, Tidmarsh. This is a nasty business. I hope you get to the bottom of it.'

'Thank you, sir,' said the local man, and watched the tall, upright figure as it walked slowly beside the girl, leading the big chestnut. When he joined Mr. Budd and the sergeant, Leek was making an examination of the dead man's clothing.

He brought to light a miscellaneous collection from the pockets, including a wallet which contained several letters addressed to 'Ted Green'. With the exception of one they were bills. The exception was evidently from the man's wife demanding arrears of maintenance and threatening legal proceedings if it was not forthcoming.

'That's the feller's name,' said Mr. Budd. 'Ted Green; and his address is 19B Angel Street, Islington. We'll have him looked up and see what's known about him.'

Tidmarsh removed his hat and scratched his head.

'Wonder why he was killed?' he muttered.

'He was killed,' said Mr. Budd slowly, 'because he saw the murderer escapin' and recognised him, that's obvious. He came and went through the garden, and this poor feller saw him leavin'.'

'But,' protested Tidmarsh, his face incredulous, 'what about the cap? Surely he wasn't dressed as a jockey?'

Mr Budd's sleepy eyes surveyed him thoughtfully.

'I don't know 'ow he was dressed,' he remarked. 'It's all very complicated. Why did he kill Corbett?'

'For the money — ' began the local man, but the stout superintendent shook his head.

'He had no reason to kill him for that,' he said. 'Corbett was going to give it to him. 'E drew it out of the bank for that purpose. 'E even sent the dogs away so as to give this feller a clear road.' He stroked his chin and frowned. 'No, there's something very queer about this business. I wonder why that girl, Miss Westmore, was comin' to see Corbett?'

'She told you,' said the superintendent.

'She told us nothin'!' declared Mr. Budd. 'What she told us was somethin' she thought up on the spur of the moment, and wasn't the real reason at all. When her father turned up she was scared all the time, in case we should mention somethin' about them two horses that never existed.'

Tidmarsh was a little shocked.

'Miss Westmore can't have anything to do with this murder,' he said. 'Her father's a J.P. and — '

'I once,' interrupted Mr. Budd, 'got a man hung who was a Member of Parliament. J.P.s and M.P.s and all the other letters of the alphabet don't make any difference when it comes to murder. We'll get back to the house and send for your Divisional Surgeon to have a look at this feller.'

'D'you want me any more, sir?' inquired the stable-boy.

The stout man shook his head.

'Not at the moment,' he answered, and Pinder hurried away to his duties, eager to recount his morning's adventure to his friends.

When they got back to the house Tidmarsh telephoned to the station while Mr. Budd questioned the Glossops. He elicited nothing from either of them beyond what he already knew. They had heard no sound during the night, and neither had any of the other members of the establishment. Glossop confirmed Pinder's story that Corbett had had trouble with the little tout, but that was all the information they could offer.

Mr. Budd went out to the stables and questioned the rest of the staff, with no better result.

The Divisional Surgeon arrived and testified, after an examination of the body of Green, that the little tout had died round about the same time as Corbett. The usual police photographs were taken and the whole place closely examined for finger-prints. But nothing came to light. The murderer had killed and gone without leaving anything behind that was likely to identify him.

It was late in the afternoon when Mr. Budd and the melancholy sergeant entered the train at Lewes to return to London. For the greater part of the journey the stout superintendent apparently slept, and they had passed Croydon before he suddenly opened his eyes and addressed his subordinate.

'This is goin' to be a big thing,' he said, 'bigger than what you imagine.'

Sergeant Leek, who was incapable of imagining anything, stared at him in silence.

'There's somethin' I didn't mention to Tidmarsh,' continued Mr. Budd, 'and I don't suppose he noticed it.' He took the silk jockey cap from his pocket and sniffed it gently. 'It's very faint,' he said, 'but you can smell it plainly.'

'What?' asked the sergeant.

'Scent,' replied Mr. Budd. 'Smell it yourself.'

He held it out and Leek took it, putting it gingerly to his thin nose.

'Take a good sniff,' said Mr. Budd

encouragingly, 'it won't gas you. Now, I'd like to know what that perfume is.'

'I can tell you that,' said the lean sergeant surprisingly.

'Oh, you can, eh?' Mr. Budd's sleepy eyes were very wide open. 'What do you know about perfume?'

The sergeant's sallow face reddened.

'I was engaged once,' he said. 'It was very sad — '

'It must have been ghastly!' put in Mr. Budd rudely. 'What's that got to do with it?'

'She was a housemaid up at 'Ampstead,' explained Leek reminiscently, 'and she 'ad expensive tastes. One of 'em was perfume, and she used this same scent. Jockey Club, they call it.'

'Very appropriate,' murmured Mr. Budd, and closed his eyes to grapple better with the problem which the sergeant's information had supplied him.

While he had been talking to Pamela Westmore he had noticed a faint and elusive fragrance — the same perfume as that which clung to the black silk cap he had discovered in the dead man's hand.

8

Blackmail

The Press seized with avidity on the bizarre aspect of the two murders and gave the story front-page prominence with scare headlines in leaded type.

Mr. Benjamin Cowan read the various accounts with interest and some unease. He had taken every precaution, but there was always the possibility that he had overlooked something which might lead the police to the real truth, and not even the comforting thought that he was eight thousand pounds better off entirely obliterated the gnawing fear at his heart. Had he known of the finding of the black cap he would have had even more cause for fear, but that discovery had been kept out of the papers.

The scheme which had been born when Corbett showed him the letter had been carried out successfully, but the memory of that moment when, flying through the darkness with the dead body of the trainer behind him, he had come face to face with Green, the little racing tout, would disturb his waking hours for a long time to come. It was a threatened disaster that if he had not dealt with it swiftly might have brought him to the trap.

He shivered, and his daughter eyed him speculatively across the breakfast table.

'What's the matter?' she asked. 'You look ghastly this morning.'

'I didn't sleep very well,' he grunted, which was true, for he had passed the night tossing restlessly to and fro, wondering fearfully whether he had overlooked anything that might lead to the discovery of his presence at Ditchling on the night Corbett had died.

Iris dropped her eyes to the letter she was reading.

'Pamela Westmore wants to know if we'd care to stay with them during the racing at Brighton,' she said. 'What do you want me to do?'

A spark of interest came into his dull eyes.

'Accept, of course,' he answered promptly.

She made a grimace.

'I shall be bored to death,' she grumbled. 'I hate the Westmores, and they hate us. Why they ask us Heaven alone knows. I suppose you've got some pull.'

'Never mind what pull I've got, do as you're told!' snarled her father. 'You do pretty much as you like most of the time, and when I want you to do something you'll do it without grumbling, see?'

'I hear,' she replied coolly, 'though personally I think you're crazy. A man of your age chasing after a girl like Pamela Westmore is ridiculous.'

'She's twenty-three!' he protested.

'And you're well on the way to sixty,' retorted Iris. 'Talk about May and December — ' She shrugged her shoulders. 'Do as you like and make a fool of yourself if you wish to, I suppose it's no concern of mine.'

'Then mind your own business!' he snapped.

She looked at him curiously. There was

no affection between these two, and they made no effort, when they were alone, to pretend there was. In public, on the rare occasions when they were together, they counterfeited a more normal relationship, sprinkling their conversation with mechanical terms of endearment, that in reality deceived no one.

In a way Cowan was proud of his daughter, proud of her appearance and attractiveness, and the admiration she received. But it was the same feeling that he possessed for the luxurious appointments of his flat, and was engendered by no trace of the love which should exist between father and child.

Iris frankly despised her father. She looked upon him as a means of livelihood, a necessary evil which had to be tolerated because it supplied the wherewithal to purchase those things which, to her, made life worth living.

'If you're contemplating marrying Pamela Westmore,' she said, after a pause, 'you'd better prepare yourself for a disappointment. You haven't an earthly. I've seen her looking at you sometimes as though you were a snake escaped from the zoo, and I'm not surprised after that Wharton business.'

Cowan sprang to his feet and brought his fist down with a crash on the table.

'Will you be quiet!' he stormed angrily. 'When I want your advice I'll ask for it. What I intend to do is my business, understand? If I want to marry Pamela Westmore I'll marry her, without consulting you!'

'And presumably,' said Iris, 'without consulting her! Well, I suppose you're quite right, it's no concern of mine, though I should hate to have Pamela Westmore for a step-mother.'

He strode from the room angrily, slamming the door behind him, and it was not until he had reached the palatial offices of Paddocks that he had succeeded in partially mastering the rage which consumed him.

A visitor was waiting to see him, and he greeted the undersized little man who was shown into his office with a scowl.

'Well, what do you want?' he growled ungraciously.

'Have you seen the papers?' said Joe Wills. 'Have you seen about Corbett?'

'Of course I have,' said Cowan. 'I'm very sorry to hear about it, but it's nothing to do with me.'

'It's to do with me, though,' said the jockey quickly. 'Did you read about that money, eight thousand quid, that's missin'? Well, part of that was mine.'

'All of it was mine,' snarled the bookmaker, 'but I'm not kicking up a fuss about it.'

'I don't suppose you are,' said Wills. 'You got plenty more, but I ain't. Corbett was keeping that for me because I ain't got a banking account. And now it's gone.'

'Well, that's your misfortune,' said Cowan, helping himself to a cigar from the drawer in his desk. 'What d'you expect me to do about it?'

The jockey looked quickly round and lowered his voice.

'I'll tell yer what,' he said. 'I can't afford to lose that money. I don't get so many mounts as I used to. I was looking to that as a kind of nest-egg.'

'You don't get mounts,' said the

bookmaker calmly, 'because you're a crooked rider.'

'Maybe I am,' snarled the jockey. 'You ought to know. Both Corbett and I 'ave done enough dirty work for you in our time.'

'And been well paid for it!' said Mr. Cowan. 'What's all this leading to, Wills?' He could give a pretty shrewd guess, and the jockey's next words confirmed his supposition.

'It's leadin' to this,' said Wills. 'I don't know who this Jockey feller is who did in Corbett and the other chap and I don't much care. All I know is that he's got my money, money which I can't afford to lose, and you've got to see me right about it.'

'Why should I?' demanded the book-maker. 'It's not my fault you lost your money.'

'It doesn't matter whose fault it is!' There was a threatening expression on the wizened face. 'You'll either make good that four thousand or else I'm going to squeal about the Wharton business. That's straight!'

'One of the few straight things connected with you, I should imagine,' said Cowan, glaring at him. 'So you're under the impression that I'm going to replace this money you've lost?'

'I know you are!' answered Wills. 'Unless you want to see yourself in Queer Street.'

'And what about you?' inquired Cowan. 'You can't squeal on me without incriminating yourself. If you make the Wharton business public your career as a jockey will be finished for good.'

'I shan't lose any sleep over that,' said Wills. 'I'm nearly finished as it is. I don't get many horses worth riding now, so what are you going to do about it? Four thousand quid and I'll keep me mouth shut.' The cunning eyes surveyed the man before him questioningly, but Cowan didn't answer immediately and the jockey added another inducement.

'There are a lot of people who'd like to know the truth about the Wharton business,' he said meaningly. 'That girl he was engaged to, what's-her-name, she'd be pleased to listen to what I had to say.'

The blood mounted slowly to Cowan's face, but he checked the sudden flood of temper that swept over him, and his voice when he spoke, although it shook a little, was normal.

'Four thousand pounds is a lot of money,' he said slowly. 'I can't give it to you immediately.'

Wills's eyes glittered greedily at this sign of capitulation on the part of his victim.

'I don't want to be 'ard,' he said generously. 'Give me five 'undred on account and the rest in three weeks' time. You'll be at Brighton for the races?'

Cowan nodded.

'Give me the balance then,' said. the jockey. 'I'm ridin' Blonde Baby in the Balcombe Stakes.'

The bookmaker examined the unlighted cigar which he was twisting between his stubby fingers.

'All right,' he said. 'Come in this time to-morrow morning and I'll give you the five hundred.'

'And the balance at Brighton?' said Wills.

'And the balance at Brighton,' agreed Mr. Cowan.

The elated Wills took his departure, and when he had gone the bookmaker lighted his cigar and grappled with this new and not altogether unexpected drain on his resources. Wills, like Corbett before him, would never be satisfied with four thousand, that was only the preliminary. He would come again and again, increasing his demands at every visit.

Mr. Cowan was not unversed in the methods of blackmailers. There was only one way to put a stop to their activities. Joe Wills must go the way Corbett had gone.

9

The Confession

The attention he devoted to his business throughout the rest of the day was mechanical. The greater part of his mind was concentrated on the elimination of the threatening Wills. But there was no 'Jockey letter' here to offer a screen, as in the case of Corbett, and he found the problem less easy of solution.

Tired, irritable and still a little worried concerning the Ditchling affair, he went home to his dinner in an unenviable mood. Iris was out, a fact for which he was rather thankful than otherwise, and during his solitary meal he eagerly read the evening editions of the newspapers which he had brought in with him.

The Ditchling murders still occupied a prominent position, and he was thankful to see that no fresh discovery had come to light. The letter from the mysterious individual signing himself 'The Jockey' had been reproduced and the papers made up for their lack of fresh information with columns of speculation concerning his identity.

At eleven o'clock Mr. Cowan went to bed, an uneasy, worried man. His lack of sleep on the previous night and his strenuous mental exertions of the day had combined to render him dog-tired, and his head had barely snuggled itself into the soft pillow before he was asleep . . .

He awoke with a start, his heart thumping wildly. He could see nothing, hear nothing, and yet instinct told him that he was no longer alone.

'Who's there?' he asked hoarsely, and out of the blackness that surrounded him came a high-pitched, squeaky voice.

'Keep quiet! Don't move, don't speak!' it said.

A cold perspiration of terror broke out on his forehead and the palms of his hands went damp. He heard a soft movement, and then with a click the shaded lights over his bed came on. At the sight of the figure that stood above him he nearly fainted. Black, from head to foot. His eyes blinking in the sudden light, took in every detail. The black silk jacket and black sleeves; the close-fitting silk cap with the broad peak; and where the face should have been a handkerchief of black silk concealing nose and mouth and chin . . .

'Who are you?' he croaked with difficulty, for his throat had gone dry in his fear.

'I am the Jockey,' came the squeaky whisper, and he saw the long-barrelled automatic that was held menacingly in one black-gloved hand. 'I am the Jockey. And I have come to demand a certain thing of you, Benjamin Cowan.'

Almost paralysed with fright, the man in the bed lay staring dumbly up at his weird visitor.

'At the present moment,' continued the figure, in that curious, whispering squeak, 'the police and the public are holding me responsible for your crimes. I am accused of the murder of Simon Corbett and the other man, Green, whereas it is you alone who are guilty of their deaths. You took advantage of my letter to Corbett to extricate yourself from an unpleasant position at my expense. I have come to-night to put that right.'

Cowan licked his dry lips as the eerie voice ceased for a moment.

'You have done many disreputable things in your life,' continued the Jockey, 'but this is the first time you have been guilty of murder.'

Cowan found his voice, a voice that was so curiously unlike his own that he started at the sound of it.

'You are mistaken,' he said huskily. 'I did not kill Corbett — '

'Don't lie!' interrupted the black-clad figure. 'It is useless. I was a witness to the murder of Simon Corbett as I was a witness to the murder of Ted Green. You killed Corbett and stole the money which he had drawn from the bank in accordance with my instructions. You killed him because he was blackmailing you over the conspiracy that sent poor Norman Wharton to a suicide's grave. You killed Green because, as you fled from the house, he recognised you, and you were afraid that if he was allowed to live his evidence might send you to the trap. I know all these things because I was present and saw them.'

'Who — who are you?' stammered Cowan.

'I am Justice!' said the Jockey sternly. 'I am the instrument chosen to purge a clean and honest sport of the parasites which infest it. Men such as you, and Corbett and Wills, who think of nothing but personal gain. Racing is a noble sport defiled by such men, men who cannot be touched by the Jockey Club because there is no evidence against them. To all such men I represent Nemesis. One by one I shall deal with them until the Sport of Kings is fit to be called by that name.'

'You're mad!' breathed Cowan.

'Is it mad to kill the worm that gnaws at the heart of the rose?' asked the Jockey. 'Is it mad to destroy the vermin that eat away a thing of beauty and reduce it to an ugly ruin? If it is then I agree that I am mad.'

'What — what do you want of me?' quavered the bookmaker fearfully.

'I want of you two things,' answered the Jockey. 'Your signature to this document and the money you took from Simon Corbett.'

From the bosom of the silken jacket he produced a paper and held it out. With a shaking hand Cowan took it, and as he read the opening words he face went grey.

'To all whom it may concern. I, Benjamin Cowan, of Park View Mansions, W. I, hereby declare that I am responsible for the murder of Simon Corbett and Edward Green on the night of — '

Rapidly he read the rest of the typewritten sheet and pushed it away.

'I'll not sign this!' he breathed huskily. 'I should be crazy to sign such a thing. Crazy!'

'You will sign!' whispered the high-pitched voice remorselessly. 'You will sign unless you wish Justice to be carried out here and now. You will sign if you want to live to see another dawn!' The muzzle of the pistol pressed lightly against his forehead.

'You daren't shoot,' he gasped. 'The report would wake the house.'

'It would wake it too late to be of service to you,' said the Jockey. 'Now sign!'

The terrified man in the bed felt a pen pushed gently into his hand.

'It will be useless to you if I do,' he whispered between his chattering teeth. 'A confession signed under compulsion is valueless . . . '

'I have indisputable evidence to back it up,' said the other, 'should I have occasion to use it. Sign!'

Benjamin Cowan's eyes roved wildly round the room, his numb brain strove desperately to think of some way out of this awful predicament.

'Sign!' repeated the Jockey inexorably, and the pistol pressed a little harder into his temple.

With despair in his heart Cowan obeyed. The Jockey picked up the fatal document and examined the scrawled signature.

'And now the money,' he said.

'I haven't got it here,' began the bookmaker. 'It's in my safe at the office.'

'You brought it here when you came back after killing Corbett!' said the Jockey. 'You locked it in the wall safe in this room, and it's there now. Get it!'

Realising that it was useless to protest, Cowan swung his trembling legs out of the bed. Shakily he went over to the dressing table where he had put his keys, picked them up and crossed to the picture that concealed the small wall safe. With difficulty, for his hands were shaking so violently that he could scarcely control them, he unlocked and opened the thick steel door. The big package of notes, intact as he had taken them from Corbett's desk, lay within, and he withdrew them, handing them to the figure at his side.

'There you are!' he said thickly. 'Take them, damn you!'

He saw the gloved hand reach out to grasp the packet, and then something snapped in his head. A little moaning cry escaped his thick lips and he collapsed in a heap on the soft carpet . . .

The Jockey stared down at the unconscious figure dispassionately for a moment, and then, crossing to a chair by the window, picked up a long, light overcoat. Leisurely he pulled it on, fastening it carefully up to his chin. Removing the black silk cap and the handkerchief that concealed his face he stowed them away in one of the pockets, withdrawing from the other a cloth cap with which he replaced his Jockey head-gear. Into the pockets of the light coat went also the pistol, the package of notes and Benjamin Cowan's signed confession.

Without a further glance at the crumpled, motionless figure of the book-maker, the night visitor stepped to the window, swung himself across the low sill, and descending by the iron fire-escape by which he had entered, vanished into the darkness of the courtyard below.

10

Introducing Mr. Richard Templeton

Mr. Richard Templeton came down the broad steps of the huge building in which the *Daily Sphere* was prepared for the morning delectation of its two and a half million readers, and pausing on the pavement, with hands in his pockets, gloomily cursed all news editors, sub-editors and proprietors of newspapers. A passing office boy on an urgent errand for his employer stopped to listen, his mouth open and his eyes wide.

'Coo!' he muttered at last, in admiration, and the reporter turned a frowning gaze in the direction of the interruption.

'What is your job?' he demanded, and the boy, a little frightened, retreated a couple of paces.

'I work for Smelley's Paste,' he answered.

Mr. Templeton nodded approvingly.

'Stick to it, my lad,' he advised. 'It is better to be connected with a useful and unromantic commodity like paste, smelly or otherwise, than to be at the beck and call of those whose lives are dedicated to the providing of sensational news with which to fill the leisure hours of a satiated and hypercritical public.'

'Yes, sir,' mumbled the dazed office boy, completely ignorant as to what he meant.

'Remember what I have said,' admonished Mr. Templeton loftily, and turning away, slouched up the sloping narrow street towards the main thoroughfare.

He was tall and loosely built, his ungainly figure clad in the baggy flannel trousers and worn tweed jacket which, except on the rare occasions when for professional purposes he grumblingly donned evening clothes, was his habitual attire. A tiny smear of ink streaked the side of his freckled nose and his unruly shock of reddish-brown hair blew about inelegantly in the wind.

Everybody in the 'Street' knew Dick Templeton. It was said of him that he loved crime for crime's sake and that he was a walking encyclopædia concerning every murder that had been committed during the past century. With his horn-rimmed glasses settled comfortably on the bridge of his broad nose he continued on his way, his long legs covering the ground at an amazing speed, the gloomy expression on his face enhanced by a ferocious scowl.

The cause of Mr. Templeton's annoyance was a recent interview with the News Editor, a thin, soured, unimaginative man, whose outlook on life was bounded entirely by headlines and column space.

'You've fallen down badly over this Jockey business,' said Mr. Pilchard, when Dick had turned in the results of his excursion to Ditchling. 'You've got nothing here that isn't in all the other papers. I want something exclusive. It isn't the murders that make this a big story, it's this Jockey fellow. He's going to appeal to the public's imagination. Can't you find out something about him?'

'The entire police force are attempting

to do that,' answered Dick, who was both tired and irritable. 'How do you expect me to be more successful than they?'

Mr. Pilchard grunted.

'You call yourself a reporter, don't you?' he inquired sarcastically. 'And you ask me that. The police force are not on the staff of this paper, but you are. Go out and get a scoop!'

He pointed significantly to the door, and Dick, who was well acquainted with his moods, knew that this was not the moment to argue.

He had left the office angry and bad-tempered, and it was not so much because the News Editor had hauled him over the coals as because he knew that Mr. Pilchard was right. There had been nothing in the copy he had turned in which the other papers hadn't got, and this rankled. Dick Templeton prided himself on always being a little ahead of his brethren of the pen. In this case, however, his usual luck had deserted him. He had arrived at Ditchling after the majority of his fellows had covered the ground, due to the fact that he had been on another case when the *Sphere* had hurriedly sent for him. He arrived after Mr. Budd had left, so that as yet he had had no opportunity of trying to squeeze any information that might be going out of the stout superintendent. Not that he had a great deal of hope in this direction. He knew the sleepy-eyed man rather well; had been concerned with him on several other cases, and he was aware that getting Mr. Budd to divulge anything he didn't want to was on a par with trying to cross the Atlantic in a canoe. However, since he had missed him at Ditchling he concluded that it would be just as well if he looked him up at the Yard on the off chance that he might be in an expansive mood.

He reached the big building on the Thames Embankment towards noon and sent up his card to the stout superintendent.

Mr. Budd was sitting hunched up in the padded chair behind his desk when the messenger arrived with the slip of pasteboard and eyed it frowningly.

'It's that man Templeton,' he grunted

to Sergeant Leek. 'I was wonderin' how long it would be before he turned up. Shouldn't have been surprised if we'd found him waitin' at Ditchling for us. Tell him I can't see him.' He turned sleepily towards the waiting messenger and the man departed.

The stout man was not in the best of moods that morning, as Sergeant Leek had already discovered. He had spent the greater part of the previous night in thinking over the facts in his possession and trying to evolve a workable theory, without result. There were so many things that required explaining. Queer things that didn't make sense. For instance, that business of the dogs. It was conceivable only supposing Corbett to have decided to accede to the demands contained in the Jockey's letter. In that case he would naturally have sent away the dogs so as to give the unknown blackmailer a chance of keeping the appointment without disturbing the household. This was not unnatural, for if the Jockey's threat held any substance the dead trainer would have been only too anxious to avoid any possibility of his being molested.

That he had intended to hand over the money was evident from the fact that he had drawn it out in pound notes from his bank. But why, if this was the case, had the Jockey killed him? Certainly not for the money. That was his without the risk of murder. Had Corbett become fractious at the last moment, or more likely pierced his visitor's disguise, and, refusing to part with the money, put forward a counter-threat of exposure?

This seemed probable, but Mr. Budd was not at all sure that it was the right explanation. There was the question of the cap, too, that had been found in the other man's hand. How had it got there? It was possible that it had been snatched off in a struggle between the two men, but this meant that the Jockey must have been dressed in clothes consistent with his pseudonym. What didn't fit in at all was the scent — that illusive perfume which had clung to the black silk cap and which Mr. Budd had detected also lingering about Pamela Westmore. Jockey Club, Leek had said it was, and this he had confirmed in a consultation with the perfume expert. And yet Jockey Club was not the type of scent that a girl like Pamela Westmore would use. It was a cheap perfume, sold in quantities at the sixpenny stores — this again he had learned from the perfume expert — and not at all in keeping with a lady like Colonel Westmore's daughter. Yet he was certain he had not been mistaken. His nose was keen, and although the scent had been very faint it was unmistakably the same as that on the black silk cap.

Mr. Budd was not at all satisfied. As the assistant-commissioner had said at the beginning of the inquiry, there was too much of the mystery-novel element about the whole affair, and the stout superintendent disliked this departure from reality. He was more at home in a straightforward case in which there appeared no mysterious letters signed by extravagant nom-de-plumes . . .

'The Jockey!' he muttered disgustedly. 'No respectable criminal would lower himself to be so childish.'

'Maybe he's a fan of this feller — '

Sergeant Leek mentioned the name of a popular novelist who specialised in sensational literature.

'Maybe he is,' agreed Mr. Budd. 'It jest shows you how these books can corrupt honest-to-goodness, straightforward crooks. Not content with givin' away secrets of police procedure and puttin' everyone wise to finger-prints and suchlike they're now corruptin' the criminal classes.'

He glowered at a report that lay on his blotting pad. It had come in that morning and concerned everything that was known about the unfortunate Ted Green. Apparently he had a police record, and had several times been convicted under the Betting Act. He was generally known in the district in which he lived as a 'bad character', but there was nothing at all helpful as far as his death was concerned. No possible suggestion of a line of inquiry that might lead to the identity of his murderer.

Mr. Budd lit one of his evil-smelling cigars and filled the office with a cloud of rank smoke.

'The inquest on these two fellers takes

place the day after to-morrow,' he grumbled, 'and we've got nothing to put before the Coroner.'

'We can ask for an adjournment,' suggested Leek brightly.

'I know that!' said his superior tartly. 'We *shall* ask for an adjournment — with the usual bunk about followin' up an important clue. That's all very well for the public, it looks mighty fine in print, but it means nothin'.'

'Maybe something'll come to light,' said the sergeant hopefully.

'Yes,' said Mr. Budd. 'Perhaps you'll suddenly become intelligent or the Commissioner'll dance the can-can down Whitehall, both are equally likely.'

Leek sighed patiently and said nothing.

'In my opinion,' said the superintendent, 'this is going to prove to be one of them unsolved crimes that the newspapers are so fond of rehashing at intervals. All we can hope for is that this Jockey feller doesn't die out with the Corbett affair. If he pops up again over somethin' else we may stand a chance. If he doesn't — ' He shrugged his broad shoulders, and closing his eyes relapsed into silence.

At one o'clock he rose ponderously to his feet, brushed the accumulated ash of the many cigars he had smoked from his capacious waistcoat and took down his hat.

'I'm going out to make an inquiry,' he announced briefly and untruthfully, and leaving his office made his way down the stairs.

11

The Man in the Flat

There was a little tea-shop just round the corner from the Whitehall entrance which Mr. Budd patronised regularly every day at the same hour, except on those occasions when business took him away. He invariably sat at a small table near the pay desk and always ordered the same thing — a pot of strong tea and two rounds of buttered toast. This was his usual luncheon, for in spite of his size he was an abstemious man and held a theory that over-indulgence in food clogged the workings of the brain. Long usage had accustomed the waitresses to expect him, and the little table was kept vacant.

He settled his huge bulk in the inadequate chair and his toast and tea was brought to him without his having to order it. Slowly and methodically he poured out the hot, strong beverage, added milk and four lumps of sugar, and after a preliminary sip to find out if it met with his approval, began to munch stolidly at one of his rounds of toast.

Dick Templeton who, for the past hour, had been waiting patiently at one of the other tables concealed behind a newspaper, for he was aware of Mr. Budd's habits, saw the arrival of the stout man, and rising to his feet crossed the restaurant and dropped into a vacant chair opposite the detective.

Mr. Budd surveyed him without enthusiasm.

'Oh, it's you,' he mumbled thickly, his mouth full of buttered toast. 'It's no good your botherin' me, Templeton, I've got nothin' to give you.'

'It is more blessed to give than to receive,' quoted Dick with a grin. 'Surely you know that, Budd?'

'What are you going to give me?' asked the superintendent, noisily gulping his tea.

'The quotation doesn't apply to me,' answered the reporter. 'In this case I am the receiver.'

'You're welcome to all you can receive from me,' grunted Mr. Budd. 'I suppose it's this Jockey business you're on, eh?'

'Of course,' replied Dick. 'Am I likely to be concerned with anything less than the latest and greatest sensation?'

The stout superintendent picked up another piece of toast and eyed it carefully.

'You think you're a smart fellow, don't you?' he said. 'Well, I don't think you're goin' to get very far with this business.'

'Does that mean that the police are stumped?' asked Dick quickly.

'It doesn't mean nothin',' retorted Mr. Budd. 'I'm just expressin' an opinion.'

'I'll bet you,' said the reporter extravagantly, 'that I'll find the Jockey before you do.'

And neither of them guessed how soon his boast was to be substantiated.

'I don't bet,' said Mr. Budd shaking his head sadly. 'Not since I had a dollar each way on a horse called Laughin' Water.'

'And lost it?' Dick grinned as he put the question.

'That horse,' said Mr. Budd, producing an enormous handkerchief and wiping his lips, 'was entered for the three-thirty at Gatwick. It might have won the last race if they'd put the startin' time back an hour. Laughin' Water!' He sniffed disgustedly. 'I'll bet nobody else was laughin' at the end of that race except the horse.'

He poured himself out a second cup of tea, and Dick, lighting a cigarette, leaned forward.

'Seriously, Budd,' he said. 'Can't you give me anything about these murders?'

The stout man shook his head.

'I don't want a lot of stuff published,' he growled, 'that's goin' to put this Jockey feller wise to anythin' we know.'

'I won't publish anything without your permission,' broke in Dick. 'I promise you that. Now, come on,' he went on persuasively. 'Remember what I've done in the past. Wasn't it me who gave the tip over that Hampstead business? Didn't I put you wise to Jimmy Snoddin's graft?'

'Maybe,' said Mr. Budd. 'I'm not denyin' that you're a bit smarter than some of the other reporters I know, but in this business I've got nothin' to give you.'

'Now don't be obstinate!' persisted

Dick. 'Look here, I'll make a bargain with you. Let me in on what you know and I'll tell you everything I discover before I give it to the *Sphere*. That's fair, isn't it?'

Mr. Budd considered the proposition. There was no denying that in the past Dick Templeton had been useful. In his capacity as Crime Reporter on the *Sphere* he came across many out-of-the-way bits of information which had proved considerably helpful to the police. The stout superintendent had more than once admitted this. Perhaps in this present instance his co-operation would be more of an asset than a liability. One thing, his word was to be trusted. If he gave a promise that he would publish nothing without permission and would turn over anything he discovered to the police, he would keep that promise.

'I'll tell you what I'll do,' said Mr. Budd cautiously. 'I'll tell you all I know up to now, but some of it's not for publication. You understand that?'

'That's O.K. with me,' said Dick, delighted at having secured what he wanted.

'But,' continued Mr. Budd warningly, 'I won't promise that I'll go any further than that. I'm not goin' to say that I'll make you a present of all the information I acquire. I'll have to use my own discretion about that.'

'Which means that I'm not bound to disclose everything I discover,' retorted Dick.

The stout superintendent frowned and pursed his lips.

'Well, that doesn't necessarily follow,' he said slowly. 'Still, we'll talk about that later. Maybe we'll swop what we discover, maybe we won't. It all depends. I'll tell you just what we've got up to now.'

It didn't take long, and Dick was more than disappointed when the stout man concluded his brief recital. With the exception of the perfume which he had not known anything about he was already in possession of most of the facts.

'Can't I mention this perfume?' he pleaded, but Mr. Budd was adamant.

'You cannot!' he declared. 'It's the one thing I don't want to leak out.'

'All right,' grumbled Dick. 'You haven't

given me much, have you?'

'I haven't given you anything,' said the fat detective complacently. 'But I've told you all I know at the moment, and if you can suggest anything I'll be pleased to hear it.'

They discussed the matter for nearly an hour, exchanging views, but the results gained were microscopic. At a quarter past two they parted outside Scotland Yard, having reached a more or less tacit understanding to work in conjunction. Dick was disappointed at the result of the interview. The only thing fresh he had learned he was prohibited from making use of. The perfume on the black silk cap could have been worked up into nearly a column, and would temporarily at any rate, have assuaged Mr. Pilchard's greed for fresh news. All the same, it suggested a line which might be followed up.

The possible connection of Pamela Westmore with the case would supply just that touch of human interest that was lacking.

Dick spent the rest of the afternoon and the greater part of the evening mooning about the London parks, evolving in his mind a plan of campaign. He dined at a little restaurant in Old Compton Street, lingering over the meal.

It was late when he paid his bill and set off towards the small ground-floor flat at the back of Russell Square where he lived, but he had come to a decision. On the morrow he would go down to Ditchling again and try and see what he could learn regarding this girl who used the same scent as that which clung to the black silk Jockey cap, and which was the only relic that that mysterious individual had left behind.

He lived alone and the flat was in darkness when he opened his small front door and stepped into the tiny lobby. His hand was reaching for the switch when a high-pitched, squeaky voice startled him in the darkness.

'Don't put on the light,' it said. 'I want a word with you and I should prefer to talk in the dark.'

'Who the devil are you?' gasped the astonished Dick.

'The Jockey!' was the reply.

12

The Scoop

THE JOCKEY!

EXCLUSIVE INTERVIEW

(Special to the *Daily Sphere*)

The Jockey, the mysterious individual who figured so prominently in the recent murders at Ditchling, visited the flat of our Crime Reporter at a late hour last night and made the following remarkable statement:

'I AM NOT A MURDERER!
I HAD NO HAND IN THE KILLING
OF EITHER SIMON CORBETT OR
TED GREEN.'

'I had just come in,' writes Richard Templeton, staff reporter on the *Sphere*, 'and my flat was in darkness.

I had stretched out my hand to put on the light when I was accosted by a high-pitched, obviously disguised voice. 'I am the Jockey,' it said, 'and I want a word with you. I should prefer to conduct the interview in the dark, and I warn you that I am armed. I have no wish to use violence, but in the event of your attempting to detain me I shall not hesitate to do so.'

'The man then made the statement referred to above.

' 'I am being credited,' he said, 'with the murder of a trainer named Simon Corbett and a little racing tout called Ted Green. I am not guilty of either crime, although I was in the vicinity of the house when the murders were committed. I wish to make it clear, through the medium of your paper, that I am not a murderer, and that is the object of my visit to-night. I admit being the writer of a letter which demanded eight thousand pounds from Simon Corbett. This was the first in a campaign which I have planned against those people who, by dishonest practices, are besmirching a fine and noble sport. There are many such people. Although the majority of those connected with racing are honourable men, there are black sheep as there are in any other form of human activity. I have a list of these black sheep, and one by one I shall deal with them until the sport of racing has been cleansed. They work so cleverly that in many cases the vigilance of the Jockey Club is of no avail. The evidence necessary for that body to take action is often lacking. I have set myself up to deal with these people and, in most instances, I shall attack them in the only way that will make any impression on them — their pockets!

''Through the columns of your paper I wish to issue a warning to all those who, by swindling and worse, have amassed fortunes from the Sport of Kings. Their fortune will be taken from them and in flagrant cases, their lives. For although I am no murderer I represent Justice, and where, in their greed, these men have caused the forfeit of a life, so in return shall their life be forfeit. Tell them to take heed, for Nemesis is about to overtake them.'

'I cannot describe,' says our reporter, 'the sincerity with which my mysterious visitor infused his speech. I received the impression that I was listening to a man of high ideals. Whose identity lies concealed behind the pseudonym of the Jockey I have no idea. From the beginning to the end of the interview I never saw my visitor, only heard that eerie voice speaking to me out of the dark- ness . . .'

There was much more, for Dick Templeton had let himself go, and the delighted Mr. Pilchard had spread the story over three quarters of the front page.

'This is the greatest scoop we've had for years!' he enthused — a rarity, for he was usually a taciturn man. 'Every other paper in the 'Street' will be green with envy!'

Mr. Budd read the account and was not so enthusiastic.

'What's all this bunk?' he inquired over the telephone, having, after some difficulty, got into communication with Dick.

'It's not bunk!' retorted the reporter. 'It's true.'

'Do you mean to tell me,' said the stout man, 'that you had this Jockey feller in your flat last night and let him go?'

'I let him go because I couldn't help myself,' said Dick. 'I know when to argue and when to keep quiet, and one of the times is when I'm facing a loaded automatic.'

Mr. Budd made a disparaging noise.

'I never thought you was a coward, Templeton,' he said contemptuously.

'There's a difference between being a coward and a suicide,' said Dick. 'I'd like to have seen you in the same position. What would you have done?'

'I'll bet the feller wouldn't have got away,' said the Rosebud. 'So all this stuff you've published is true, eh?'

'Nearly all of it,' said Dick. 'I've dressed it up a bit. But the majority of it is solid, rock-bottom fact.'

'This feller really said all this?' asked the superintendent.

'Yes,' answered the reporter. 'So far as he's concerned I've quoted him word for word.'

'And you believe it?' Mr. Budd sounded a little sceptical. 'You believe all this nonsense about Justice and cleanin' up racin' and so forth?'

'Much as it may surprise you,' said Dick, 'I do!'

'H'm!' said Mr. Budd, noncommittally. 'Well, I'd like to see you sometime. Maybe you'll be along this way?'

'I'll be in the tea-shop at four o'clock,' said Dick promptly, and his caller rang off.

The *Sphere's* published interview with the Jockey caused something of a sensation in racing circles. Lord Mortlake read it at his club, murmured something about 'ridiculous nonsense' and turned to the more congenial columns of *The Times*. Sir Godfrey Latimer adopted a more open mind.

'There may be something in it,' he remarked to Bastion at lunch, 'but you never can tell how much is true and how much is manufactured at the offices of these 'rags'.'

Like a good many people he was under the impression that the greater part of the news served up in the more sensational newspapers was manufactured on the premises. Thus did he slander an honest profession.

Mr. Walter Pyecroft read the account in the garden of his little cottage in Surrey and smiled at the reference to the Jockey Club. Many people read it and inwardly quaked, for to them the warning of the Jockey represented an intangible fear that might at any moment take shape and substance.

Among these was Benjamin Cowan. Since that dreadful night when he had awakened to find the sinister figure at his bedside the bookmaker had lived in a sweat of terror, and his peace of mind was further disturbed by the knowledge which an inspection of his bank balance had revealed to him. In spite of the huge profits which poured into the coffers of Paddocks, Mr. Cowan was by no means as rich as people supposed. Many were the drains on his resources, and the final demand made by the little jockey, Joe Wills, would necessitate some ingenuity on his part to meet. The five hundred he had managed to rake up, but it had left him overdrawn beyond his limit, as the letter which he had opened that morning from his bank manager reminded him.

Unlucky speculations; a bad season at the races; and a hundred and one unmentionable calls on his purse had contributed to his precarious position. It was necessary, within the next few weeks, that he should find money, a large sum of money, and this worry combined with that other dread that never left him sapped at his vitality and reduced him to a nervous, irritable creature scarcely capable of attending to the daily routine of business that came his way.

He looked an old man as he sat in his sumptuous office, glowering at the desk in front of him. His sallow cheeks were

116

flabby and there were pouches under his eyes; the hand that carried the cigar back and forth as he smoked spasmodically trembled visibly. He was afraid, desperately afraid, and his greatest fear was of the man who had forced him to sign that confession. Whenever he thought of that the perspiration broke out on his forehead and his throat went dry. While that paper remained in existence he would never know a moment's peace.

The Jockey had it in his power to send him for that nine o'clock walk from which there is no return, and Mr. Cowan never passed a police station without shivering inwardly. It was not the confession alone that frightened him, it was the fact that the man had said he possessed other evidence to back it up. The confession obtained, as it had been, under compulsion, might have been set aside, though in the event of its being made public it was bound to lead to ugly inquiries and that was the one thing that Benjamin Cowan could not afford. He was mixed up with too many shady concerns and lived too near the edge of things to risk an examination into his affairs. Although up to now he had been clever enough to retain the veneer of respectability, a police inquiry, which would be the inevitable result of any breath of suspicion against him, would lay bare secrets which he preferred to remain hidden.

There was only one way out of his difficulty, one logical way, that was. He must find the Jockey, regain that confession, and destroy the man who had brought it into being. But this solution was not so easy as it sounded. He had no inkling of the real identity of the man on whose shoulders he had thought it so simple to shift the responsibility of his own crime, and, without any clue, to find him was like looking for one particular blade of grass in a five-acre field. He might be anyone.

He dropped the butt of his cigar into the chromium ashtray and lighted another. What was the best way to begin his search? He had so many other matters to attend to that it was impossible to devote all his time to this, though it was the most urgent of them all. Something must be done about Wills. It was impossible to submit to his demands for long. The balance of the four thousand pounds was due at Brighton, and if it wasn't paid he was well aware that Wills would keep his word and divulge his share in the conspiracy against Wharton, which would mean utter and complete ruin so far as Cowan was concerned. And even if it was paid it wouldn't satisfy the greed of the man for long. He would come again and again, increasing his demands each time. Something must certainly be done about Wills. But what?

The solution which he had found in the case of Corbett was too risky to try again. It must be something subtler.

He passed his hand wearily across his forehead. On the top of all these worries he had the question of money to consider. That was almost as urgent as the other two matters. If he could only be certain that Shy Lad would win the Balcombe Stakes at Brighton his immediate financial difficulties would be over, for he had backed the horse to win him twenty thousand pounds. If Blonde Baby was out of the race it was almost a certainty, for he had an uneasy feeling that Blonde

Baby was the better horse at the weight.

Could anything be done with Wills? Wills was riding the big bay mare and a little careful manipulation might ensure that Shy Lad passed the stick first.

The bookmaker considered this suggestion and mechanically shook his head. It was unsafe to approach Wills. Knowing what he did, the jockey, even if he considered the suggestion that he should pull his mount, would expect so much for doing it that it wouldn't be worth while. No, he must take the risk. Perhaps a 'saver' on Blonde Baby would help to minimise his loss, and there was a good chance of Shy Lad winning. With the exception of the bay mare there was nothing that could touch him.

His mind swung back to the Jockey and he racked his brains to try and find a starting point from which he could begin his search for that mysterious individual.

'Crabthorne.' He spoke the name aloud, and the frown cleared from his face. He was the very man! Why hadn't he thought of him before? If the Jockey was discoverable, Crabthorne would find him.

13

The Inquiry Agent

He stretched out his hand and picked up the telephone, giving a Terminus number.

'Is Mr. Crabthorne in?' he asked the clerk who answered the call. 'Put me through to him, will you. Benjamin Cowan speaking.' There was a slight delay, and then he heard the voice of the man he was seeking.

'I want to see you, Crabthorne,' he said, cutting short the rather oily greeting of the other. 'I want to see you urgently.'

'Come right away, Mr. Cowan. It's always a pleasure to see you,' said Crabthorne unctuously.

'I'll be with you in twenty minutes,' said the bookmaker, and hung up the receiver.

He rang for his secretary, curtly informed the girl that he would be out for the greater part of the afternoon, and was carried downstairs by the lift, where the uniformed commissionaire procured him a taxi.

In a little back street behind Southampton Row he alighted and entered a narrow doorway, on the lintel of which was a dingy brass plate bearing the insignia 'Marius Crabthorne. Inquiry Agent. Second Floor.'

There was no lift, and he climbed the worn stone staircase to a bare landing from which two doors opened, one a glass door on which in black letters was the word 'Inquiries'. Pushing this open he entered a small office which had been divided by a counter on which stood a bell. In answer to the shrill summons of this a pale-faced, spectacled youth appeared round the corner of a partition. He was shabbily dressed, with a dirty collar and soiled cuffs, and his jet-black hair shone with the grease he had used to plaster it down.

'Mr. Crabthorne's expecting you, sir,' he lisped, when Cowan mentioned his name. 'Will you come in?'

He lifted the flap of the counter and escorted the visitor across the small outer room to the door of an inner office, ushering him deferentially into the presence of the head of the firm.

Mr. Crabthorne rose from behind an untidy desk and extended a not over-clean hand.

'Come in, Mr. Cowan,' he said, in a rich, oily whisper. 'Come in, sir. It is a great pleasure to see you again after so long.'

Cowan grunted, touched the extended fingers, and looking round disparagingly, sat down in a dingy, uncomfortable armchair that stood in front of the desk.

'Are you busy at the moment?' he asked abruptly.

Mr. Crabthorne shrugged his plump shoulders.

'Unfortunately, no,' he replied. 'Business is very slack, Mr. Cowan. We have one or two little matters on hand, but nothing to speak of.'

'That's good,' grunted Cowan, 'because I want you to look into a little job for me. It's a full-time job.'

The short, fat figure of the inquiry agent slid into the chair behind his desk.

'However busy we were we should always be prepared to do any little job for you, Mr. Cowan,' he said. 'What is the trouble? Nothing serious, I hope?'

'It's very serious,' replied the bookmaker. 'You've read about this — this crook who calls himself the Jockey, I suppose?'

Mr. Crabthorne's rather shifty eyes narrowed.

'Who hasn't, Mr. Cowan?' he replied. 'Is it in connection with him that you've come to see me?'

The bookmaker nodded.

'Yes,' he answered. 'I want you to find him, Crabthorne. Find out who is behind this ridiculous masquerade.'

The inquiry agent pursed his lips doubtfully.

'It will be a difficult job, Mr. Cowan,' he began.

'I know that,' broke in his client, 'but you're to spare no effort or expense. It is essential for certain plans of mine that I know who it is who conceals his identity under the pseudonym of the Jockey.'

'I will do my best,' said Mr. Crabthorne.

'And you will treat the commission as

confidential,' went on Cowan quickly. 'Nobody must know that I have consulted you in this matter, you understand?'

'The things that pass in this office,' said Mr. Crabthorne, 'go no further. I am a man of integrity, Mr. Cowan.'

He made the outrageous statement without batting an eyelid. And outrageous it was, for Benjamin Cowan knew enough about this man to send him down for ten years on a charge of blackmail, and Mr. Crabthorne knew that he knew.

'You can draw up to a reasonable amount for expenses,' continued the bookmaker, 'but there must be no delay in starting your campaign. I want this man found at the first possible moment.'

'The whole resources of my establishment will be utilised immediately to that end,' said Mr. Crabthorne grandly. 'But, as I have said, Mr. Cowan, it is not going to be an easy task. Can you give me any hints? Have you any suspicions — '

'I can give you nothing,' said Cowan. 'You have all sorts of out-of-the-way sources of information, use them. That's why I have come to you.'

'I shall leave no stone unturned,' said the inquiry agent. 'If it is possible to find this man he will be found. You could not have come to anyone better.'

He spoke the truth, as the bookmaker was well aware, for Mr. Crabthorne had many contacts and heard many things that went on in that nebulous and ever-shifting strata of society which is commonly classified as 'The Underworld'.

'I'll leave it to you,' said Cowan. 'Report to me daily, and if you make any discovery, immediately, no matter what the hour.'

He took a cheque-book from his pocket, uncapped his fountain-pen and scribbled quickly.

'That will do to be going on with,' he said, tearing out the cheque and passing it across to the inquiry agent, and Mr. Crabthorne's eyes glistened greedily as he noted the amount. 'If you want any more let me know, and I shall want a detailed account of expenses, you understand?'

'Naturally,' murmured Mr. Crabthorne. 'We are business men.' He was an expert at rendering an expense account. Long practice had enabled him to produce a total that was staggering in its dimensions.

'Get busy, then,' said Cowan, and took his departure, a little relieved now that he had started a campaign against the man who held his safety in the hollow of his hands.

His relief would have been tempered with a different feeling had he been aware of the man who had followed him from the unsavoury street in which Mr. Crabthorne had his office to the main thoroughfare and watched him get into a taxi. For the Jockey was aware of his visit to the inquiry agent and had guessed the reason which had prompted it.

14

The Man in the Moonlight

During the days that followed many people received communications from the Jockey, couched in the same terms as that which had preceded the death of the unfortunate Simon Corbett. But few of these letters reached the Press or the police for their recipients were chary, after the statement published by the *Sphere*, of admitting that they were one of the victims marked down by the mysterious individual who had taken it on himself to mete out Justice to the unlawful. By doing so they tacitly acknowledged that they had been guilty of nefarious practices, and preferred, with however bad a grace, to pay and keep silent. It was a difficulty which Mr. Budd had foreseen, and which he mentioned to Dick Templeton during one of his many interviews with that enterprising reporter.

'That was the reason he gave you that freak interview,' he grunted. 'He knew what effect it would have on the people he was after. Naturally you can't expect these fellers to come forward and lay information. It'd be as good as signing confessions that they were swindlers. If he made a mistake and sent a letter to someone who had nothin' to fear it would be different. But these people can't afford to risk the inquiry that would follow if they mentioned the matter to the police. I expect dozens of people have had letters that we know nothin' about.'

He was a little extravagant in his estimate. So far the Jockey's demands had embraced only half a dozen, and of these there was one who took his courage in both hands and brought the epistle he had received to Scotland Yard.

Sir Trevor Bleck was well-known on every racecourse in England and his reputation was not of the best. On more than one occasion he had only escaped a 'warning off' notice by a hair's-breadth, for he cared nothing for racing as a sport and only saw in it a profitable means of adding to a depleted income. He was a tall, thin man, with a smear of moustache under his jutting nose and a monocle that his friends swore had been in his left eye when he was born.

'It's up to you to do something,' he drawled when he interviewed Mr. Budd in the latter's office at the Yard. 'Whether there's any truth in these allegations this fellow makes I'm not prepared to discuss, but if he thinks I'm going to hand over ten thousand pounds without a protest he's a fool! And if you don't catch him you're a fool, too!'

The stout superintendent made no reply to this offensive remark but read the letter which lay before him on his blotting pad. It began abruptly, and without preliminary:

'For some years now you have made a considerable sum of money by swindling the racing public and honest bookmakers. I estimate the fortune you have acquired in this way to be approximately two hundred thousand pounds. As a first

instalment I shall require you to pay ten thousand pounds in treasury notes and in a manner I shall stipulate later in the personal column of the Sphere. You will be well advised to comply with these instructions, otherwise I shall have no compunction in removing such a dangerous and useless specimen of humanity as yourself.

'The Jockey.'

'When did you get this?' asked Mr. Budd.

'This morning,' answered his visitor, 'and I've come straight round to the proper quarter. I'm the wrong man to be intimidated by threats of this sort. What do you intend to do about it?'

'We can't do anythin',' said the Rosebud, 'until we see what he's got to say in the 'Personal' column of the *Sphere*. I'll have a watch kept on that from now on.'

Sir Trevor Bleck yawned.

'Well, it's up to you,' he declared, levering his long length out of the chair in which he had been seated. 'I look to you to protect both my personal welfare and my banking account.' He nodded curtly and followed the messenger who had come to show him out.

Mr. Budd eyed the closed door sleepily after he had gone, and his sympathies at that moment were entirely with the Jockey.

'A nasty piece of work!' he murmured reflectively, and thrusting a finger and thumb into his waistcoat pocket produced one of his unpleasant cigars, and a second or two later he was filling the office with clouds of pungent smoke, as though to fumigate it after the presence of his visitor.

Sir Trevor Bleck, completely ignorant of the impression he had engendered in the mind of the stout superintendent, strolled leisurely up Whitehall, crossed Trafalgar Square, walked up the Haymarket, and entered the American Bar of a restaurant near Piccadilly Circus. Several cronies who were grouped at the crescent-shaped counter hailed him as he came in. They were mostly men of his own type, and under the mellowing influence of a number of cocktails Sir Trevor related the story of the Jockey letter and what he had done about it.

'The fellow's nothing more nor less than a common blackmailer!' he declared. 'All this high-falutin' nonsense that was published in the *Sphere* is all rot. But he isn't going to blackmail me!'

The sycophants among his audience murmured words of praise, and by the time Sir Trevor left the bar and went in search of lunch at one of the few clubs of which he was still a member he began to feel that he was a very fine fellow indeed.

The result of his incautious remarks appeared in the evening newspapers. There had been a reporter present, and he had taken advantage of the piece of news which had been so gratuitously offered. Bleck read the account as his car carried him homeward that evening to his pleasant house in Surrey, and he was a little worried as to whether he had not been ill-advised to make public the line of action he had taken. It didn't trouble him very much, however, for he was one of those men who can conveniently put aside anything unpleasant at will, and during dinner and afterwards his mind was wholly concentrated on a new idea which had occurred to him for increasing his bank balance during the racing at Brighton.

He had two horses entered for the Sussex Handicap, one of which had been made favourite. The other was a long price, and it was with this that he intended to win. He was too clever a man to resort to 'pulling' the better horse. His methods were more subtle. He had on his pay-roll a man who was the most expert doper of horses in existence. He had, in fact, served several terms of imprisonment for this, and he could fake a four-year-old so that it could be substituted for a three-year-old and run in a three-year-old event so that the substituted horse could not be distinguished from the animal actually entered for the race. There was a certain drug completely undetectable which, administered subcutaneously a few minutes before the 'off', was sufficient to assure that the horse would not be the first to pass the post. And it was Sir Trevor Bleck's intention to utilise this in the Sussex Handicap.

His house at Weybridge was small but beautifully appointed and stood on a hillside in a pleasant setting of trees, lawns and colourful flower-beds. It was a warm, moonlight night, one of those nights in early June when the moon is so bright that one can see almost as clearly as at midday, and Bleck, after writing several letters, elected to stroll out into his garden to smoke a final cigar before turning in.

The scent of roses mingled with the fragrant smell of the tobacco as he strolled across the broad lawn with the huge cedar tree in the centre that sent long, black shadows reaching across the grass. It was very still and peaceful, for there was no wind, and a sense of complete content enveloped him as he moved leisurely towards the clipped yew hedge that marked the entrance to the rose garden. Passing through the arch he descended the shallow steps beyond and continued his way under the pergola, already showing signs of the blaze of colour which was to come. Beyond the rose garden was a second smaller strip of lawn, bordered by a thick shrubbery.

The moon lit up the shaven grass, turning it to dove grey, and pausing in the middle Sir Trevor stood drinking in the beauty of the night. There was a streak of the genuinely artistic in him which caused him to appreciate such things.

For a long time he stood motionless, bathed in the blue-white of the moon, and then, with a last draw at the stub of his cigar he threw it away and turned to go back to the house. Turned, and stopped dead with a sharp intake of the breath.

Between him and the entrance to the rose garden stood a figure — a figure that showed up sharp and clear in the bright moonlight, a figure dressed from head to foot in black. Black riding breeches, black jacket; black silk cap with a broad peak. A figure without a face, for beneath the peak of the cap was nothing but a black patch.

'Good evening, Sir Trevor,' said the

Jockey, in his curious, weird, high-pitched voice, and the startled man he addressed saw the long-barrelled pistol that he held in his gloved right hand. 'I have come for that ten thousand pounds I mentioned in my letter.'

Bleck swallowed, and his momentary fear departed.

'Oh, you have, eh?' he said harshly. 'D'you think I usually carry ten thousand pounds about with me when I take an evening stroll?'

'No!' was the answer. 'But I don't think that will prove an insurmountable obstacle. Your action in going to the police this morning has precipitated my plans, and for any consequences that may ensue you have only yourself to blame.'

The sinister figure advanced slowly.

'If,' sneered Bleck, 'you can extract ten thousand pounds from me you're a clever man, Mr. Jockey.'

The Jockey bowed as if in acknowledgment of the compliment, and now he was standing only a few feet away.

'I think I shall succeed,' he said. 'During the course of your racing career,

Bleck, you have doped many noble animals to satisfy your greed for money. Try a little yourself!' His left hand shot forward and Bleck caught a momentary glimpse of something that glittered in the moonlight.

A hoarse cry left his lips and he started back, but he was too late. The hypodermic syringe in the black-gloved hand entered his arm. He felt a sharp twinge of pain and then a sudden numbness; the beauty of the night dimmed, the bright disc of the moon began to whirl madly and then a black wave of unconsciousness swamped his brain, and as his knees crumpled under him the Jockey caught him and eased his fall.

*　　*　　*

As the Piccadilly Branch of the United Bank opened its doors on the following morning a man who had been waiting stepped up to the counter and presented a cheque and a letter to the cashier. The cashier scrutinised both, went away with a murmured apology, and after a short delay came back.

'How will you have this, sir?' he inquired politely.

'In tens,' answered the early caller.

The cashier produced stacks of notes and rapidly counted them. It took him some time to complete the transaction, but when he had entered the numbers, he pushed two thick packets under the grill.

'Ten thousand pounds,' he said pleasantly. 'You'll find that correct, sir.'

The man who had presented the cheque signed by Sir Trevor Bleck, and the letter of authority to cash it, rapidly checked the money and put it carefully away in his pocket.

'Thank you,' he said. 'Good morning.'

'Good morning, sir,' said the cashier, and watched the stranger curiously as he left the bank premises.

He would have looked at him even more curiously had he known that that insignificant exterior concealed the identity of the Jockey.

15

The Man Who Passed By

Mr. Budd looked sleepily at the angry, almost incoherent man before him and stifled a yawn.

'Now, now, sir,' he said soothingly, much as he might have spoken to an unruly child. 'It's no good losin' your temper. It's not my fault that you've been robbed of this money. You shouldn't have talked so much . . . '

'The scoundrel drugged me and locked me up in one of my own tool-sheds!' roared Sir Trevor Bleck, his thin face red with rage. 'He tied me up and forced me to sign a letter and a cheque . . . '

'Yes, yes! You've told me all that before,' sighed the Rosebud wearily. 'Did you have your cheque-book on you?'

'No!' snarled the baronet. 'The villain had a cheque form with him.'

'And while you were still tied up in the

tool-shed,' murmured the stout superintendent, stroking the lowest of his battery of chins, 'he cashed the cheque and cleared off with the money. H'm! Of course, armed with your letter of authority it was a walk-over.'

'I might have been in that damned shed yet,' stormed Bleck, 'if I hadn't managed to get my mouth free of the gag and attract the attention of one of the gardeners. The place is right away from the house and never used . . . '

'Of course, he knew that.' There was a touch of admiration in Mr. Budd's voice that annoyed his hearer. 'Clever!'

'Damn his cleverness!' cried Sir Trevor furiously. 'He's got ten thousand pounds of my money and I rely on you to get it back!'

Mr. Budd raised his eyebrows slightly.

'We'll do our best,' he replied, 'but we can't do miracles, sir. The money was drawn in tens, you say?'

'Yes!' snapped Bleck.

'Then the bank will have the numbers, and we may be able to trace them,' said Mr. Budd, but there was not much hope in his voice, and his pessimism was, to a certain extent, justified.

During the next few days the greater part of the money which the Jockey had filched from Sir Trevor Bleck's account drifted back to the bank, but it was paid in mostly by bookmakers and had been passed on various race courses, so as a clue to the identity of the man who had stolen it, it was useless.

The newspapers got hold of the story and made much of it, with the result that for a long time afterwards Sir Trevor Bleck had to submit to the chaff and ridicule of his friends and acquaintances. But he appeared to have accepted the situation more or less philosophically.

'I'll get even with that fellow one day!' he asserted. 'No one's yet got the better of me without being sorry for it!' There was a look on his face and an expression in his cold eyes that convinced his hearers that he meant what he said.

Mr. Benjamin Cowan, who knew him rather well, succeeded in obtaining a copy of the numbers of the stolen notes on the pretext that some of them might come through Paddocks, and this he took round to Marius Crabthorne.

'It may help you,' he said, and the inquiry agent, whose efforts to discover anything concerning the Jockey had so far met with failure, received the suggestion much as a drowning man might have clutched at the rotting branch of a tree that offered possible salvation.

'I'm leaving London for two or three days to-morrow,' said the bookmaker, 'and if you want to get in touch with me my address will be 'Downlands, Ditchling'. I'm staying with Colonel Westmore for the Brighton races.'

Mr. Crabthorne made a note of the address and his client took his departure.

Pamela Westmore had received Iris Cowan's effusive letter accepting her invitation with mixed feelings, for she loathed both the stout bookmaker and his daughter.

'The Cowans come down to-morrow,' she said, coming into the long library at Downlands where her father was reading.

'Do they, my dear?' The elder man looked up from his book. 'By Jove, so they

143

do!' He sighed, and then brightened a little. 'Well, they'll only be here for two or three days, anyway, so we'll have to make the best of it.'

'Why should we have to make the best of it?' demanded the girl frowning and nibbling at her thumb. 'Why do we have to invite them at all? You know you don't like Mr. Cowan, and I hate that over-dressed daughter of his. Why do we have to ask them here?'

'Policy, my dear,' answered the colonel. 'I don't want them here any more than you do, but — well, I'm under a certain obligation to Cowan and I suppose in the circumstances one has to hold the candle to the — er — devil.'

Pamela's frown deepened. She was well aware of the obligation he referred to, for it was one of the darkest shadows that overhung that pleasant house nestling at the foot of the Sussex downs. Like the majority of his type Westmore was a bad business man. Some years ago a friend of his, little better versed in the intricacies of business than himself, had, in all good faith, recommended what he fondly imagined was a sound speculation. A new goldfield had been discovered and an imposing company floated. The experts' reports were encouraging and the shares soared. Westmore had raked together every available penny and invested it in the concern, and then the mine had petered out and the shares had dropped to practically nothing. The company went into liquidation and the colonel found himself faced with ruin. It was Benjamin Cowan who had come to his assistance. A keen follower of racing, Westmore had met the bookmaker at a sporting club. Cowan had considered the old man rather a bore, and was not particularly interested in him until one day at Newmarket he had been introduced to Pamela, and then his outlook changed.

A man in whose life women had played no very large part he had conceived for the girl a passion which was frightening in its intensity. This is not an uncommon occurrence in men of Cowan's age, and from the moment that he first set eyes on Pamela Westmore she had filled his thoughts almost to the exclusion of anything else. He sensed her dislike of him from the beginning, and knew that in the ordinary course of events he stood no chance whatever of gratifying his desires. But this had only served to intensify his determination to win her. The fact that she was engaged to Norman Wharton was no deterrent in his eyes.

Systematically he set to work to eliminate the man who stood in the way of his objective, and the conspiracy which had resulted in Wharton's suicide was conceived and carried out entirely with that end in view.

With Westmore more or less under his thumb, for he held a mortgage on Downlands and had advanced the colonel a sum of money which it was next to impossible the old man could ever repay, and Wharton out of the way, Cowan had high hopes of gratifying his aspirations. But he was too clever a man to precipitate matters. No word had passed his lips that might suggest to Pamela the state of his feelings. He treated her politely and courteously, ignoring the dislike which she scarcely made an effort to conceal. In some extraordinary way the knowledge that she hated him added to his desire. One day, when he had achieved his object, he would break her spirit; would force those cool, contemptuous eyes, the expression which made him writhe inwardly, to look upon him in a different manner.

But although he had said nothing Pamela had guessed what was passing in his mind; knew exactly the reason why he took so much trouble to engineer these invitations and on every conceivable excuse sought her company. And the knowledge not only annoyed but frightened her, for beneath the bookmaker's rather flabby exterior she sensed the ruthlessness of his nature, and was under no delusions concerning the difficulty of escaping from any snare which this man might set.

Although she had not actually been in love with Norman Wharton, the two had grown up together, and their eventual marriage had been more or less looked upon as a foregone conclusion. She had liked him intensely and his tragic death had left a blank in her life which no one else could fill. She had never believed that he had been guilty of the charge brought against him by the stewards of the Jockey Club. Her natural intuition had told her that the evidence had been faked by Cowan, and the reason why, and from that moment her dislike of the man had turned to hatred and loathing. She found difficulty in even being civil to him; would have refused to allow him past the doorway but for the trouble she knew it would bring upon her father. And this loathing extended to Iris. That exotic creature, with her drawling voice and languid, affected manner, got on her nerves to such an extent that more than once she could have screamed. That Iris returned her dislike she knew. The girl hated her for the breeding which she herself did not possess, the easiness of manner which came natural to Pamela, but which she had had to acquire and had not been altogether successful.

'I wish we'd asked some other people as well,' said Westmore thoughtfully, 'it would have relieved the strain a little, what?'

Pamela shrugged her shoulders.

'It might have been a good idea,' she admitted. 'Anyway, we shan't be in much, that's one consolation.'

'No,' murmured her father. 'And Cowan will be returning to Town after the two days' racing. Have you seen anything more of that reporter fellow?'

The girl shook her head.

'No,' she answered, 'though Cresset tells me he's staying in the village.'

The colonel raised his eyebrows.

'Staying in the village, is he?' he remarked. 'How did Cresset know?'

'He tried to get into conversation with Cresset at the Ditchling Arms,' replied Pamela. 'Not, so far as I can gather, with much success.'

Westmore's thin lips twisted into a faint smile. The elderly and dignified butler was not the type of man with whom anyone would find it easy to strike up a promiscuous acquaintance.

'I wonder what he's staying for?' he muttered, but the girl could offer no explanation.

Richard Templeton had called to see

her some days back and put several questions concerning her discovery of the dead body of the little tout, but since then she had seen nothing of him.

The questions had struck her as being rather feeble and irrelevant, as indeed they were, for Dick had merely utilised them as an excuse for making the girl's acquaintance. And the object of making that acquaintance had been achieved. Pamela Westmore certainly did *not* habitually use Jockey Club, or at any rate she had not been using it that morning, for the perfume that clung to her was of a more subtle and delicate fragrance.

Westmore saw the worried little frown between her eyes that his reference to the reporter had engendered and wondered at its cause. But he said nothing, and would have received an evasive reply if he had, for the secret which Pamela Westmore kept locked in her breast was known to only one other person, and it was the knowledge of this secret that caused her uneasiness at the presence of the reporter in the neighbourhood. It was impossible that he could suspect anything. It was only her conscience that prompted her fear.

She tried to reassure herself with this argument, but the doubt lingered and gave her a certain amount of disquiet. Nobody had questioned her explanation concerning the reason for her visit to Corbett that dreadful morning when she had discovered the dead man by the hedge. They had apparently accepted the story which she had made up on the spur of the moment about the two horses which the trainer had offered for sale. If they had questioned her or if the matter had come to the ears of her father — She shivered a little! It would have been awkward, more than awkward, for she dared not tell the truth.

Cresset, a plump, dignified man with a bald head, brought in tea and she put her fears and misgivings out of her mind and busied herself with the tea-things. Whatever danger there might be was remote at present, and it was foolish to meet trouble half-way.

She had some letters to write that evening, and after tea went up to her own pleasant little sitting-room leaving her father to continue his book. This was her favourite apartment and she sometimes spent hours sitting at the window looking out across the garden to the miles of undulating country that spread before her. Life at Downlands was very quiet, and a girl less fond of the country than Pamela would have found it dull. But she loved the old house in which she had been born, loved its weather-beaten bricks, its clinging ivy, its broad lawns and brightly-coloured borders, and found plenty to occupy her time.

She finished her correspondence. One letter was a little difficult and took some time, and she was standing by the window and looking out at the long shadows cast by the setting sun when she saw something moving slowly across the distant meadow. On a table near her was a pair of race glasses, and taking them from their leather case she put them to her eyes and adjusted them until the moving object showed up sharp and clear. It was a man, and a stranger.

She watched him idly until he was lost

to view behind a belt of trees, and then, putting away the glasses, she set about preparing for the visitors who would arrive on the morrow.

The Jockey passed on his way, enjoying to the full the pleasures of the summer evening, and completely unaware that he had been seen by the girl who, at that moment, was occupying his thoughts. Not that he would have been in the least disturbed if he had known, for there was nothing to connect the respectable gentleman who strolled leisurely across the downs with the mysterious, spectacular individual to whom the newspapers had given so much prominence.

16

Mr. Cowan Shows his Teeth

Mr. Cowan and his daughter arrived at eleven o'clock on the following morning in a large and opulent Rolls, and Pamela, as she received them, thought that Cowan had never looked so unprepossessing. Never a very healthy-looking man, he now had the appearance of someone who was in the grip of a wasting disease. His usually sallow face was grey; heavy pouches hung beneath his dull eyes, and the skin around his chin and mouth hung loosely. Iris, on the other hand, was radiant. Her undoubted prettiness was accentuated by the expensive frock she wore, and Pamela, as she replied to the girl's effusive greeting, thought she looked more attractive than she had ever seen her.

'It's so nice to get away from all the noise and rush of London,' said Iris in her cultivated drawl. 'Really, I envy you people who live in the country, so peaceful and quiet.' Since there was nothing to prevent Iris living in the country if she wanted to, Pamela made no reply. 'I'm looking forward to the racing so much,' went on the girl. 'It should be perfect in this weather.'

'The going 'ull be a little hard,' grunted Cowan. 'A couple of days' rain would have done all the good in the world.' His eyes as they watched Pamela lost something of their fishlike dullness.

Cresset took them to their rooms, and when Cowan came down there was no sign of Pamela although he searched for her everywhere. She did not put in an appearance again until lunch-time, excusing herself on a plea that she had had certain household duties to attend to.

The conversation during the meal was confined almost strictly to the prospect of the two days' racing, but when it was over Cowan drew Westmore aside.

'I'd like a word with you in private,' he said.

The colonel sighed resignedly.

'Come into the library then,' he muttered, and led the way into the big, book-lined room.

The bookmaker seemed a little ill at ease, and Westmore wondered at the reason. He made no effort, however, to give his guest an opening, and Cowan had to search round for the best means of approaching the subject which was nearest to his heart.

'I want to have a talk with you about — about that loan,' he began at last. 'It's an unpleasant subject, and I wouldn't bring it up only — well, I've had some rather serious losses lately and I've got to find a large sum of money immediately.'

The old man's eyes clouded.

'I'm afraid I — I can't do anything about it at the moment,' he said. 'You know how I'm situated, Cowan. Money's the very devil.'

'Yes, I know.' Cowan's voice was sympathetic. 'I was just wondering if we couldn't come to some arrangement, that's all.'

'What arrangement?' asked Westmore.

The bookmaker cleared his throat.

'Well, I'll be quite candid with you,' he said. 'You know that as a security for the money I advanced, you gave me a mortgage on this estate?'

The colonel nodded.

'Well,' continued Cowan nibbling at the end of his thumb, 'circumstances have forced me to transfer that mortgage to a man to whom I owe a lot of money. It was the only security I had to offer and I had to do it. Unfortunately, since I have been unable to meet my obligations, he threatens to foreclose.'

'I see.' Strive as he might Westmore could not keep the dismay from his voice. If Cowan was speaking the truth, and he had no reason to doubt it, the position was a serious one. The sum the bookmaker had advanced was beyond anything that he could hope to raise, and unless it was paid off, this man who held the mortgage would foreclose, and that would mean the loss of the house which he loved.

'Can't you see this fellow,' he suggested, 'and come to some arrangement? If I have any luck to-morrow I may be able to settle up part of the money . . . '

'I've already seen him,' said Cowan untruthfully, for the man he had mentioned existed only in his own imagination, 'and I think that the matter could be settled amicably if — ' He paused.

'If what?' asked Westmore.

Cowan avoided his eyes.

'I have certain securities,' he said, speaking slowly and distinctly. 'By selling them at a considerable loss I could, at a pinch, raise sufficient money to settle this matter. But you realise that there is no reason why I should do this unless — well, unless it was worth my while.'

'I don't quite understand you,' said Westmore.

'Let me put it more plainly.' The bookmaker spoke rapidly, as though anxious to get an unpleasant matter settled as quickly as possible. 'It would certainly cripple me to meet this mortgage, but I am prepared to do it — for your daughter's sake.'

Westmore looked up sharply and his eyes hardened a little.

'I have a great admiration for her,' went on Cowan, before he could speak. 'I think you are aware of that, I think she is aware of it also. One of my greatest ambitions is to make her my wife.'

'Have you mentioned this — this ambition to her?' inquired Westmore coldly.

The bookmaker shook his head.

'No, I have said nothing yet,' he answered.

'Then, don't you think,' said the colonel, 'that, since the matter chiefly concerns her, it would be better if you approached her first?'

'There are reasons why I have not,' said Cowan. 'I may be wrong, but I am under the impression that Pamela dislikes me.' He waited for a denial of this statement, but receiving none he continued: 'She is under the impression, I think, that I was responsible for — for the disgrace of young Wharton, whereas, as a matter of fact, I only did my duty.'

'Is it necessary to discuss that?' said Westmore. 'If Pamela dislikes you there's an end of the matter.'

'Not entirely,' said Cowan. 'I suppose you have some influence with her?'

The other's thin lips tightened.

'Do you suggest,' he asked, 'that I should use my influence to force my daughter to marry you against her will?'

'No, no!' Cowan waved aside the suggestion instantly. 'But I thought you might prepare her — suggest to her what an advantage it would be. I know I'm older than she is, but at the same time it is not always the young men who make the best husbands. I don't wish to be in any way offensive, and you'll realise it's a difficult matter to speak about, but should anything happen to you Pamela will be more or less destitute. You are practically penniless. Beyond this house, which is mortgaged up to the hilt, you have very little to leave her. Surely it would be a relief to your mind to know that she was provided for — that she could continue to live in the manner to which she had been accustomed.'

'Let us speak plainly,' said Westmore, and there was an edge to his voice which Cowan did not like. 'Your suggestion

160

amounts to this. That in return for bringing my influence to bear on my daughter, and more or less coercing her into a marriage with you, you are prepared to wipe out the loan between us and satisfy your friend's demands concerning this mortgage. Is that right?'

'That's right, though you've put it rather bluntly,' said Cowan.

'And if I don't?' queried Westmore.

The bookmaker shrugged his shoulders.

'Then I'm afraid,' he said, 'things will have to take their course. As I explained to you I am, for the moment, temporarily in need of a large sum of ready money. The amount you owe me would be sufficient to put me straight. Naturally, I couldn't sue my future father-in-law — '
He stopped, but his meaning was plain.

Westmore's forehead wrinkled in a worried frown and he stroked his lean jaw.

'I'll speak to Pamela,' he said, 'but you must understand that I have no intention of attempting to force her to do anything against her will.'

'If you put it in the right way,' said Cowan, 'she'll realise the advantages of my offer. Anyway, talk to her.'

He left the older man and went in search of the girl who had been the subject of the conversation. He found her sitting beneath the cedar tree in the garden chatting to Iris, or rather listening while Iris did the chatting. She rose quickly as Cowan dropped into the chair by her side.

'Excuse me,' she said hurriedly, 'but I have some household accounts to attend to.'

She was gone before Cowan could make any rejoinder, walking swiftly towards the house with her long, graceful stride. The bookmaker scowled.

'Anybody 'ud think I'd got the plague!' he muttered.

His daughter's eyes danced with amusement.

'What else can you expect?' she asked. 'You're not exactly a romantic figure, are you? I tell you you're wasting your time bothering about that girl. She'll never have anything to do with you.'

'Won't she?' muttered Cowan. 'We'll see about that!'

Iris lifted a shapely shoulder.

'You're a fool!' she said bluntly. 'But I suppose you won't take advice.'

'When I want a thing,' said her father, 'I get it. And I'm going to get Pamela Westmore, remember that!' He got up and strode savagely across the close-cut grass towards a winding path that led through a mass of shrubbery.

The girl's open dislike of his society annoyed him, but at that moment he had other things to think about. She could safely be left until later. He had waited so long that a week, or a month for that matter, would make little difference. At the present moment he was chiefly concerned with his arrangements for the morrow. For he had discovered the solution to at least two of his more pressing problems: the elimination of the blackmailing Wills and the acquiring of the ready money which was so necessary to his peace of mind. And both these desirable achievements could be accomplished at one stroke.

17

The Warning

It was immediately after breakfast that the telegram arrived, and Benjamin Cowan read it with a frowning brow, although its advent had been expected and, indeed, arranged for before he had left London.

'I'm terribly sorry,' he said, looking up at his host and hostess, 'but I shall have to go back to Town immediately. Some urgent business has cropped up which necessitates my personal attention.'

'Don't apologise,' said Westmore, and the tone of his voice was anything but complimentary. 'It's a pity, because you'll miss the first day's racing.'

'I'm afraid it can't be helped,' said the bookmaker. 'I shall be back later on this evening.'

Pamela said nothing. The prospect of being relieved of the company of this man was so pleasant that she could have blessed the sender of the telegram, whoever it was. Iris eyed her father suspiciously.

'You never said there was any likelihood of your being called back to Town,' she said sharply.

'I didn't know there was,' he answered. 'This is quite unexpected, I assure you. However, it won't affect you. I am sure you can manage to enjoy yourself without me.'

'You'd better leave me some money before you go,' said the girl. 'I've only got a couple of pounds, and that won't take me very far.'

'You see what it is to have a spendthrift daughter,' said Cowan heavily humorous as he took his wallet from his pocket and extracted three ten-pound notes. 'There you are, my dear, that'll see you through the day, and if you're clever you'll treble it by to-night.'

His car was brought round at eleven-thirty, and as Pamela watched the back of the big machine disappear down the drive a weight seemed to lift from her shoulders and she could have sung with joy.

They drove over to Brighton, reaching the course just before the first race. Although the meeting cannot be called one of the classical events of the Turf, it is certainly popular, as the multitudes who thronged the stands and enclosures testified. The actual racing track has been much improved in recent years and the new stands are exceedingly comfortable. To Pamela the noise and colour and excitement were a never-failing delight. She loved racing, and her eyes sparkled and her cheeks were flushed with excitement as she stood inside the entrance to Tattersall's and looked around her at the familiar scene. Iris was just as interested, but masked her emotions behind an expression of studied boredom.

'Look!' Pamela touched her father's arm. 'Isn't that the detective who came down about the murder?'

Westmore, who was studying his race card, glanced in the direction she indicated, and caught sight of a stout figure moving slowly through the crowd.

'Yes, I believe it is,' he answered. 'I wonder what he's doing here?'

'Even detectives must have some time to themselves,' said Pamela. 'Probably he's got a day off.'

Her conjecture was wrong, however, as Dick Templeton, who had also spotted the Rosebud, discovered when he greeted him.

'Hullo!' he said, coming up behind the big man. 'What are you doing here? Trailing pickpockets?'

Mr. Budd turned round and surveyed him with a sleepy eye.

'Oh, it's you!' he grunted. 'At the present moment I'm lookin' for my sergeant.'

'Is Leek here too?' asked Dick in surprise.

'He *was* here a minute or two ago,' answered the superintendent, looking round the crowded ring. 'The way that feller's never where you want him is surprisin'.'

'There he is,' said Dick, and pointed out the lean figure of Leek, who was talking to one of the bookmakers.

Mr. Budd grunted.

'I might have guessed that's where he'd

be,' he muttered. 'Wastin' his money gamblin'. D'you know anythin' for the first race?'

'High Jinks!' said Dick promptly. 'You can put your shirt on it! Come with me, I'm just going to back it myself.'

Mr. Budd followed him ponderously as he made his way over to the bookmakers' stands. Dick secured the odds of six to one and put on a pound each way.

'Going to back it?' he asked, as he received his check.

'Might as well.' The stout superintendent fumbled in his pocket and produced a crumpled pound note which he eyed doubtfully. 'You sure it's a good horse?'

'It's a certainty!' declared Dick optimistically, and even as he spoke the price came down to fives.

Mr. Budd invested his pound and turned away with a sigh, fingering the little ticket he had received in exchange.

'I suppose that's gone!' he growled. 'Racin's the quickest way of spendin' money I've ever come across.'

'Better come up on the stands,' said Dick. 'It's getting near the 'off'.'

The melancholy sergeant joined them as they walked back towards the stands.

'I didn't back anything,' he said mournfully, in reply to Mr. Budd's queston. 'I heard somebody in the crowd say that 'Igh Jinks was a good thing, but when I spoke to that there bookmaker he didn't seem to think much of the horse's chances.'

'H'm!' grunted the superintendent, and looked at Dick. 'There you are! If you've let me in for a quid I'll never forgive you.'

'High Jinks is the best thing in the race!' asserted Dick. 'Bar a miracle he'll pass the post first.'

Leek's long face lengthened.

'Perhaps I'd better have a bit on after all,' he said, and looked towards the line of bookmakers.

'You'll have to hurry up then,' said Dick. 'They're going to the tapes now.'

The sergeant drifted away as the horses engaged in the first race moved towards the starting gate.

'What are you doin', wastin' your time here?' said Mr. Budd, when they had elbowed their way through the crowd and

169

found a place on the stands.

'I'm here on business,' replied the reporter. 'I've got a hunch that the secret of the Jockey lies somewhere in the neighbourhood of Ditchling.'

The stout man glanced at him curiously.

'Maybe you're right,' he commented. 'I suppose by Ditchling you mean Pamela Westmore?'

Dick nodded.

'Yes,' he replied. 'She's here, so's her father and the daughter of that bookmaker fellow, Benjamin Cowan.'

'And so is somebody else!' remarked Mr. Budd, and following the direction of his eyes Dick saw a short, stocky man crossing the enclosure. 'Now I wonder what *he's* doin' here?'

'Who is it?' asked the reporter.

'Not a nice feller,' said Mr. Budd. 'A man called Crabthorne. He's a private detective now, but he used to be a crook — and still is as far as I know. He's been 'inside' once, and ought to be 'inside' now if all the rumours about him are true.'

Unaware of this slanderous statement

concerning his character, Mr. Marius Crabthorne elbowed his way through the crowds towards the stands, and he was not a little elated, for chance had put in his way a clue which he hoped would eventually lead him to the identity of the Jockey.

'He's a new one on me,' said Dick. 'By the way, what are you doing here, Budd?'

The Rosebud fingered his chin.

'I'm here,' he said slowly, 'because I got a letter from this Jockey feller.'

Dick's eyebrows shot up.

'You got a letter?' he said interestedly. 'What about?'

'It wasn't very informative,' replied the superintendent, and produced it from his breast pocket.

The reporter read the single line of typewritten characters:

'Watch Joe Wills. He's riding in the Balcombe Stakes at Brighton.
                    'The Jockey.'

Dick pursed his lips.
'What's the idea?' he inquired, but Mr.

Budd shook his head slowly.

'I dunno,' he answered. 'But I thought it was worth while followin' up. Remind me to tell you somethin' after this race.'

A bell clanged as he finished speaking and the old familiar roar welled up from the crowd.

'They're off!'

The cry was followed by the almost uncanny silence that told of thousands of people focusing their glasses on the field, of thousands doing their best to make out the varied colours with their naked eyes, all with the same object — to determine just how the horse that was carrying their money was faring.

The race was a five-furlong event and was over almost before it began. A flash of colours, a streak of grey, black and brown; the bunch of horses came flashing by, their jockeys crouching. High Jinks was a black horse and it was a grey which Leek saw drawing out from the bunch as he came up to where the reporter and Mr. Budd were standing.

'Saved me money,' he said with a note of satisfaction. 'I was too late to get it on.

Bit of luck for me. I didn't see High Jinks among that lot.'

'You wouldn't,' said Mr. Budd. 'It was ahead of 'em!'

'And won by six lengths!' put in Dick with satisfaction. 'As soon as the numbers go up we'll go and draw our winings, Budd.'

The sergeant's melancholy face was expressive of his disappointment.

'Well, what d'you think of that!' he grumbled lugubriously.

'Never mind,' said Dick cheerfully. 'Put all you've got on Blonde Baby in the Balcombe Stakes and you'll go home a richer man than you came.'

He hurried away with the stout superintendent to collect their winnings, and as they turned away after being paid out they saw Westmore and his daughter talking to a slim man with glasses.

'Who's that?' asked Mr. Budd.

'A fellow called Pyecroft,' answered Dick. 'He's the Secretary of the Jockey Club. There's Sir Godfrey Latimer over there, one of the stewards.'

The superintendent's sleepy eyes turned

towards the immaculately dressed, cynical-faced man whom Dick indicated.

'H'm!' he said. 'Remember I told you to remind me about somethin' after the race?'

Dick nodded.

'Well, this is it,' said Mr. Budd. 'Remember the Wharton business, that feller who was warned off and shot himself — ?'

'Yes?' Dick looked at him questioningly. 'I remember, it happened a year ago. What about it?'

'This,' said the stout man. 'Corbett was mixed up in that business and he's dead. Joe Wills was mixed up in it, and I've got this letter in my pocket from the Jockey tellin' me to watch him. That girl Westmore was engaged to Wharton, and somehow or other she's mixed up with the Jockey. Funny, isn't it?'

18

The Balcombe Stakes

The reporter's eyebrows almost met in the concentration of his frown.

'What are you gettin' at?' he demanded.

'I'm not gettin' at anythin',' said Mr. Budd. 'I'm only mentionin' things that strike me as queer. I'll tell you what I think,' he continued. 'It won't take long. I think that if we knew more about that Wharton business we'd know more about the Jockey.'

'Oh!' breathed Dick. 'What makes you think that?'

'Just an idea,' said Mr. Budd. 'A hunch I suppose you'd call it. I get 'em now and again, and more often than not they're right.'

'It's worth looking into,' said the reporter.

'I'm lookin' into it,' said the Rosebud.

'What about this next race? If you've got any more suggestions like High Jinks let's hear 'em.'

'I've nothing good until the Balcombe Stakes,' said Dick. 'But if you want to gamble you might put a bit each way on Abbot's Slipper in the next race.'

Mr. Budd shook his head.

'I don't gamble,' he said, 'I only bet on certainties. What's this Blonde Baby you're talkin' about?'

'She's a four-year-old, owned by Orfford and trained by Winters,' said Dick. 'Why don't you look at your card? What d'you think they print it for?'

Mr. Budd consulted his programme.

'Ah, yes, here she is,' he said, and his lips pursed in a low whistle. 'Joe Wills is ridin' her.'

'And she'll win,' said Dick. 'Unless he tries some of his crooked business. There's nothing to beat Blonde Baby at the weight unless it's Shy Lad, and I think the other horse is better at the distance. It's a mile and two furlongs race, and Blonde Baby's got more stamina.'

Mr. Budd eyed him admiringly.

'It's surprisin',' he murmured, 'what a lot you know about racin'. I think I'll keep my money for Blonde Baby.'

The next race was a Selling Plate, and was won by the favourite. Dick and the superintendent had backed nothing, but Sergeant Leek, who had secured two to one, was as jubilant as his melancholy nature would allow. He was so pleased with himself that he almost smiled.

The big event of the day was imminent and the increasing excitement among the crowd became infectious. Dick and his two companions strolled into the paddock and watched the Parade.

'There's Blonde Baby,' said the reporter, pointing out the big bay mare, 'and that black horse is Shy Lad, the grey is Sky Sign.' He went through the card, naming the fourteen horses entered for the race.

From the cheaper enclosure the voices of the bookmakers blended in a blatant and never-ceasing roar, for the betting was fast and furious. Five minutes before the race Blonde Baby was so hot a favourite as to be almost unbackable. At five to four and evens she did not appeal to the bulk of the punters and the majority were putting their money on Shy Lad. From seven to one he was backed down to fours. Other runners, Sky Sign, Noble Duke, Lonely Boy and even the greatest long shot in the race, Apple Chutney, were coming in for a great deal of attention.

The horses were being saddled when the reporter, the stout superintendent and the lean sergeant went back to the stands. Mr. Budd watched the scene interestedly. One of the men employed by the bookmakers to keep them posted at the earliest possible moment as to what was going to the gate for the various races came hurrying through the crowd.

'One, two, four, six down to eleven and fourteen!' he shouted.

'What's he mean?' murmured the stout superintendent.

'Runners!' answered Dick shortly.

A man in the enclosure took from his pocket a folded wad of oblong strips of paper, telegrams. The stout detective saw them transferred to a companion, who hurried away and was lost in the crowd.

'Those wires are being sent off at the last moment,' said Dick, 'so that even if some are received at the starting price offices before the next race there will be no time to get the money back to the course and spoil the price.'

'I see,' murmured Mr. Budd, though he only had the vaguest idea of what the reporter meant.

'Here they come!' said Dick suddenly, and focused his glasses on the course as the horses began to move slowly towards the mile and two furlongs starting gate. He picked out the royal blue with scarlet sleeves and cap worn by Joe Wills on Blonde Baby and near to him the orange and black colours of Shy Lad. The horse was being ridden by Johns, a jockey who had something of a reputation for bringing off close and sensational finishes.

It seemed an age to the waiting crowd before the string of horses reached the curve and took their places behind the tapes. The bookmakers were still shouting hoarsely, taking last-minute bets, and the subdued murmur which is one of the characteristics of a racing crowd before the start and is the prelude to the roar which marks the 'off' formed a background oddly like the beating of countless drums.

The horses drew into a straight line. Shy Lad was restive, apparently living up to his name. A hush fell suddenly as the thousands of watching eyes became fixed, waiting expectantly for the flag to drop and the field to get off. But at the last moment, when the starter had almost got the horses in line, Shy Lad once more whipped round.

'Are they never goin' to start?' asked Mr. Budd.

'It's Johns' mount that is causing the delay,' muttered Dick. 'They're quiet now.' His glasses were levelled unwaveringly at the line of colour behind the tapes. 'They're in line. Yes. They're off!'

His last words were caught up and repeated by thousands of eager racegoers, but it was a false start, for no bell confirmed it. Once again Shy Lad had proved fractious. Again the horses lined up at the tapes, Shy Lad still rearing and plunging, but Johns got him quiet. The flag dropped, the tapes flew up, and the bell clanged.

'They're off!'

This time the combined roar was like a peal of thunder, and its volume enhanced the temporary silence of doubt and uncertainty that followed.

The bunched mass of horses came thundering round the curve in front of the starting gate.

'Who's leadin'?' demanded Mr. Budd. 'I can't make out these colours, they all look alike to me.'

'Apple Chutney's got off in front and is leading the field,' said Dick. 'Whether he'll keep his position is another matter.' He could see now the emerald green and white of Apple Chutney's jockey showing a clear four lengths in the lead, the other horses so far in a close group behind him.

Approaching the bend that led into the straight, Noble Duke drew out and challenged. Joe Wills, crouching low on Blonde Baby, was lying behind Sky Sign, with Shy Lad a length in the rear. For a moment Dick's glasses rested on him. He saw that Johns was nursing the horse, and that he looked to have an immensity of reserve speed in hand. Blonde Baby, hugging the rails, drew level with Apple Chutney and passed him.

The crowd roared their encouragement. They turned into the straight, and seizing his opportunity Johns brought Shy Lad out towards the centre of the course. The black horse passed Sky Sign, and slowly but surely decreased the distance between it and Blonde Baby. Apple Chutney was still going strongly, but Dick was of the opinion that the rise before the post would prove too much for him.

Noble Duke had dropped behind. The spurt which he had put on and gained second position had only been temporary. The jockey was using his whip, but the horse had no reserve with which to respond.

'It's Blonde Baby's race!' said Dick. 'Blonde Baby wins!'

The big bay was in front now, with Shy Lad five lengths behind. Apple Chutney obviously hadn't the staying power to stay the distance. Johns was crouching over

Shy Lad's neck and the black horse was creeping nearer to Blonde Baby with every stride.

They were at the downhill stretch now and approaching the rise to the post.

'It'll be a close race,' said Dick, 'but Blonde Baby 'ull do it! Blonde Baby!'

'Shy Lad!' shouted the crowd. 'Come on Shy Lad!'

Joe Wills was still clinging to the rails, and he darted a glance over his shoulder. He saw Shy Lad coming up to his flank like an onrushing express train, and an ugly look crept into his eyes. Wills was a clever race cooker, and more than once had artistically 'pulled' a horse under the very eyes of the stewards and got away with it.

He did something of the sort now. It was just the merest tug on his off-side rein, a jerk that hurt Blonde Baby's sensitive mouth. The horse threw up its head irritably. In a flash it was sprawling out from the rails and swerving clean into the course of Shy Lad. Johns was compelled to swerve out in his turn and lost ground by doing so.

It was between Blonde Baby and Shy Lad now, the field was nowhere. Apple Chutney had shot his bolt and was becoming a very tired horse indeed.

'Blonde Baby!'

From all directions the roar rose confidently.

'The favourite wins! He's walked away with it!'

'I think he has,' breathed Dick excitedly and then: 'No, no, look! Here comes Shy Lad! By Jove, what a horse!'

Foot by foot Johns was making up the lost ground, and then Wills, for the first time, used the whip. A slight flick and Blonde Baby seemed to streak through the air. The two lengths that separated him from Shy Lad increased to three to four.

'Blonde Baby!' shouted the crowd hysterically. 'Blonde Baby wins!'

And then it happened.

Joe Wills gave a sudden convulsive start and seemed to collapse limply on his mount's outstretched neck. The next second he had rolled from his saddle, was carried along the ground, one foot caught in the stirrups for five or six yards, and then left, a motionless heap, his blue and scarlet jacket making a patch of colour on the emerald grass, while the riderless horse passed the post five lengths in front of his black rival, Shy Lad.

19

The Silent Death

The excited roar from the multitude of spectators rose to a deafening clamour as they saw what had happened, and then became suddenly hushed only to break out again in a dull murmur of sound. In that moment of almost complete silence the rest of the field thundered past the motionless figure of the fallen jockey, the flying hooves of the horses missing him by inches. An attendant near the Judge's box skilfully caught Blonde Baby by her trailing bridle and as he brought the big horse to a standstill there was a concerted rush from the stands to the rails.

Mr. Budd, Dick and the lean sergeant were in the van of the chattering crowd, maintaining this position only by sheer physical force. By the time they reached the rails a squad of uniformed police were engaged in keeping the curious throng back and several more were grouped round Joe Wills. Mr. Budd ducked under the rails and was stopped by a burly constable.

'It's all right,' gasped the stout superintendent, panting from his exertion, 'take me to your inspector.'

The man hesitated, and impatiently Mr. Budd dragged his warrant card from his pocket and thrust it under the constable's nose.

'That'll show my authority!' he grunted, and as Sergeant Leek and Dick joined him: 'These people are with me.'

'Sorry, sir,' muttered the constable. 'There's the inspector, over there.' He pointed to the group by the huddled figure of the jockey, and Mr. Budd went over. 'What's the trouble?' he asked. 'A heart attack or somethin'?'

The uniformed official looked at him suspiciously.

'Who — ' he began, but before he could finish the question Mr. Budd produced his warrant card again and the other's manner changed. 'Thought you was just one of the crowd, sir,' he said apologetically, touching his hat. 'No, I don't think it was a heart attack. Look here!'

Mr. Budd looked and pursed his lips. Joe Wills lay face downwards and on the grass near his head was a crimson patch.

'Blood!' muttered the big man.

The inspector nodded.

'I've sent for a doctor and the ambulance,' he remarked.

'You're not suggesting,' put in Dick, 'that it wasn't an accident?'

Mr. Budd eyed him, and there was a queer look on his face.

'Remember that note I got?' he asked.

The reporter started. For the moment he had forgotten the message that the superintendent had received from the Jockey: 'Watch Joe Wills. He's riding in the Balcombe Stakes at Brighton.'

Was this the reason why it had been sent? Had this sinister and mysterious individual who signed himself 'The Jockey' known when he had sent this message what was going to happen? Was it possible that he could have been responsible —

Mr. Budd, watching Dick's face, guessed what was passing in his mind.

'Curious, isn't it?' he said. ' 'Watch Joe Wills', and this is what has happened.'

He turned away before Dick could speak and bent over the pathetically small figure of the jockey. Lifting the head he stared at the tiny hole in the right temple from which the blood had trickled sluggishly.

'Shot!' he breathed incredulously.

The uniformed inspector's expression was one of unfeigned astonishment.

'Shot?' he echoed. 'Impossible! There was no report — '

'All the same he was shot!' said Mr. Budd with conviction. 'That's a bullet hole, 'an there's no gettin' away from it.' He let the limp head fall back to its original position and straightened up. 'The right temple,' he said thoughtfully. 'That means that the person who shot him was somewhere in the crowd over by the rails.' He nodded towards the sea of curious faces that thronged the cheap enclosure. 'H'm! Interestin' and peculiar. I don't remember in the whole of my experience a similar thing happenin'.'

'It's never happened before,' said Dick, and the excitement in his voice was audible, for already he was visualising the startling headlines that would herald his account of the crime in the *Sphere*. 'It's unique!'

'What d'you think they'll do about the race?' put in the lugubrious voice of Leek.

'They'll either declare it void,' said Dick, 'or award it to Shy Lad. The fact that Blonde Baby passed the post riderless disqualifies her.'

The sergeant's melancholy face brightened.

'I 'ad a quid each way on Shy Lad,' he murmured with a note of satisfaction, 'at seven to one.'

'You'll be able to retire,' grunted Mr. Budd, 'and live on your ill-gotten gains.' He turned as the stewards of the Brighton meeting, accompanied by Sir Godfrey Latimer and the thin-faced secretary, Pyecroft, came up to them.

'What happened? What was it?' inquired Major Wright. 'Did the man have a heart attack or something?' He addressed his question to the inspector, his eyes roving quickly over the others.

'No, sir. He was shot!' answered the uniformed man.

The steward's eyebrows went up.

'Shot!' he snapped. 'Nonsense, how could he have been shot?'

'It's true, all the same,' put in Mr. Budd. 'The doctor 'ull bear out what the inspector says when he arrives.'

'Who are you, sir?' demanded the major, a stoutish, red-faced man.

'I am a superintendent of the C.I.D.,' answered the Rosebud, yawning, and at that moment the doctor and the ambulance arrived.

A brief examination confirmed the fact that Joe Wills had been shot. He had been shot through the right temple, the bullet lodging in his brain, and the doctor affirmed that he had been dead before he touched the ground.

'I know it sounds incredible,' he said to the amazed stewards, 'but it happened all the same.'

'But there was no sound!' protested Sir Dennis Croft, another of the Brighton stewards. 'There would have been a report, and we should have heard it.'

'Maybe,' said the inspector, 'the shouts of the crowd drowned it.'

Mr. Budd disagreed with this suggestion.

'They wouldn't!' he declared. 'If there had been a report it would have been heard. I should have heard it, and I heard nothin'!'

'It's absurd, man,' muttered Major Wright. 'You can't shoot a man without a report — '

'Were you in the War, sir?' asked Mr. Budd sleepily.

'Yes! Of course I was!' snapped the major. 'What's that got to do with it?'

'There was a type of German air-pistol used on certain fronts durin' night raids,' went on Mr. Budd dreamily, 'called a Deloraine. It wasn't much good and was eventually given up because it was ineffective beyond a range which the German authorities thought was too short.'

'Are you suggesting, Superintendent,' put in Sir Godfrey Latimer quietly, 'that this fellow was shot with an air-pistol?'

'Yes, sir,' said Mr. Budd nodding, 'and I'm only suggestin' it remember. I'm not sayin' it's a fact.'

'The man who fired it must have been a remarkably good shot,' said Pyecroft, peering at them through his glasses. 'It would have been difficult enough if Wills had been a still target but he was on the horse — '

'Yes, you're right,' declared Croft. 'A remarkable shot.'

'But not impossible,' said Mr. Budd. 'There's half a dozen men at the Yard I know personally whose shooting's sufficiently good to have done it.'

'Well,' Major Wright frowned and consulted his watch, 'we'd better get him off the course. It's getting near the time for the next race.'

'There's no reason why he shouldn't be moved,' murmured Mr. Budd, and at a signal from the inspector the ambulance men came forward, and picking up all that remained of Joe Wills laid him on the wheeled conveyance they had brought with them.

'What are you going to do about the Balcombe Stakes?' asked Latimer. 'Declare the race void?'

The Brighton stewards consulted hurriedly.

'I don't think so,' said Major Wright. 'No, let it stand. Award the race to Shy Lad.'

Johns and the other jockeys had already gone to weigh in, passing the group with curious eyes, and some seconds later the numbers went up and the gratified people who had backed the black horse went to collect their money.

The bookies were already shouting the odds for the next race when Mr. Budd, accompanied by his two companions, followed the stewards to their room behind the stands.

'If it had to be anybody,' said Latimer, when they entered the oblong apartment, 'I'm glad it was Wills. He was a good jockey, but he didn't bear a very enviable reputation. Half a dozen times he's been on the verge of being 'warned off'.'

'It's a nasty thing to have happened, whoever it was,' grunted Major Wright.

'It's going to be pretty difficult to catch the fellow who did it I should think.'

Mr. Budd thought so too, but he kept the thought to himself. It was not his job to go after the murderer of Joe Wills. That was the duty of the Brighton police. The only interest he had in the murder was what connection, if any, the Jockey had with the crime. He produced the letter he had received from that mysterious individual and caused something of a sensation.

'B'Gad!' exclaimed Major Wright. 'D'you think he's the fellow who did this?'

'I don't think anythin',' said Mr. Budd carefully.

'It's hardly likely, surely,' said Sir Godfrey Latimer. 'If he was coming to commit murder he'd scarcely warn Scotland Yard of the fact.'

'You can't tell what a fellow like that 'ud do,' growled Croft. 'Look at that interview he gave to the *Sphere*. The man's crazy, anyway, and you can't predict what a crazy man 'ull do.'

'Whoever killed Wills, sir,' said the

inspector, 'must have been among the crowd at the rails. My men are questioning the people who were in the neighbourhood of the place from which the shot must have been fired to see if anyone noticed anything.'

There was a tap at the door and a sergeant came in.

'What is it, Berry?' asked the inspector. 'Any fresh information?'

The sergeant shook his head.

'Nothing about the shooting, sir,' he answered, 'but we've caught a 'wizzer', Harry Dew, a little dip we've had our eye on for some time. Caught him in the act! I've got him outside, would you like to see him?'

'Yes, bring him in,' said the inspector, and murmured an apology to the stewards as the sergeant departed.

Two constables came in escorting a small, frail-looking man with a thin, unhealthy face and delicate-looking hands.

'Now then,' said the inspector, 'what have you got to say for yourself?'

'It's all a mistake,' growled the prisoner

sullenly. 'A man had dropped his wallet and I was just going to return it to him when these 'flatties' pounced on me.'

'He had his hand in the man's pocket, sir,' volunteered one of the policemen.

'That's perjury!' exclaimed the little man. 'I never 'ad me 'and in 'is pocket. 'E'd dropped the wallet and I was just picking it up — '

'Your name's Harry Dew, isn't it?' interrupted the inspector.

'And what if it is?' said Mr. Dew in an injured voice. 'I'm respectable, I am. Can't a feller come and 'ave a day at the races without bein' persecuted by the police? It's an outrage, that's what it is!'

The inspector smiled hardly.

'You're an outrage, Harry!' he said without animosity. 'You've got a record against you as long as my arm and you stand there and try and bluff it out. Have you searched him?'

The sergeant to whom the question was addressed nodded.

'Yes, sir,' he said. 'Three wallets, a couple of watches and a bundle of notes.' He produced the articles as he spoke and laid them on the table in front of his superior. The inspector glanced at them and then looked reproachfully at the prisoner.

'Looks as though you'd had a good day, Harry,' he remarked. 'Too bad!' He examined the wallets. 'George Brown,' he muttered, 'Merple Road, Lewes. Alfred Green, Station Street, Brighton. Benjamin Cowan, Park View Mansions, W.I. Well, it'll be easy to find the owners — '

'Benjamin Cowan!' ejaculated Sir Godfrey Latimer. 'That's the bookmaker, the fellow who runs Paddocks. That's rather curious.'

'Why is it curious, sir?' asked the inspector.

'This pickpocket was operating in the cheap enclosure,' explained Latimer. 'If Cowan was here at all, and I haven't seen him, he'd be in Tattersall's.'

Mr. Budd, who had apparently fallen asleep, suddenly opened his eyes very wide.

'This feller you're talkin' about, Mr. Cowan,' he murmured, 'wasn't he one of the witnesses in that Wharton scandal a year ago?'

Sir Godfrey Latimer's face clouded.

'One of the principal witnesses,' he replied.

'H'm!' said the fat superintendent. 'I thought so. Queer! And you haven't seen him here to-day?'

Latimer shook his head.

'He was called to town early this morning.' It was Pyecroft, the secretary, who spoke in his low pleasant voice. 'I was talking to Colonel Westmore and his daughter a few moments ago. Cowan is staying with them. He had a wire this morning calling him to Town on business.'

'Oh, he had a wire, did he?' Mr. Budd's eyes had nearly closed again, a sure sign that his brain was working rapidly. 'He had a wire. Most peculiar!'

'What's peculiar about it?' demanded Major Wright a little irritably. He was not at all impressed by the sleepy-eyed, lethargic man before him.

'There's this peculiar about it,' said the fat superintendent slowly. 'If Mr. Cowan went to London this morning and didn't attend the races how was this feller able to 'dip' him?'

'"Dip' him? What d'you mean, 'dip' him?' grunted the major.

'The superintendent means pick his pocket,' translated the inspector concealing a smile. '"Dip' is a slang term.'

'Oh!' Major Wright frowned. 'Yes, there's something in that. Perhaps he didn't go to Town after all.'

'In which case,' said Latimer, 'he'd have been in Tattersall's; he wouldn't have been in the cheap enclosure.'

'He isn't here at all, I'm sure,' put in Pyecroft. 'His daughter's here with the Westmores, but Mr. Cowan went to Town.'

'Well, here's a little problem,' said Mr. Budd thoughtfully. 'Mr. Cowan goes to Town and his pocket's picked on Brighton racecourse. Interestin' and peculiar!'

20

Sir Godfrey Latimer's Hat

'What's at the back of your mind?' asked Latimer curiously.

'A lot of things,' answered the stout superintendent. 'There's so many things at the back of my mind that they're all keepin' each other from comin' to the front. I suppose there's no doubt that that wallet is the property of Mr. Cowan?'

'None at all!' said the inspector. 'His name and address is stamped in gold on the inside flap.'

The big man stretched out a fat hand and picked up the leather notecase. It was an expensive affair of crocodile skin bound at the edges with gold. In an inner compartment were several ten pound notes, half a dozen pound notes, some cards and two letters. Mr. Budd examined the notes with close attention, sighed, put them back, and coolly extracted the letters from their envelopes. They were uninteresting. One was a bill from a wine merchant and the other an acceptance to an invitation to lunch from somebody who signed himself Geoffrey.

Mr. Budd closed the wallet and looked at the inspector.

'Can I borrow this?' he asked. 'I'd like to return it to its owner if you've no objection.'

'I don't think there's any objection,' said the inspector.

The stout superintendent thanked him.

'D'you remember where you got this?' he asked, addressing the silent and sullen-faced little pickpocket.

'I didn't get it anywhere,' declared Mr. Dew stubbornly. 'It's a frame-up, that's what it is! All these things were put in my pocket by the police themselves!'

'Now then, Dew!' warned the sergeant. 'Don't you go saying things like that. It won't do you any good.'

'The truth never did anyone any 'arm,' said Mr. Dew virtuously. 'You know as well as I do that I wouldn't pinch nothin'!'

'We'll see what the magistrate has to say to that,' broke in the inspector. 'Answer the superintendent's question!'

'I 'ave answered it,' said the little wizzer defiantly. 'I know nothin' about those clocks and the wallets, and the person what says I do is a liar!'

Patiently they tried to extract further information from him, but without result. Steadfastly he stuck to the fact that the police had framed him, and eventually Mr. Budd gave it up.

'They're all alike,' he said. 'You can't get anythin' out of 'em.'

Mr. Dew, still protesting his innocence, was forcibly removed, and the big man rose ponderously to his feet.

'I don't think I can be of much use to you,' he said wearily, 'but if you discover anythin' connected with the killin' of Wills I wish you'd let me know.'

The inspector promised, and, accompanied by the impatient Leek, Mr. Budd left the stewards' room.

'You won't be wanting me for a minute or two, will you?' asked the sergeant as they came out into the open air.

203

'I don't know what I have you with me at all for,' said Mr. Budd. 'You're no ornament and you're no good any other way. What's the idea? What d'you want to do now?'

'I thought I might collect my winnings on Shy Lad,' explained Leek. 'There's seven pounds due to me — '

'Go and get it,' said Mr. Budd, 'and then find the refreshment tent and drink yourself to death.'

The sergeant looked at him indignantly.

'I'm a teetotaller,' he said, 'you know that! Not a drop of intoxicating liquor has ever passed my lips!'

'They sell milk,' said Mr. Budd, and turned to greet Dick Templeton, whom he saw hurrying towards them after having telephoned the news of the tragedy to the offices of the *Daily Sphere*.

'Anything fresh?' asked the reporter.

Mr. Budd nodded.

'Yes,' he said. 'I'll tell you somethin' peculiar.'

Dick listened to his brief account of the arrest of Mr. Dew and the discovery of the wallet in his possession.

'Funny, isn't it?' concluded Mr. Budd. 'Here's a man in London who has his pocket picked in Brighton. It don't make sense.'

'Cowan must have been here,' said the reporter, and Mr. Budd sighed gently.

'Astoundin' discovery by well-known newspaper reporter!' he murmured. 'How you do it beats me! Of course Cowan was here, that's the only explanation. But he wasn't here as Cowan, otherwise he'd have been with his daughter and his friends at Tattersall's. And if he wasn't here as Cowan why was he here at all? Why did he want to pretend he'd been called back to London on business and then sneak into the cheap enclosure like a criminal?'

Dick, with a puzzled frown, remained silent.

'You can't tell me,' said Mr. Budd. 'I thought you couldn't. And I can't tell meself, but that's obviously what happened. Cowan wanted everybody to believe that he was in Town, when in reality he was here. I'd like to know what the object was. I'd also like to know somethin' else, who's this feller Sir Godfrey Latimer when he's at home?'

Dick looked at him startled.

'Sir Godfrey Latimer?' he echoed. 'He's one of the stewards of the Jockey Club.'

'What else is he?' asked the stout superintendent. 'What's he do for a livin'?'

'He doesn't do anything,' answered the reporter. 'He's a man of independent means.'

'Got a good reputation?' said Mr. Budd.

'The highest reputation!' said Dick. 'What are you getting at? What bee have you got in your bonnet now?'

'I don't wear a bonnet,' said the stout superintendent, 'and I know nothin' about bees. But I'll tell you what I'm getting at, and it's not for publication in that scurrilous rag of yours, understand that!' He paused and softly stroked his cascade of chins. 'When we was in the stewards' room' — he jerked his head in the direction of the building — 'this feller Latimer took off his hat. He took off his hat and he set it down on the table near where I was sittin'.' He paused again and Dick broke in impatiently:

'Well, what about it? Why shouldn't he take off his hat?'

'No reason at all,' said Mr. Budd slowly, 'only he uses some sort of dressin' for his hair, and the scent struck me as bein' familiar.'

The incredulous Dick stared at him.

'You don't mean — ' he began, and Mr. Budd nodded.

'Jockey Club,' he said; 'the same as on the black cap in Green's hand, same as on that girl.'

'Sir Godfrey Latimer!' breathed Dick. 'It's impossible! It must be a coincidence.'

'Maybe,' said Mr. Budd yawning, 'but it's interestin' and peculiar all the same.'

21

Mr. Cowan Gets a Shock

Mr. Benjamin Cowan got out of the taxi which had brought him to the entrance of the block of flats in which he lived, flung some coins to the driver, and, hurrying into the vestibule, was carried up to his own floor in the automatic lift.

He was worried and ill at ease, and there was a vague fear in his heart as his trembling hand fitted the latchkey into the lock. A servant came forward and took his hat and gloves.

'Will you have dinner at the usual time, sir?' asked the man.

Cowan stared at him dully for a moment uncomprehendingly.

'Eh, what's that?' he asked. 'Oh, yes . . . Bring a tray to my study . . . I've got a lot of work to do and I don't want to be disturbed.'

He crossed the room quickly, opened

the door of his room, entered and locked the door behind him. Only when he was alone did he utter a sigh of relief. On a table near his desk stood a tantalus and some glasses, and going to it he poured himself out a drink, gulping the spirit eagerly. It sent a glow through him and steadied his nerves. There was no reason for fear — reason rather for congratulation. He had carried out his scheme successfully, rid himself of a man who would have drained his resources to the limit, and in doing so netted a considerable profit for himself. The disqualification of Blonde Baby and the awarding of the race to Shy Lad meant that he was richer by over twenty thousand pounds. The scheme had been a clever one and he had carried it out successfully — completely successfully, except for that one unforeseen incident which had brought that icy touch of fear to his heart.

Why had he been such a colossal fool as to carry that wallet with his name and address in it when he had adopted his disguise to put his plan into execution?

Still, it was one of those things that couldn't possibly be foreseen. How could he have known that he would be selected as the victim of a pickpocket?

All the same it was worrying and dangerous, although the danger might not be so great as he imagined. In all probability the wallet was destroyed by now. Pickpockets did not keep those things for long; they only kept the negotiable valuables, and got rid of anything incriminating at the first opportunity. It was more than likely that his fears were groundless.

He helped himself to another drink and felt better. There was nothing to connect him with the shooting of Wills, nothing at all. His chauffeur could testify that he had driven him to London and left him at his flat. Nobody had seen him leave by the fire-escape three-quarters of an hour later, and if they had no one would have recognised him in the disguise he had adopted. He had boarded the train at Victoria for Brighton, travelling third class, and had been driven to the course in a charabanc in company with fifty or sixty other people.

The actual shooting of Wills had been carried out without anyone in the vicinity being any the wiser. The powerful air-pistol which he had used had been concealed within a large box camera and nobody suspected that the man who was apparently taking a snapshot of the finish of the race was in reality responsible for the accident which had caused such a sensation. He had got rid of both the pistol and the camera in a ditch near the course before taking the train back to Town, and there was nothing to remotely connect the immaculate Benjamin Cowan with the rather commonplace individual whose identity he had assumed for the purpose.

There was no reason why anyone should suspect him. It was only the discovery of his missing wallet that sent a qualm of fear through him. But for that he would have felt completely assured of his safety.

He had planned the whole thing so carefully, so well, that it was impossible for his crime to be brought home to him.

The suitcase he had deposited in the 'left luggage' department at Victoria before taking the train to Brighton contained a complete change of clothing, and on his return he had collected this, and in the cloakroom had removed the moustache that had constituted his simple disguise, dressed himself in his usual clothes and packed the ones he had worn in the suitcase. When he had emerged and entered the taxi he was once more himself.

It was only that infernal wallet that bothered him, and it continued to worry him, try as he might to put it out of his mind. It was the worst of bad luck!

He sat down in the chair behind his desk and chewed thoughtfully at his nails. Supposing the man who had picked his pocket should be arrested and the wallet found on him, how would he be able to explain it away? It was an unlikely contingency, but Mr. Cowan was a man who liked to take into account unlikely contingencies. It was this attention to detail that had raised him from a Whitechapel gutter to his present position.

Supposing such a thing to have happened the police would require an explanation. They would quickly discover that he was not supposed to have been at the Brighton races at all, and would naturally wonder how, in these circumstances, his wallet could have been there.

With his brows drawn together and his fingers fidgeting with his lips he concentrated all his thoughts on discovering a solution to the problem should it arise. So far as he knew he might never have to answer the question, but it was as well to be prepared. What sort of explanation could he put forward if it became necessary? His life might depend on his having a ready and convincing story.

An idea occurred to him and he thought it over carefully. Yes, that was the way out. It couldn't be proved, certainly, but on the other hand the police couldn't prove that it wasn't true.

A weight lifted from his mind, and there was a slight smile on his thick lips as he stretched out his hand for the telephone.

'Give me Toll,' he said when the operator answered, and a few seconds later was speaking with the butler at Downlands.

'I'm under the impression, Cressit,' he said, 'that I must have left my wallet behind this morning. I shall be down later on to-night and if you find it you might keep it for me.'

'I should naturally do so, sir,' said the dignified voice of Cressit, and Mr. Cowan rang off with the pleasurable feeling that he had established one point in his favour, he had notified the fact that the wallet was missing.

He was feeling more cheerful as he ate the meal which his servant presently brought to him. Things were going extremely well. Corbett was no longer a source of danger, Wills was beyond troubling him any more, and he was richer to the extent of some twenty-odd thousand pounds. Colonel Westmore, too, had listened to his suggestion concerning Pamela much more reasonably than he had expected. So far as his wishes lay in that direction he was under the impression that they would be gratified. He knew the girl too well to imagine that she would for a moment allow the estate to pass out of her father's hands. However unpleasant the alternative, and Mr. Cowan made no secret to himself that marriage with him *would* be an unpleasant alternative, she would prefer it to losing the house which she loved. There was only one disturbing element in his mind — The Jockey!

He went cold at the thought of that confession which still remained in existence. Once that was destroyed he would have nothing further to worry about. His financial difficulties were only temporary, and the twenty thousand pounds which he had won would go far towards relieving his immediate difficulties.

He wondered if Crabthorne had succeeded in obtaining any information at all concerning the identity of the mysterious individual who had filled him with terror on the night when he had stood by his bedside and forced from him the confession of his guilt.

A glance at the clock showed him that it was too late to ring up the inquiry agent's office. He would have gone, and the bookmaker had no idea of his private address. Well, he could leave that until he came back to Town.

He finished his meal and rang the bell, and when his man entered gave him instructions concerning the car.

'Tell Roberts to have it here at nine o'clock,' he ordered. 'I shall be leaving then, and if there's anything important you can telephone me to Colonel Westmore's house. You know the number.'

'Yes, sir,' said the manservant.

'Don't worry me unless it *is* important,' said Cowan, piercing the end of a cigar. 'I shall be back the day after tomorrow in any event.'

The man departed, and when he was alone the bookmaker took out his betting book and totted up his winnings. The amount he had won on Shy Lad came to just over twenty-three thousand pounds and he gave a grunt of satisfaction as he put the book away.

He had dined early and there was an

hour to fill in before the car would arrive to take him back to Ditchling. He was debating with himself how he could best fill in the time — there were several books in the cosily furnished room but Mr. Cowan was not a reader — when he heard the bell ring softly, and frowned. Who the deuce could be calling? He expected no one and was not in the mood to see anyone whoever they were. Most probably it was some friend of Iris's . . .

He heard a murmur of voices, and presently there came a tap on the door and his servant entered with a card.

'Will you see Superintendent Budd, of Scotland Yard?' he asked.

Mr. Cowan felt his heart leap.

'What's that?' he rasped. 'Who did you say?'

'Superintendent Budd, sir,' said the man. 'He wants to see you, and he says it's rather urgent.'

'I can't see anyone — ' began Cowan, and then as a thought struck him: 'All right, ask the superintendent to come in.' Better to see the man whatever it was about, he thought. No good trying to stall him, and he would rather know what it was that had brought this police official to his flat . . .

Mr. Budd came heavily into the room, his sleepy eyes taking stock of his surroundings.

'Sorry to trouble you, Mr. Cowan,' he murmured. 'Nice place you've got here, comfortable and luxurious. It's a funny thing, but those two don't always go together. Some people have got comfortable places and others have got luxurious places, but very few people have got both luxurious *and* comfortable.'

'No, quite,' said Cowan. 'What did you wish to see me about, Inspector?'

'Superintendent, sir,' corrected Mr. Budd gently, removing his hat and gazing into the interior. 'Superintendent.'

'I'm sorry,' said the bookmaker.

'No need to apologise,' said the Rosebud, still inspecting the interior of his hat and looking rather as though he might be expected to produce a rabbit at any moment. 'I've come in connection with a small matter concerning some property of yours.'

'You've found the wallet?' said Cowan quickly.

Mr. Budd was a little taken aback. He had not expected that.

'Yes, sir,' he said. 'You were at Brighton races to-day?'

The bookmaker shook his head.

'No, I was not,' he answered. 'I intended to be, but I was unfortunately called to Town this morning. What makes you think I was at Brighton?'

'Well, sir,' said Mr. Budd, 'a pickpocket was arrested on the course, and the police found in his possession a wallet with your name and address in it. I don't see very well how it could have come into the pickpocket's possession unless you'd been there.'

'Extraordinary!' said Cowan. 'That really is extraordinary! He was arrested on Brighton race-course you say?'

'He was,' said the stout superintendent, and although his eyes were still half closed he was watching the bookmaker closely.

'Amazing!' said Cowan. 'I missed the wallet when I got to London, but I was

219

under the impression that I had left it at Downlands, Colonel Westmore's house, where I was staying. As a matter of fact I phoned through to the butler a little while ago asking him if he found it to keep it until I returned.'

'You phoned a little while ago,' said Mr. Budd. 'You didn't phone immediately you discovered your loss?'

'No,' said Cowan frankly. 'To be perfectly candid, Inspector — '

'Superintendent,' murmured Mr. Budd.

'I'm sorry, Superintendent,' apologised the bookmaker. 'To be perfectly candid when I missed the wallet I was so certain that I'd left it at the house that I didn't bother very much.'

'I see.' The big man pursed his lips. 'Well, since it was found in the possession of this pickpocket you couldn't have left it at the house, could you?'

'No, obviously,' said Cowan. 'I must have lost it when I stopped at that shop in Lewes to buy some cigars.' He made the assertion confidently for this part of his story was true, at any rate, and could be checked up.

'You stopped at a shop in Lewes?' repeated Mr. Budd. 'You think you lost your wallet then, sir?'

'It's more than likely,' answered the bookmaker. 'I was in rather a hurry. I must have dropped it instead of putting it back in my pocket as I thought.'

Mr. Budd sought inspiration from the interior of his hat.

'And somebody picked it up and took it to the races,' he murmured.

Cowan watched his face, but it was completely expressionless, and there was no indication of what was passing in the detective's mind. He was not particularly impressed by this sleepy, bovine looking man. He neither looked nor spoke as if he possessed a great deal of intelligence, and Cowan, like a great many more people before him, was deceived by outward appearances.

'Naturally,' said Mr. Budd, after a pause, 'you reported your loss to the police?'

Cowan shook his head.

'No, I didn't,' he replied. 'Until you told me the wallet had been found in the

221

possession of this pickpocket I was convinced I had left it behind at Colonel Westmore's house.'

'I see.' The stout superintendent appeared infinitely bored with the whole matter. 'Well, I can understand, after your explanation, how it might have come into the possession of somebody on Brighton race-course.'

'Of course,' agreed the bookmaker, 'it's quite simple. Obviously this person who picked it up was going to the races and took it with him.'

'Yes, that's understandable,' murmured the Rosebud. 'What I can't quite understand though is the ticket.'

'Ticket? What ticket?' asked Cowan sharply.

'The return half of a railway ticket,' said the superintendent, and the lids drooped so low over his eyes that they were mere slits. 'The return half of a railway ticket dated to-day and issued at Victoria Station.'

Cowan's heart jumped. He felt the colour drain from his face. He had forgotten that! After giving up his ticket at

Brighton he had put the return half in his wallet. He remembered it now. Coming back he had had to buy another with the loose change he luckily had in his trousers pocket.

'Extraordinary!' he said, speaking with an effort. 'The ticket certainly didn't belong to me.'

'No,' said Mr. Budd, 'I suppose it didn't.'

'Of course it didn't! It must have been the property of whoever picked up the wallet,' went on Cowan quickly.

'I suppose it must,' agreed the big man, 'though it's queer all the same, don't you think so, sir?'

'I don't see anything queer about it — ' began Cowan.

'It's queer,' interrupted Mr. Budd, 'that someone who had travelled from Victoria to Brighton to go to the races should have been at Lewes. You read about this shootin', I suppose?'

'Shooting? What shooting?' said Cowan.

Mr. Budd yawned into his hat.

'It's in all the evenin' papers,' he said. 'This jockey what was shot durin' the

223

Balcombe Stakes to-day.'

'Oh, that! Yes, I read something about that.' Cowan was elaborately unconcerned. 'Extraordinary thing. Quite, as far as I know, without precedent.'

'He was a friend of yours, wasn't he?' asked Mr. Budd.

'Well, hardly.' The bookmaker was uneasy, but he strove to speak naturally. 'I knew him of course, I know most of the jockeys, but I wouldn't call him a friend.'

'I see,' said Mr. Budd. 'Well, I don't think I need trouble you any more for the moment, sir, I'll just return your property and go.' He plunged a fat hand into his pocket and withdrew it holding a notecase.

'Thank you,' said Cowan. 'I'm extremely obliged to you, Superintendent, and perhaps you'll accept a little present for your trouble?' He slipped one of the notes out of the wallet and held it out, but Mr. Budd made no effort to take it.

'That's very kind of you, sir,' he murmured, 'but we're not allowed to accept presents for doin' our duty.' He turned towards the door. 'Good evenin', sir. Perhaps I'll see you again one of these days.' It was a conventional remark, but something in the tone caused Cowan to look at him sharply.

'I shouldn't think it was very likely,' he said. 'I don't make a habit of losing things, Superintendent.'

'No, I suppose you don't,' remarked Mr. Budd wearily. 'Bookmakers seldom do, do they? By the way, talkin' of losin', did you win much on the Balcombe Stakes?'

'Nothing to speak of,' muttered Cowan. 'Why?'

'I just asked out of natural curiosity,' said Mr. Budd. 'I'm interested in racin' and I wondered. Nothin' to speak of! Well, I suppose it's all a question of degree. If I'd won twenty thousand pounds on a race I should feel like shoutin' it from the housetops let alone speakin' about it. But to a rich man like you I suppose it don't mean much. Good night, sir.'

He left Mr. Cowan with a vague sense of uneasiness. How had the man been aware of the sum he had won on Shy

Lad? The bets had been distributed among a number of bookmakers, and unless careful inquiries had been instituted it would have been impossible to discover exactly the sum involved. Which meant that inquiries *had* been instituted, police inquiries, for to no other source would the information have been divulged.

Mr. Cowan was a worried man as he took his seat in the car that was to transport him to Ditchling, and the worry remained with him for the greater part of the journey, until it was dispersed in the anticipation of meeting Pamela Westmore and turning to reality the dream which had for so long occupied his mind.

22

A Question of Proof

Mr. Marius Crabthorne returned from Brighton well satisfied with his excursion. Not only had he won a modest sum of money on the day's racing but the following-up of the slender clue which had come into his possession concerning the identity of the Jockey had been successful beyond his wildest hopes.

He got out of the train at Victoria Station and was so elated that he indulged in the unwarranted extravagance of a taxi to take him to the small flat at the back of Tottenham Court Road in which he lived. He occupied the top floor of a building which had once been an ordinary lodging-house until the tenants, unable to pay the accumulated arrears of rent, had been ejected by the landlord, and that enterprising gentleman had converted his property into alleged self-contained flats. This scheme had been carried out by the simple expedient of erecting a partition across each landing, inserting a door, and so shutting off the rooms beyond from the rest of the establishment.

Mr. Crabthorne twisted his key in the lock of his particular door and let himself in. He found himself in a dark and tiny hall consisting of that part of the landing which had been enclosed, and fumbling along the wall pressed a switch. A dingy light came on, revealing three doors, two on his right and one facing him. The one facing him gave admittance to his sitting-room; the others led respectively to his bedroom and a box-like compartment that combined kitchen and bath.

He hung up his hat on a peg, passed into his sitting-room, helped himself to a whisky and soda and sat down in the shabby armchair before the fireless grate. He had much to think about. Days of patient and untiring effort had enabled him to follow up a slender clue provided by the list, which Benjamin Cowan had given him, of the numbers of the notes stolen from Bleck. One of these had come into the possession, by a piece of extraordinary good luck, of a small bookmaker with whom Mr. Crabthorne had a modest account. The inquiry agent had supplied this man with a copy of the list in the vague hope that it might yield results, and much to his surprise it had. With great trouble and labour he had succeeded in tracing the note back to the person who had originally passed it, and the astounding possibility which this discovery had opened up amazed him. It seemed impossible that the person to whom he had traced the note could be the Jockey, and yet there was no concrete reason why not.

Two things occupied Mr. Crabthorne's mind. One was turning a possibility into a certainty and the other was what to do with the knowledge when he had obtained the proof he wanted. The second of these was not as easy as it appeared. Morally, of course, the information should be placed at the disposal of his client, Benjamin Cowan. Benjamin Cowan had engaged him to do a certain thing, and, when he had consolidated his suspicion, his duty was to place the result in front of Cowan. But Mr. Crabthorne was not troubled by scruples concerning his duty. The only thing that bothered him at all was how much he could make over the business. Could he make more from the Jockey by keeping his secret than he could from Cowan by divulging it?

However, there was time enough to think about that when he had obtained his proof, irrefutable proof that could not be denied. And that brought him to his first problem. How was this proof to be obtained? It was one thing to be suspicious and quite another thing to back that suspicion with solid facts.

It took an hour and a half and four large whiskies and sodas to provide him with a solution, and then, rising to his feet, he put on his hat and went out.

There is a little restaurant near Warren Street Station in which Mr. Crabthorne was a familiar figure. Entering this establishment he sought out the Italian proprietor. Mr. Monelli, fat, greasy, and with his obese figure enveloped in a dirty apron, rubbed the thick hair on a forearm when the inquiry agent put his question.

'I have not seen him for one, two, three days,' said Mr. Monelli shaking his head. 'He 'as not been in 'ere.'

Mr. Crabthorne frowned.

'Is 'Slick' about?' he asked.

The Italian nodded.

'Yes, 'e is 'ere,' he replied, jerking a dirty thumb towards the back of the restaurant. ''E is round the corner.'

The place was shaped like an L. Threading his way through the dozen or so small tables that occupied the longer arm Mr. Crabthorne turned the angle and glanced about him. This part of the restaurant was small in comparison to the other, consisting of three tables set in what was little more than an alcove. The man he sought was sitting in a corner, a cup of coffee before him, studying an evening paper. He looked up as the inquiry agent pulled up a chair and sat down in front of him.

''Evening, Mr. Crabthorne,' he said.

'Good evening, Slick,' said Crabthorne.

231

'D'you know where I can find Lew?'

'Depends on what you want him for,' said 'Slick' Fawley noncommittally. ''E don't come in 'ere now, 'ad a row with one of the boys.'

'One of Sellini's lot?' asked the inquiry agent.

The other nodded.

'Yes,' he answered. 'Something to do with a dame. Lew muscled in on a blonde that 'Clarky' Farrel had got hold of. Stupid thing to do. She was a nice bit of stuff I'll admit, but Lew ought to 'ave known better than to start messing round with any skirt belonging to Sellini's crowd. It was asking for trouble.'

'Women were always Lew's failing,' said Mr. Crabthorne, shaking his head. 'Where can I find him, Slick? I've got a job for him.'

The sharp-featured, cunning face opposite him came nearer.

'Do you know Luigi's, back o' Old Compton Street?' whispered the pickpocket.

'Painted red with blue curtains?' said Mr. Crabthorne.

232

'That's the place,' Slick nodded quickly. 'You'll find Lew there.'

The inquiry agent slipped a ten shilling note from his pocket and slid it across the table.

'Thanks, Slick,' he said, and rising to his feet made his way back to the exit.

'You finds him?' asked Mr. Monelli from behind the narrow counter as he passed.

'Yes, thanks,' said Crabthorne, and with a nod left the restaurant.

Luigi's was a slightly more pretentious place, and as he entered Mr. Crabthorne saw the man he was seeking sitting by himself at a table a few yards away from the door.

Lew Sleator was a youngish-looking, slim man, rather flashily dressed and with a prematurely bald head. His narrow face was sallow and his eyes were so close to the bridge of his thin nose that they gave the illusion of a permanent squint.

'Hullo, Mr. Crabthorne!' he greeted as the inquiry agent approached the table. 'It's many moons since I seen you.'

'I'm a busy man, Lew,' said Mr.

Crabthorne genially. 'How's the world treating you?'

The burglar shrugged his shoulders.

'So, so,' he answered. 'Mustn't grumble.'

A waiter came bustling up and Mr. Crabthorne ordered coffee.

'I've got a job for you, Lew,' he said, lowering his voice when the man had departed. 'There's fifty quid down, and if it's successful another thousand.'

Lew Sleator carefully replaced the pepper pot with which he had been seasoning his dish of macaroni.

'Sounds good to me,' he remarked. 'What's the job?'

Mr. Crabthorne lowered his voice until it was only just audible to the man in front of him.

'I want to collect some evidence,' he said, 'and I'm looking to you to get it for me.' He broke off and waited while the coffee he had ordered was set before him, and then, while Lew Sleator ate his macaroni he spoke rapidly in the same low tones he had adopted before. The interest on the sallow face of the man opposite him increased as he proceeded.

'It's a pretty big thing you're on, isn't it?' he said when Mr. Crabthorne had finished.

The inquiry agent nodded.

'One of the biggest I've ever tackled,' he answered. 'But there's money in it, Lew, there's money in it for both of us if we can only prove that my suspicions are correct.'

'When d'you want me to do this?' asked the burglar.

'As soon as possible,' said Mr. Crabthorne. 'The quicker we know the quicker we can 'touch'.'

'I'll have to 'feel' the house,' muttered Sleator. 'It's too risky to go on a job like that without.'

'You go about it your own way,' said Crabthorne, 'but remember this: Make it look like an honest-to-goodness burglary.'

'I get you.' The burglar's mouth creased into a grin. 'You don't want this person to suspect anything.'

'That's right,' said the inquiry agent. 'Now, you know what you're looking for?'

'You bet your life I do,' said Sleator. 'When can I 'touch' for that fifty?'

'Come round to my office in the morning, ten minutes after the banks are open, and I'll have it waiting for you.'

'That's O.K. with me,' said Lew Sleator. 'I ought to be able to do the job say' — he wrinkled his forehead and gazed at the ceiling — 'say Saturday night.'

'That'll do,' said Mr. Crabthorne.

He gulped the coffee, paid his bill, and leaving the restaurant made his way thoughtfully and complacently homewards. That night he slept the sleep of the just, unaware that he had started a chain of circumstances that were to result not only in the destruction of his fondest hopes but ultimately to bring about his death!

23

Mr. Budd Discourses

Mr. Budd left Benjamin Cowan's flat and sought a bus that would carry him back to Scotland Yard with a thoughtful expression on his heavy face. He was not at all satisfied with the bookmaker's explanation as to how the wallet had come into the possession of the little pickpocket, Harry Dew. There had been a discrepancy in Cowan's statement which the stout superintendent had noticed, but on which he had made no comment. He had said that until he had learned that the wallet had been found in Harry Dew's possession he had been convinced that he had left it behind at Colonel Westmore's house. And yet during his journey to Town he had remembered stopping at a shop in Lewes and buying cigars which he had paid for with part of the money contained in the wallet. If his story was true, then, when later he missed it, he must have remembered this fact and could not possibly have been under the impression that he had left it at the Westmore's house.

Mr. Budd got ponderously down from the bus that had stopped at the corner of Whitehall, his mind still occupied with the result of his recent interview. He was practically certain that Cowan had been lying, and this conviction was not entirely due to the slip which the bookmaker had inadvertently made. Long experience had enabled the Rosebud to read faces, and the subtle expression that accompanied a lie were as obvious to him as a printed page.

The question that bothered him was why had Cowan lied? And the only reasonable answer was that he had never lost the wallet at all, but that it was from his pocket that Mr. Dew had filched it on the racecourse. Which meant that although Cowan had supposedly spent the day in Town he had in reality done nothing of the sort, but had returned to Brighton by train, using the ticket the return half of which Mr. Budd had discovered in the stolen wallet.

The stout man sighed wearily as he nodded to the man on duty at the door and slowly ascended the stone steps to his office. Although in his own mind he was sure that Cowan had been at Brighton during the murder of Joe Wills he realised how difficult it would be to prove it. And even if it could be proved, there was still no concrete evidence to show that it had been the bookmaker who had fired the shot which had killed the jockey.

He entered his bare, cheerless office and Sergeant Leek looked up from the book he had been frowningly studying.

'According to all the laws of racing,' remarked the lean sergeant, as his superior hung up his hat, 'Beauty Queen should win the Sussex Handicap to-morrow.'

Mr. Budd looked at him severely.

'What do you know about the laws of racin'?' he demanded.

'I've been studying form,' said the sergeant, 'and it's a certainty.'

'Like Laughin' Water I suppose,' grunted the superintendent as he squeezed himself

239

into his chair. 'What's all that stuff you've got there?'

Leek looked guiltily at the collection of literature on his lap.

'I thought I'd get one or two racing papers,' he mumbled. 'This book 'ere is *Racing Up to Date*. It tells you what won and what didn't.'

'I can tell you what didn't,' said Mr. Budd, 'without wastin' time lookin' up books.' He thrust his stubby fingers into his waistcoat pockets and produced one of his black cigars. 'I suppose you think because you won seven pounds on Shy Lad that you're an expert?'

'I know a good horse when I see one,' said Leek complacently.

'I'll bet you do!' grunted Mr. Budd lighting his cigar and blowing out clouds of pungent smoke. 'I'll bet you do! You know there's a head at one end and a tail at the other and that's about all!'

'It isn't the head or the tail that counts,' said Leek, 'it's points. Now, take Beauty Queen — '

'We won't take Beauty Queen or any other queen,' said Mr. Budd. 'What d'you think this is, the Sportin' Club? This is a respectable Government office dealin' with thieves and murderers and black-mailers. If you want to take up racin' you'd better send in your resignation. Until then put away all that rubbish and listen to me.'

Leek sighed resignedly.

'What you going to talk about?' he asked.

'I'm goin' to talk about the job we get paid for doin',' said Mr. Budd severely. 'Of course I know it's not so important as whether Beauty Queen will win the Sussex Handicap to-morrow, but still, if you can spare a moment or so from you racin' activities I'd like you to pay attention.'

'All right,' said the sergeant, 'I'm listening.'

'I suppose,' continued the stout super-intendent, 'it's useless my suggestin' that you might say 'Sir' occasionally? I know that my rank doesn't mean a thing to you, but still it's an old custom, and these traditions ought to be respected.'

'I'm sorry, sir,' said the sergeant patiently.

'That's better!' Mr. Budd nodded approvingly. 'That's much better! Now I'm beginnin' to feel that we really are in Scotland Yard and not in a racin' stable. I've just come back from an interview with Cowan and I'm not satisfied.' He explained at some length the result of his visit to the bookmaker. 'Of course, so far as the killin' of Joe Wills is concerned,' he concluded, 'it's nothin' to do with us, that's the affair of the Brighton police. But where it touches on this Jockey feller, that *is* our business.'

'I don't see that it does,' said Leek.

'You don't see anythin',' said Mr. Budd disparagingly. 'You never did see anythin'. If the Jockey came in here now and stood under your nose you wouldn't see him. I'll tell you somethin'.' He leaned back in his chair and closed his eyes. 'This shootin' of Wills may not have anythin' to do with the Jockey, but there's a connection all the same, and the connection is Cowan!'

'You mean Cowan is the fellow who shot him?' asked the sergeant.

'I mean nothin' of the sort!' growled

242

Mr. Budd irritably. 'Why do you go jumpin' to conclusions?'

'Well, I thought — ' began the injured Leek.

'You didn't! You never do!' Mr. Budd snapped him up before he could finish the sentence. 'And when you do it's wrong. The connection between Cowan and this Jockey feller dates back, in my opinion, to that business with Wharton. I've got a hunch that's the kernel of the whole thing.'

Leek made no effort to interrupt him as he paused, but waited in silence for him to go on.

'The people,' continued the superintendent dreamily, 'who were chiefly concerned with the Wharton business were Joe Wills, Corbett and Cowan and two of 'em are dead. Doesn't that suggest anythin'?'

'They was murdered,' said Leek brightly, and Mr. Budd heaved a long sigh.

'I wonder sometimes,' he said, shaking his head, 'how you ever got into the police force at all! Of course they were murdered! Everybody knows they were murdered! Were you under the impression

243

they died of old age?'

'No,' said Leek, 'but — '

'Well then, don't interrupt me by sayin' things that are so obvious a child of six could see 'em!' grunted Mr. Budd witheringly. 'What I was gettin' at was this: was the thing that started the Jockey on this cleanin' up racin' stuff the Wharton case? It's queer when you come to think of it. Three people gave evidence against Wharton at the Jockey Club inquiry and two of 'em are dead.'

'And that fellow Green,' put in Leek, 'don't forget him. He had nothing to do with the Wharton business, did he?'

'He had nothin' to do with anythin',' said Mr. Budd. 'He was killed because he saw the murderer of Corbett, and he had to die to shut his mouth. That's the only way he comes into it, I'm pretty sure of that. What I'm not sure of is who killed Corbett.'

'The Jockey!' said the sergeant with conviction.

'Did he?' murmured Mr. Budd musingly. 'That's just the question. *Did* he kill Corbett? He says himself he didn't when he had that interview with Templeton.'

'Naturally he wouldn't admit it,' said Leek.

'No, I'm not takin' so much notice of that,' the superintendent went on. 'What I *am* takin' a great deal of notice of though, is the motive. He had no motive for killin' Corbett. It's all very interestin' and peculiar. Let's take it, for the sake of argument, that this Wharton business was a 'frame-up'; that Cowan, Corbett and Wills hatched up a plot among themselves to get him 'warned off'.'

'What for?' inquired Leek.

'Never mind what for,' said Mr. Budd impatiently. 'I don't even know that they did, I'm just assumin' it. Supposin' for some reason or other they did, where does that get us?'

'It doesn't get me anywhere,' said the miserable Leek, glancing furtively at the clock.

'It gets us,' said Mr. Budd, as though he hadn't spoken, 'to this: That Wharton was an innocent man who suffered and committed suicide, remember that, owin' to a conspiracy which these three people

245

had hatched against him. Now, supposin' he had some great friend or relation, wouldn't they want to try and get their own back for what these fellers had done? Mightn't that have brought the Jockey into existence?'

'I suppose so,' said Leek gloomily, thinking of the supper which awaited him at his lodgings and which seemed to be receding further and further into the dim future with every passing minute. 'But what about Bleck? He hadn't anything to do with the Wharton business, had he?'

'No,' agreed Mr. Budd, 'he hadn't. But isn't it conceivable that this feller we're supposin', incensed at the treatment which Wharton had received from a bunch of crooks, had made up his mind to prevent such a thing happenin' again, and decided not only to avenge Wharton but to stop anyone else sufferin' the same way as he did?'

'A minute ago,' said Leek, 'you was saying the Jockey had no motive for killing Corbett, and now you're giving him one.'

'I'm givin' 'im a motive to try and

extract eight thousand pounds out of Corbett,' corrected Mr. Budd, 'but am I givin' 'im a motive for murder? I don't think so. How many crimes of vengeance can you remember in this country durin' the past twenty years?'

'No, that's right,' said Leek. 'But you don't want to find a motive for a man trying to extract eight thousand pounds from another, the money's sufficient motive.'

'Maybe you're right,' said Mr. Budd, to Leek's surprise. 'Maybe you're not. What I'd like to know is where Corbett got that eight thousand?'

'Out of his bank,' said Leek.

'I know!' retorted Mr. Budd wearily. 'But how did it get in his bank? Durin' the last nine months before his death Corbett had practically no horses under his care. His reputation was a bad one and most of his old clients had taken their horses elsewhere. Where did he get the eight thousand he drew out and the four thousand that remained?'

'Perhaps he saved it,' said the sergeant.

'A year ago,' said Mr. Budd, 'he was on

the verge of bankruptcy, and durin' the past twelve months he didn't do enough business to earn a tenth of that sum. Where did it come from?' He flicked the ash from his cigar and leaned forward. 'I'll tell you where I think it came from,' he went on. 'Cowan!'

'Why should Cowan pay Corbett twelve thousand pounds?' said Leek, wrinkling his forehead.

'Because Corbett knew the truth about the Wharton business!' said the superintendent softly. 'And threatened to squeal.'

'But he was in it as much as Cowan if it was a 'frame-up'!' protested Leek.

'But it wouldn't have done him as much harm as Cowan,' said Mr. Budd. 'If he was goin' bankrupt and givin' up his racin' stables it wouldn't have hurt him to be 'warned off', and that's all that would have happened to him. But it would have smashed Cowan. It was very lucky for Cowan that Corbett died. If I'm right it saved him a lot of money.'

Leek shook his head helplessly. Mr. Budd had talked so much and jumped from one subject to another so quickly that he was both dazed and bewildered.

'It seems to be a bit of a mix-up, doesn't it?' he said.

'It *is* a mix-up,' agreed the big man. 'A hell of a mix-up! But maybe we've pulled one or two ends out of the tangle.'

The lean sergeant was not so sure on this point.

'I'm havin' inquiries made into Wharton's past,' murmured the superintendent, 'and I think we shall find somethin' there that'll help us. There's no doubt there's a connection between the Jockey and Wharton. You remember what that girl said about his racin' colours?'

'That may have been a co-in-ci-dence,' said Leek. 'You can't put too much reliance on that.'

'I'm not puttin' any reliance on anythin',' said Mr. Budd. 'What I'm doin' at the moment is just tryin' to straighten things out. I'm considerin' all the points and tryin' to see how they might fit.'

Leek privately considered that they didn't seem to fit very well, but he thought it better not to mention this.

'Nothin' clarifies a case more,' continued the Rosebud, 'than talkin' about it. Every time you talk about it you bring some additional thing to light, and maybe at the end you get at the truth. I'll admit while you're doin' so it seems a bit of a jumble, but that can't be helped.' There was a tap at his door and he looked round. 'Come in,' he said, and a sergeant entered carrying a folder. 'Oh, it's you, Gotch,' said Mr. Budd unnecessarily. 'Well, how d'you get on?'

'I've checked up on Wharton, sir,' said Sergeant Gotch, laying the folder on the desk in front of his superior. 'Though I think there must be a mistake somewhere.'

'Mistake? What do you mean?' asked the superintendent sleepily.

'Well, I was given to understand, sir,' said the sergeant, 'that this man, Wharton, was the son of Colonel Henry Wharton, the race-horse owner.'

'That's right,' said Mr. Budd, 'he was. His father died when he was five years old and he inherited the property.'

'Well, there's something queer somewhere, sir,' said Gotch. 'Colonel Wharton married a Miss Eleanor Board. I've traced up all that, you can see it in the folder.'

'Well, what about it?' said Mr. Budd. 'Why shouldn't he have married this girl Board?'

'No reason at all, sir,' said the sergeant, 'only there were no children.'

The sleepy expression on the stout superintendent's face vanished. He sat up with a jerk, his eyes wide open and alert.

'Are you sure of that?' he asked.

'Positive!' said Gotch. 'There's no doubt about it. I've been all through the records at Somerset House. The marriage certificate's there all right but there's no birth certificate.'

'Maybe the baby wasn't registered,' suggested Mr. Budd frowning, 'maybe it was born abroad.'

Sergeant Gotch shook his head.

'No, sir, I thought of that,' he answered. 'Wharton was twenty-eight when he died, that means he was born in 1907. In 1907 Colonel Wharton and his wife were living in Surrey at their country house at Shere. They were married in 1906, but there was no child.'

'No child,' repeated Mr. Budd thoughtfully. 'Then who,' he added softly, after a long pause, 'was Norman Wharton?'

24

Pamela Surprises her Father

Benjamin Cowan reached Downlands at a little before eleven, to find his daughter yawning in the drawing-room and Westmore on the point of going to bed.

'Sorry I'm late, but I couldn't get back before,' he apologised. 'Where's Pamela?'

It was the first time he had spoken of the girl by her Christian name and the old man raised his eyebrows.

'She was tired,' he said shortly, 'and went to bed early. By Jove, Cowan, you ought to have been here to-day! We had some excitement at Brighton.'

'I read about it in the evening newspapers,' said the bookmaker. 'A dreadful thing!'

'We've had the police here making inquiries about you,' continued Westmore, and Cowan started.

'Inquiries about me?' he said sharply.

'What inquiries?'

'A man was arrested on the course,' explained the colonel, 'and — '

'Oh, I know all about that,' interrupted Cowan, and Iris looked at him quickly as she heard the note of relief in his voice. 'They found a wallet of mine in his possession and wondered how he came by it. A fellow from Scotland Yard called at my flat just before I left. There's no great mystery about it. I lost the wallet on the way up to London — must have dropped it in a shop at Lewes — and I suppose this fellow whose pocket was picked found it and took it with him to the races.'

'I told the inspector you weren't here,' said Westmore, 'and he's calling again to-morrow.' He yawned. 'Well I think if you'll excuse me I'll go to bed, too. Good night, Cowan. Good night, Miss Cowan.'

'Good night,' said Iris, but the book-maker followed him out into the hall.

'Did you speak to Pamela?' he asked.

Westmore shook his head.

'I haven't had an opportunity yet,' he

answered. 'We were too busy discussing the shooting of this unfortunate jockey. There's no particular hurry, is there?'

'Well, I'd like you to do so as soon as possible,' grunted Cowan, a little annoyed, for he had hoped and expected that the way had been smoothed for him.

'I'll try and see her in the morning,' said the colonel. 'But I warn you that I'm not going to press her in any way.'

'I'm not asking you to,' answered the bookmaker. 'All I'm asking you to do is to put the situation before her, and if she's a sensible girl that's all that will be necessary.'

'All right, I'll do that,' said Westmore, and with a curt nod went upstairs.

Cowan returned to the drawing-room. Iris was standing in front of the glass over the mantelpiece touching up her lips with red.

'Thank goodness we've only got another day here!' she said petulantly. 'I've been bored to tears.'

'Are you ever anything else?' grunted Cowan, dropping into an easy chair.

'Yes,' she answered. 'I'm all right when

I'm with my own friends, but this sort of company doesn't suit me. Did you really go to Town to-day?'

'What do you mean?' he demanded harshly. 'Of course I went to Town! What makes you think I didn't?'

She shrugged one bare shoulder.

'I don't know, I just wondered,' she said. 'When that detective came about the wallet I thought — '

'Who asked you to think?' he snarled. 'I spent the day in Town on business, don't forget that.'

'All right,' said the girl. 'You needn't be so touchy. What's the matter with you? Did you have a bad day?'

'I'm sorry, Iris.' His tone was more conciliatory. 'I'm a little worried, I've got a lot of things to think about.'

'Who hasn't?' she retorted. 'By the way, while I remember it, you'll have to let me have some more money. I lost every penny I had to-day.'

He frowned.

'Why don't you bet more sensibly,' he grumbled. 'If you put your money on horses that had a chance of winning you might make a bit instead of losing.'

'There's no excitement in backing certainties,' she answered. 'If you've got your money on an outsider and it wins, it's worth while.'

'If it wins,' growled Mr. Cowan. 'Backing outsiders is a mug's game, unless you've got inside information. How did Westmore get on?'

'Pamela won a few pounds,' said his daughter uninterestedly, 'but her father lost.'

'Good!' said the bookmaker with satisfaction, and she looked at him curiously.

'Why do you say that?' she asked.

'Because,' replied her father, 'as long as Westmore remains practically penniless I've got him where I want him!'

'You may have got *him*,' she said, 'but you haven't got Pamela.'

He looked at her sharply.

'What do you mean?' he inquired.

'What I say,' answered the girl. 'I can't understand what you want to worry about her for.'

'There are a lot of things you can't

understand, Iris,' he said quietly, 'and that's one of them.'

He got up, and walking over to the window looked out into the bright moonlight of the summer night. Those broad acres that stretched away to the folds of the downs were practically his own property and he regarded them with an air of proprietorship. Westmore was never likely to find sufficient money to redeem the mortgage, and with the beautiful old house and its picturesque surroundings went the slim, straight girl whose antagonism he sensed; whose unspoken contempt cut like the lash of a whip. To bring her to heel; to humble her; to punish her for her insolence would be an achievement more satisfying than any he had attempted in his chequered career . . . His daughter's voice broke in on his thoughts.

'If you're going to stand mooning there I'm going to bed,' she announced, and he turned.

'I think bed is the best place for both of us,' he said, and accompanied her out into the big hall.

Cressit, who had been waiting patiently, watched them vanish round the bend of the staircase, and put out the lights. He had already completed his round of the house, and when this duty was done he retired softly to his own room, a tired and contented man, who had earned the sleep which so soon came to him.

The moon flooded the grounds with light, turning the lawn to dove grey and touching the chimneys and gables of the sleeping house with silver. It was a still night. No breath of wind stirred the leaves of the trees, no cloud marred the blue expanse of the sky. The perfume of the roses drifted heavily towards the house from the lower garden and mingled with the secent of honeysuckle and stock so that the night was drenched with a rich blend of intoxicating fragrance. Faintly a clock somewhere in the village struck one, and as it did so a moving patch of shadow began to make its way stealthily through the shrubbery towards the house.

A vivid splash of bright moonlight crossed the path, and the shadow, entering this, took shape and substance; the black silk cap with the broad peak, the black jacket with the sleeves tightly buttoned at the wrists, black riding breeches and boots . . . Black from head to foot the figure showed up sharply and clearly.

Hesitating for a second at the fringe of the lawn, it came boldly on, cautiously crossed the gravel of the path that surround the house, and stopped beneath a small window that opened into the big hall. Beyond the window was darkness, and from the pocket of the black riding breeches the Jockey drew something that glittered momentarily in the moonlight as it was raised towards the casement . . .

Colonel Westmore was usually an early riser, but this morning he was up even earlier than was his habit. Standing at the window of the sunny breakfast-room he stared out at the brightness of the morning and gnawed his lips. The excuse he had made to Cowan that he had had no opportunity to speak to Pamela had not been entirely a true one. There had been ample opportunity on the previous evening and, even if there had not, he could, had he felt so disposed, have easily engineered one. But he had not felt disposed. His one desire had been to put it off as long as possible, for it was an interview which he viewed with uneasiness. Not that he was in the smallest degree afraid of his daughter, there was a camaraderie between them that discounted anything of the sort, but he felt uncomfortable. He was well aware how she regarded Cowan, and the suggestion that she should sacrifice herself to save him and the estate was not a pleasant thing to suggest. Not that he had the slightest intention of trying to persuade her one way or the other, but he knew sufficient of her character to realise what a plain statement of the situation would entail. Sooner than lose the house in which she had been born and which she loved she would be willing to tolerate even a marriage with Benjamin Cowan. Westmore was pretty sure of this, and he shrank from putting the question to the test.

As he stood frowning out of the

window he cursed heartily, not for the first time, the day that he had come in contact with the bookmaker. It would have been far better for all concerned if the result of his rash speculations had been allowed to take their natural course. But Benjamin Cowan had been so suave and smooth, so willing to assist, so sympathetic, that almost before he had realised it, Westmore had come to the arrangement that had, for ever after, destroyed his peace of mind.

There was a streak of weakness in his character which prompted him always to take the easiest way out, and the way Cowan had offered had been very easy indeed. By the mere effort of putting his signature to a document he had been relieved of all his anxieties, that is for a time. They had returned three-fold, but this he had not anticipated. He was an optimist, a condition of mind which is largely founded on the belief that somebody else will do something, and he had been confident that before the mortgage fell due he would have been able in some way or other to have raised the money necessary to meet it. But as the time passed and no miracle happened to justify this pleasant outlook his hopes had dwindled, and now it was a question of losing everything or sentencing his daughter to a life of misery with a man she loathed.

Now that it was too late he realised exactly what Cowan had been working for all along. The story the bookmaker had told him concerning his own financial position and of some unnamed man holding the mortgage as security did not deceive him for a moment. He knew perfectly well that it was merely a screen to more or less soften the veiled threat by which Cowan was seeking to enforce his wishes. And his wishes looked like being realised. There was no hope that he could raise the fifteen thousand pounds necessary to extricate himself from his position. He had tried every possible way that offered, and some that were impossible.

Although he had no intention of coercing Pamela, he hoped at the back of his mind that she would fall in with Cowan's wishes. He loathed himself for hoping this, but he couldn't help it. The alternative prospect was more than he could contemplate with any degree of calmness. To lose everything! To be turned out of the home which had belonged to his family for generations — penniless! To live the rest of his life in some dingy lodging-house eking out his bare existence on what meagre pittance could be saved from the wreck! He shivered.

Perhaps, after all, it would not be so bad for Pamela. These marriages sometimes turned out well. She might not be in love with Cowan, but on the other hand she wasn't in love with anyone else, and she would be well provided for.

He tried to convince himself with these arguments, but was only moderately successful, and turned wearily away from the window as the girl came in.

'You're early, Pamela,' he said, and then looking at her critically: 'What's the matter?'

Her face was pale and drawn and there were purple smudges beneath her eyes. 'I didn't sleep very well,' she said.

'By Jove, you look ghastly!' exclaimed her father with genuine concern in his voice.

'That's the last thing you should ever tell a woman,' she said reprovingly. 'No matter how ill they look you should always say they're charming. I feel quite all right, a little tired, that's all.'

'Perhaps you'd rather we didn't go to the races to-day?' he suggested, but she shook her head.

'No, no, I shall be all right after breakfast,' she answered. 'Did Mr. Cowan come down last night?'

Her father nodded gloomily.

'Yes, he got here just before eleven,' he answered, and then bracing himself with an effort and avoiding her eyes: 'I — I'd like to have a word with you, Pamela.'

She looked at him quickly, attracted by the subtle change in his voice.

'Have as many words as you like,' she said. 'What about?'

'About — about Cowan.' Westmore moistened his lips. He was finding it less easy than he had anticipated.

'Must we talk about Mr. Cowan before

breakfast?' she asked. 'It's not the best thing in the world to give one an appetite.'

'You dislike him, don't you?' he said.

'I hate him!' she answered viciously.

Westmore sighed.

'I guessed you did,' he said, 'and it doesn't make what I've got to say any easier.'

She frowned.

'What *have* you got to say?' she demanded, and as he hesitated: 'If it's unpleasant you might as well say it and get it over.'

'Well, the fact of the matter is,' began her father, 'Cowan had a talk to me yesterday. You know that some time ago I was forced to accept his help.'

'You mean the mortgage?' she inquired.

He nodded.

'Yes,' he replied. 'It was — it was urgent that money should be raised quickly and that was the only way to do it. I must say in justice to Cowan he was very decent about it.'

'It suited him to be!' she remarked curtly, and as he remained silent: 'Well, go on.'

'Well, the whole point of the matter is this.' Westmore took a deep breath. 'Cowan has got an idea in his head that — that he'd like to marry you.'

'He's had that idea in his head for some time,' said Pamela calmly. 'Go on.'

'He suggested,' continued her father, avoiding her eyes and rubbing his fingers gently up and down the edge of the polished table, 'that I should have a word with you first before he broached the matter himself. He seems to be aware that you — well, that you don't exactly like him and he wondered — '

'He thought,' she broke in, as he hesitated, 'that you would act as an ambassador.'

He nodded.

'I want you to understand,' he said hastily, 'that I'm not trying to force you in any way, my dear. I told Cowan that you'd have to act entirely of your own free will. All I said I'd do was to put the position before you.'

'The position being?' she inquired.

'Well, the mortgage falls due to-morrow week,' said Westmore uncomfortably, 'and

I don't think there's any need for me to tell you that I have no more hope of raising the money to meet it than I have of flying out of the window.'

She was silent for a moment.

'Let me get this right,' she said quietly. 'Mr. Cowan has suggested that in consideration of my agreeing to marry him he will not foreclose the mortgage which he holds on this estate. Is that it?'

'He didn't put it quite so crudely as that,' muttered Westmore, 'but I suppose that is the situation.'

She gave a little hard laugh.

'Why wrap it up in sugar coating?' she asked. 'That's what it amounts to. Well, you can tell Mr. Cowan, or I'll tell him if you like, that I wouldn't marry him if he was the last man in the world or if he offered me ten million pounds as a dowry.'

For the first time since he had broached the subject he looked at her. Her face was flushed and her eyes were bright.

'You realise what this means?' he said.

'I realise what Mr. Cowan *thinks* it means,' she retorted. 'He thinks that sooner than lose this house, that sooner than see you turned out penniless, I would be willing to make any sacrifice. Well, he was right. Had it been necessary I might have agreed to his alternative. But in the present circumstances there is no need to.'

'What do you mean?' Westmore stared at her in astonishment.

'How much do you want to pay off this mortgage?' she asked, instead of answering his question.

'With the interest, just over fourteen thousand pounds,' he replied, 'and I haven't got fourteen thousand pence!'

'Wait!' said the girl. 'I'll be back in a minute.'

She ran from the room and he heard her light footsteps ascending the stairs. A few moments later she was back again and laid a thin packet on the table in front of him.

'There's fifteen thousand pounds,' she said. 'Pay off that mortgage and tell Benjamin Cowan and his unpleasant daughter that the sooner they get out of this house the better we shall be pleased!'

25

The Discomfiture of Mr. Cowan

If the table had suddenly taken unto itself legs and walked away Westmore could not have looked more astonished. His jaw dropped and he gaped in amazement at the thin package of money.

'Fifteen thousand pounds!' he croaked hoarsely, and Pamela nodded.

'Count it!' she said. 'You'll find that's the correct amount.'

'But — but — ' His astonishment was so great that he found difficulty in speaking. 'Where did you get it? How did you come by such a large — ?'

'That's my business,' she said calmly. 'The money's there, and I came by it honestly.'

'But — I don't understand!' Her father passed a hand wearily across his eyes as though he was under the impression that he was dreaming.

'There's no need for you to understand,' she said. 'All you have to do is to take that money, lodge it in your bank, ring up your lawyers and tell them to arrange to take up the mortgage.'

'Yes, yes, that's all right.' Westmore was recovering a little from his first shock. 'But you must explain. You must tell me where you got this.'

'Why must I?' The girl's chin set stubbornly. 'Whether I must or not I'm not going to. It's sufficient that it's there at a time when it's most needed.'

'You haven't — done anything foolish — ' he began.

'I haven't done anything at all,' said Pamela, 'except provide you with the necessary means of getting rid of Mr. Cowan and his family for good and all. It's no good questioning me,' she went on quickly as he opened his lips, 'because I'm not going into any more details concerning that money.'

'Will you tell me one thing,' he asked. 'This is your money?'

'Oh yes, it's mine,' she answered without hesitation. 'You didn't think I'd stolen it, did you?'

'No, no,' he said hastily, 'but — well, it's such an extraordinary thing. I can't understand it!'

'Don't worry yourself about it any more,' she said. 'Look upon it as a gift from Heaven if you like.'

'B'Gad it is!' said Westmore in something of his old voice, and stretching out his hand he picked up the packet.

There were a hundred and fifty Bank of England notes of a hundred pounds each and he gazed at them incredulously.

'Well,' he said, drawing a long breath, 'I don't know how you came by this but however the miracle happened it's going to save a lot of trouble.'

She looked at him and sighed. Fond as she was of her father she had no illusions concerning him. He had been prepared, for the sake of his own comfort, to offer her as a sacrifice; was prepared now to clutch at this means of salvation without inquiring too deeply into its source . . .

'By Jove, I'll have something to say to Cowan this morning!' he remarked as he slipped the notes into his pocket. 'I've stood about enough of this overbearing nonsense!'

'Good morning, Westmore. Good morning, Pamela,' said the smooth voice of the bookmaker as he bustled into the room rubbing his hands. 'Fine morning, eh?'

'A lovely morning, Mr. Cowan,' said Pamela, laying stress on the Mister.

The rebuff which any other man would have noticed passed Cowan by.

'We ought to have a good day at Brighton,' he said. 'I hear you weren't too lucky, Westmore. Maybe I'll be able to get hold of one or two tips. Bleck's running two horses for the Sussex Handicap. Beauty Queen, the favourite, and Golden Rain. If I know anything of Bleck's methods Golden Rain'll win. It's a long price.'

'I should think it's quite likely!' said the girl contemptuously. 'It's pretty well known that he's a crooked owner.'

'He's smart,' said Cowan, with a chuckle. 'You have to be smart to make money at racing these days.'

'I prefer to regard it as a sport and not

as a money-making institution,' said Pamela coldly, and left the room.

Cowan frowned. His skin was thick, but the snub had been so direct that it had got home.

'A bit up-stage this morning, isn't she?' he grunted, turning to Westmore.

The older man shrugged his shoulders.

'She was right, anyway,' he remarked calmly. 'Racing should be kept as a sport and not as a means for a lot of crooks to line their pockets.'

'You'd be popular with that fellow they call the Jockey!' sneered Mr. Cowan. 'That's his line of talk, though he isn't above making a few thousand himself. It's the same with all these people who preach, there's a cash end to it somewhere.'

'That may have been your experience,' said Westmore. 'I don't altogether agree with you.'

Cowan opened his mouth, realised that he was losing his temper and controlled himself.

'Everyone's entitled to their opinion,' he said with an effort. 'Have you spoken to Pamela?'

'I've mentioned your suggestion to my daughter, yes,' said Westmore.

'And what did she say?' asked Cowan eagerly.

'She refused to consider the matter,' answered the other shortly.

The bookmaker's brow darkened.

'But that's not final,' he said. 'You're not going to leave it at that. I suppose you explained the situation to her?'

'Oh yes, I explained it very fully,' said Westmore. 'And I intend to leave it exactly at that, Mr. Cowan!'

'Oh, you do, eh?' Cowan's voice was hoarse with the rage that consumed him. 'I suppose you realise the result? That mortgage falls due — '

'Ah, yes, I wanted to talk to you about that,' said Westmore easily. 'If you will instruct your solicitors to have the documents ready I'll arrange with mine to take up the mortgage on the day it falls due.'

'You'll *what?*' Cowan's eyes almost started from his head.

'I'll take up the mortgage,' said the colonel calmly.

'But — where are you going to get the money?' demanded the bookmaker. 'It'll cost you fifteen thousand pounds.'

'I'm aware of that!' retorted Westmore calmly. 'A little under, I think.'

'And where are you going to get fifteen thousand pounds?' sneered Cowan. 'If this is a joke, Westmore — '

'It's no joke,' said the other, 'I can assure you of that. And as to where I'm going to get the money I don't think that's any concern of yours. So long as it is paid to your solicitors on the day the mortgage falls due, that's all that matters.'

Cowan's face went livid. The last thing he had expected had happened. He saw all his carefully-prepared plans coming to nothing. Saw the girl he had believed to be as good as his slipping through his fingers . . .

'If you're fooling me,' he said huskily, 'if this is a trick to gain time you'll be sorry!'

'There's no trick about it,' said Westmore. 'It's purely a business transaction. And I should be glad if you would kindly adopt a different tone.'

'Oh, you would!' said the bookmaker thickly. 'I suppose you think you've got rid of me now, eh? I suppose you think I'm going to accept the situation? Well, I'm not! If you think this is going to make any difference to my intention of marrying Pamela you're mistaken. I've made up my mind I'm going to marry her and I'm going to marry her!'

'I don't think we need discuss that,' said Westmore stiffly, 'and in the circumstances I think it will be better, Mr. Cowan, if you and your daughter can make it convenient to return to Town, or at any rate find somewhere else to stay during the rest of your visit to Brighton.'

'And,' said a cool voice at the door, 'so far as any prospects you may entertain of marrying me are concerned you can put them right out of your head once and for all, Mr. Cowan.'

The bookmaker swung round to meet the steady eyes of Pamela.

'Can I?' he snarled. 'We'll see about that, my lady! I've been a good friend to you and your father.'

'That's a matter of opinion,' she said

coldly. 'What you've done you've done to suit your own ends, and they haven't turned out exactly as you expected.'

Her calm seemed to infuriate him. The change in him was remarkable. At the best he was an unpleasant-looking man, now — she shivered inwardly to see him. His jaw was out-thrust and his eyes blazed with anger.

'You think that, do you?' he said. 'Well, you wait and see! I've never been thwarted in anything I've wanted yet, and I'm not going to be over you! I'll have you and nobody else, and I'll go to any lengths to get you, you understand?'

She faced him without flinching, and her quiet disdain maddened him.

'I don't know how you've got this money, if you have got it,' he shouted, 'but it's not going to get rid of me. You can turn me out of your house but you can't turn the determination out of my mind. Ever since I first saw you I've schemed and planned to make you my wife, and I'm going to achieve that object.'

'You schemed and planned. Yes, you

did!' she said, and her voice was steady and cold as ice. 'Your scheming and planning sent Norman Wharton to a suicide's grave! Your scheming and planning nearly involved my father in a financial catastrophe, for it was through you, indirectly, that he speculated in the worthless shares of an equally worthless gold mine. You didn't think I knew that,' she continued as he started. 'I don't think my father knew it. But it was on your advice that John Codagan invested his money and passed on the information to my father. Your scheming and planning has gone wrong in spite of your cunning and cleverness. And it will continue to go wrong. There is one who is equally as clever and cunning as you. One who will bring you to ruin and possibly death — the Jockey!'

Cowan's face went grey and he flinched as though from a physical blow.

'What do you know about the Jockey?' he croaked huskily. 'What do you know about him? Answer me, you — '

'That'll do, Mr. Cowan!' broke in Westmore coldly, and with a supreme effort the bookmaker regained control of himself.

'I'm sorry,' he muttered. 'I didn't mean to lose my temper, but you rattled me.'

With a contemptuous shrug of her shoulders Pamela walked over to the fireplace and pressed the bell.

'There's no reason why we should be bad friends,' went on Cowan quickly, realising, and trying to rectify, his mistake. 'I apologise for losing my temper, but you must make allowances for my very natural disappointment. I had hoped that to-day would see the realisation of my dearest ambition — '

'There's no need for us to discuss the matter any further,' said Pamela. 'And so far as friends, bad or otherwise, are concerned, don't let that worry you. From now onward you play such an unimportant part in my life that for all the interest I have you might not exist at all.'

The grey of the bookmaker's flabby face was replaced by a dull flush, but before he could say anything Cresset appeared in the doorway.

'Oh, Cresset,' said the girl, 'will you inform Mr. Cowan's chauffeur that he will be wanting the car in an hour. Mr. Cowan and his daughter will be leaving then.'

'Certainly, Miss,' said the dignified butler, and, although his face expressed nothing, there was joy in his heart, for he disliked Mr. Cowan intensely, a dislike that was shared by all his fellow servants from the housekeeper to the scullery-maid.

'You mean that?' said Cowan, when he had gone. 'You intend to turn us out?'

'After what has occurred you can hardly wish to stay,' said Westmore.

The bookmaker bit his lips.

'Oh, I'll go,' he snarled, 'but the matter doesn't end here, understand that. I'm not the type of man to relinquish a thing once I am determined to get it. You can be as proud and disdainful as you like now, but there'll come a time when you'll be crawling on your hands and knees to me, and then it will be my turn!' He twisted on his heel and strode from the room consumed with rage and disappointment.

Westmore looked at the girl for a moment after he had gone in silence. Then he shrugged his shoulders.

'I'm very glad that's over,' he said. 'By Jove, it'll be a treat to get that fellow out of the house.'

Pamela nodded, but her own relief was tempered by a vague uneasiness. There had been something in Benjamin Cowan's eyes as he uttered his final threat that warned her that she had *not* seen the last of him. When she had first met him she had sensed the ruthlessness that lay beneath that smooth, suave exterior, and she knew that he would go to any lengths to revenge himself for the indignity which he had suffered at her hands.

26

Sir Trevor Bleck Pulls off a Coup

The second day's racing at Brighton was even better attended than the first. The weather was still glorious and the crowds that flocked in the enclosures and on the downs presented a colourful sight in the bright sunshine.

Dick Templeton, standing near the entrance to the paddock, saw the arrival of Colonel Westmore and his daughter and noted the absence of the over-dressed girl who had accompanied them on the previous day. He wondered idly at the reason, for the news of Mr. Cowan's ignominious retreat from Downlands had not as yet had time to circulate round the village. He watched the slim figure of Pamela with approval, and wondered, not for the first time, how she was mixed up in the Jockey business, and what was the explanation of the perfume which Mr.

Budd's sensitive nose had detected.

He had come to Ditchling with high hopes, which, to his chagrin, had not been realised. Unless, he thought gloomily as he watched the activity around him, he could pick up a line soon his sojourn in the pretty little village would be curtailed. Mr. Pilchard was already getting restive. But for the sensation of Wills' death on the previous day he would, undoubtedly, have been recalled, and Dick had a hunch that in the neighbourhood of Ditchling was the clue that would eventually lead him to the truth about the Jockey. And in spite of his failure so far to discover anything concrete, this hunch still remained.

It has been said that a good reporter is born, not made, and there is a great deal of truth in this statement. A newspaper man's greatest asset is instinct, and Dick's instinct had never yet failed him, although it looked like failing him now. His conviction that there was a link between Pamela Westmore and the mysterious individual calling himself the Jockey looked like proving a fallacious one. But although all his cautious inquiries had, up to the present, led to precisely nothing, he clung to his original idea with a tenacity that was characteristic. Had anyone told him that there was any other reason for his reluctance to leave the neighbourhood he would have indignantly denied it and firmly believed that he was speaking the truth. And yet there was another reason which one day he was to realise to his intense surprise and annoyance, for Dick had lived his short and busy life without heed to the softer passions, and failed to recognise the subtle and unaccustomed sensations which the sight of Pamela Westmore had inspired within him.

He kept a look-out for the fat figure of the Scotland Yard man, but neither Mr. Budd nor the lugubrious Sergeant Leek showed any signs of putting in an appearance. He saw and nodded to Pyecroft and Sir Godfrey Latimer as they passed him on the way to Tattersall's, and eyed the thin, immaculately clad figure of Sir Trevor Bleck as he entered the paddock with his trainer. The baronet passed him without any sign of recognition although Dick had interviewed him after the Jockey had so neatly succeeded in relieving him of the ten thousand pounds which he had demanded.

'Uncivil brute!' thought Dick, but his accusation was unjustified, for Bleck had been so occupied with his own affairs that he had failed to notice the reporter.

'They've made Beauty Queen favourite,' he said in a low voice. 'The present price of Golden Rain is a hundred to seven. We ought to net a nice little bit on the race.' —

His trainer nodded.

'Everybody thinks Beauty Queen 'ull win,' he grunted.

'That's what we want 'em to think,' said the baronet. 'If they started thinking anything different Golden Rain's price would shorten. I'm backing the horse to win a hundred thousand. I'm backing it by telegram at starting price. The wires will be sent off at the last moment so that even if they're received before the race there'll be no time to get the money back to the course and spoil the price. You've got the stuff all right?'

'Yes,' said the trainer. 'Freedman gave it to me last night. I'll give the horse a shot just before she's saddled.'

'Be careful,' warned Bleck. 'The confounded stewards are suspicious as it is, and they will be watching like cats.'

'You can trust me,' said Luke Walsh. 'Ain't I in fifty-fifty? By a bit o' sheer bad luck there may be something faster in the race than Golden Rain, but it won't be Beauty Queen!'

'There's nothing else in the race to touch either of them!' said Bleck confidently. 'If Beauty Queen doesn't run up to her usual form Golden Rain'll be the first past the stick.'

'I suppose you've backed Beauty Queen?' said Walsh. The baronet smiled.

'What do you take me for?' he said. 'Of course I've backed her. I've got two hundred each way on her, and so far as anyone knows, nothing on Golden Rain. I'll have to pay out four hundred, but what's that against fifty thousand.'

He stopped to talk to an acquaintance. The horses for the first race were already in the saddling enclosure, and there was a general move to the stands. Dick, rather despondently, drifted with the rest of the crowd. He could, had he liked, have joined his fellow reporters on the Press stand, but he was in no mood for their company, preferring his own thoughts.

The first race was a selling handicap and was won by a four-year-old, Knight of Arran, a popular win with the crowd.

'A good start for the day, my dear,' said a voice behind Dick. 'I got three to one in hundreds.'

Dick turned, and saw that he was standing a few yards away from Pamela Westmore and her father. The colonel murmured something to the girl and left her, and acting on an impulse Dick moved to her side and raised his hat.

'Good afternoon, Miss Westmore,' he said.

Pamela looked at him, and recognition came to her eyes.

'You're Mr. Templeton, aren't you?' she said. 'Have you found out anything more about the murder of Mr. Corbett and that poor man Green?'

'No,' he said, 'but I am still hoping to.'

'Is that why you're staying at Ditchling?' asked the girl, and he was a little staggered at her knowledge. He must have shown it, for she smiled. 'You needn't be surprised that I know you're staying in Ditchling,' she went on. 'It's quite a small village, and servants talk.'

'I suppose they do,' he said lamely, and remembered the nightly appearance of Mr. Cresset in the bar of the inn at which he had a room.

'What do you expect to find out by remaining here?' she asked. 'The Jockey is not a local institution surely.'

'Do you believe the Jockey killed Corbett?' he said quickly.

'Don't you?' she countered, and then, before he could reply: 'The police think so, don't they?'

'It's not always easy to tell what the police think,' he said evasively. 'So far as I'm concerned I'm not at all sure that the Jockey was responsible for those two crimes.'

She looked at him quickly.

'Why do you say that?' she asked.

289

'You forget,' he replied, 'that I am one of the few people who have met the Jockey.'

'Yes,' she said softly. 'Of course. I — I had forgotten that.'

'What he told me at that interview,' said Dick, 'carried a certain amount of conviction. Personally I'm inclined to believe him when he said he had no hand in the murders.'

Her face flushed and her eyes sparkled.

'I'm so glad,' she said. 'You don't know how glad I am to hear you say that!'

'Why?' His astonishment showed in his face. 'Why should it give you so much pleasure, Miss Westmore?'

'I can't explain, but it does,' she answered hurriedly. 'It's my belief, too. There's Father beckoning to me,' she added hastily. 'Good-bye, Mr. Templeton. Perhaps — perhaps I'll see you again.'

She slipped away, and he saw her join Colonel Westmore, who was standing in the middle of the ring talking to a stout, genial-faced man whom Dick recognised as Lord Mortlake. He moved across to the paddock to watch the parade for the next race a little puzzled. The girl's gratitude at his belief in the Jockey's innocence was extraordinary. What difference could it make to her whether he believed that mysterious person to be innocent or guilty?

He was so busy with his thoughts that he saw very little of the second race, and until the numbers went up was unaware which horse had won. Making his way to the bar he was thoughtfully consuming a glass of beer when he heard his name called, and turning, recognised a Fleet Street acquaintance.

'Hullo, Templeton! What are you doing here?' asked Jimmy Belmore, of the *Star*. 'Didn't know you played the races.'

'I don't as a rule,' said Dick. 'Generally too busy.'

The racing man grinned.

'I suppose you're here on the look-out for the Jockey?' he said. 'Well, if you can pick him out from among all this crowd you're clever.'

'Even if he's here,' said the reporter.

'Oh, I'll bet he's here all right!' replied Belmore with conviction. 'It's obvious he's a keen follower of racing, and a bit of a crank, too. Ye gods, if he thinks he can clean the turf of crooks he must be a super-optimist or a believer in miracles!'

'Racing is not all crooked,' said Dick.

'You're telling me!' retorted Jimmy. 'And I've been a racing reporter all my life. No, the majority of racing people are the straightest and most honourable in the land, but while there's big money to be made easily you'll always find the crooks around. There's one now!' He lowered his voice.

Dick, out of the corner of his eye, saw Sir Trevor Bleck and a couple of friends enter the bar.

'I suppose that fellow's done more crooked things on a race-course than any man alive, and yet he could sue me for slander if he knew I'd said so.'

'He's running two horses in the next race,' said Dick.

His friend nodded.

'Yes, and I wouldn't risk a penny on either,' he declared. 'You never know what's going to happen with Bleck's horses. Beauty Queen's been made favourite, but if it wins I'm a Dutchman! There'll be some sad hearts amongst the punters after the race, I'll bet! Have another drink.'

Dick accepted, and they chatted until it was almost time for the 'off'. When Belmore left to make his way to the Press stand Dick went slowly towards the paddock. The Sussex Handicap was within a few minutes of being run and already some of the horses and their jockeys were riding out of the saddling enclosure to go to the starting gate.

It was a fairly large field, fifteen horses were going down to the gate and Dick picked out the colours of Beauty Queen. The big chestnut was carrying the first colours, which is usually the only sign an owner gives of his personal fancy — the conspicuous pink and white were easily distinguishable. Among the raucous cries of the bookmakers from the cheaper enclosure Dick heard the favourite being laid at seven to four. Golden Rain was still a hundred to seven and in one or two cases twenties were being offered.

He made his way up to the Stand, the

dull roar of the multitude, the cries of the bookmakers and the hoarse shouting of the tipsters blending in a babel of sound that was like the surging of surf on a rocky coast. As he selected a good position there was a lull in the confused roar. The fifteen runners were at the starting gate and the sun glinted on countless pairs of glasses as they were focused upon them. They were getting into line and the tense excitement of the waiting crowd could almost be felt. A hush came, punctuated only by the voices of a few bookmakers here and there offering tempting odds on outsiders in an effort to try and secure money upon them to balance their books.

Then suddenly the comparative silence was rent by a mighty roar that was like the initial clap of thunder proclaiming the breaking of a storm.

'They're off!'

It was an almost perfect start. Every horse engaged in the race had jumped off together on the flashing up of the tapes.

The field bunched together, the colours for the moment indistinguishable, came round the bend from the five-furlong starting gate into the straight. Gradually from the confused mass four horses emerged and Dick identified them from the colours: Gold Dust, Air Mail, Beauty Queen and Thunder Cloud. He looked for Golden Rain, but it was still in the ruck. Beauty Queen and Thunder Cloud were leading, and a shout went up from the crowd as they saw the favourite overtaking the grey.

'Beauty Queen!'

All over the course the name thundered, for the horse had been napped by most of the newspapers and backed by the majority of the people present,

'Beauty Queen!'

The excited shout turned to a groan of dismay as the pink and white jacket began to drop back. The few supporters of Thunder Cloud roared their encouragement.

'Thunder Cloud! Thunder Cloud wins!'

And then Dick saw the orange and green worn by Golden Rain's jockey shoot out from the ruck, challenge and overtake Beauty Queen and decrease the distance between it and Thunder Cloud.

'Golden Rain! Golden Rain!'

The cry was meagre, for only a comparative few of the thousands present had backed Sir Trevor Bleck's second string. The jockey on Thunder Cloud became aware of the danger creeping up behind him, and used his whip, and he could not have made a worse error. Thunder Cloud flinched and swerved and as he did so Golden Rain shot past him . . .

Three lengths divided the two horses as the orange and green colours flashed past the post.

The win was received in almost complete silence, and as Dick made his way to the paddock to see the winner led in he heard some uncomplimentary remarks passed concerning the owner. But it was the trainer who led Golden Rain through the murmuring crowd, for Sir Trevor Bleck could not be found. He was searched for everywhere, but during the race he had vanished, and no one had seen him go.

'Ashimed to show 'is face, I should

think,' said a little Cockney. 'The twister!'

But that was not the real reason, as Dick learned later when he saw the letter which had been delivered to one of the Brighton stewards. It was brief and to the point:

'In spite of my warning Sir Trevor Bleck has continued to swindle the racing public. He will do so no more. I have removed him to a place where he will remain until such time as the punishment he deserves shall be meted out to him.'

And it was signed —

'The Jockey.'

27

The Prison-House

Sir Trevor Bleck opened his heavy eyelids and gazed dully about him. His head throbbed painfully and his tongue felt dry and unpleasant. Vaguely he wondered what had happened to bring about this queer sensation, and then he remembered the note which had been delivered to him just as he was making his way from the paddock to the stands — the note, purporting to come from Luke Walsh and requesting his presence urgently at the place where he had left his car.

The hastily scrawled message could only mean one thing — that something had gone wrong, and that Walsh wanted an immediate consultation with him in private. Hurrying to the 'Owners'' car park he had found it deserted. The various chauffeurs, including his own, had gone to watch the race, and there was no sign of the trainer.

He went over to his big, black saloon, and as he reached it the door opened and a husky voice called his name.

'What's the matter, Walsh?' he said, leaning into the interior, and that was all he remembered.

Something had pricked him sharply in the arm and his senses had fled.

He tried to struggle up, discovering in the attempt that his hands were shackled and his legs immovable. He was lying on a truckle-bed, a narrow cot of iron, in a small room devoid of furniture and containing a tiny oblong window through the heavy bars of which he caught a faint glimpse of blue sky. There was an unpleasant feeling of nausea in his stomach, the result evidently, of the drug which had been administered to him by the man who had been waiting in the car. The symptoms were so exactly similar to that other occasion when he had recovered consciousness in the disused shed on his own estate that he had no difficulty in guessing the identity of his captor.

The knowledge sent a twinge of uneasiness through him. Very well he remembered the contents of the letter which the Jockey had sent on that occasion and he had ignored its warning. He had continued with his plans for doping Beauty Queen, and this was the result. The Jockey had carried out his threat, though how the devil he had come to discover the plot was beyond Bleck's comprehension.

He was not, however, a great deal concerned with that. What concerned him mostly was his own position. He had been brought to this unknown place, which was so reminiscent of a prison cell, for a purpose, and he wondered what that purpose was. Obviously the Jockey had no intention of killing him. Had that been in his mind he could have accomplished his object without going to all this trouble. There was something else behind the reason for his abduction.

Curiously enough this did not tend to reassure him. The uncertainty surrounding his ultimate fate was a great deal more terrifying than any definite knowledge could have been. What did this unknown man intend to do with him, and how long was he likely to be kept a prisoner in this comfortless room?

From the faint sounds which filtered in through the small window he gathered that he was somewhere in the country. He heard the distant lowing of cattle and the harsh cawing of rooks, and then a noise that was nearer and of human origin, the sound of footsteps ascending a carpetless stair. They grew louder, came nearer, and stopped at the door of the room in which he was confined. There was the clink of metal and the rasp of a key and then the heavy door swung open and a figure appeared on the threshold. It was a familiar figure to Bleck's peering eyes, the figure he had seen in the moonlight on the lawn of his house at Weybridge.

'You have recovered from the effects of the drug?' inquired the thin, high-pitched voice. 'I thought it was time for you to do so.'

Bleck's fear became replaced by a wave of anger.

'Perhaps you'll kindly explain the meaning of this outrage!' he snarled viciously.

The Jockey closed the door and came over to the bed, surveying the recumbent man through the narrow slits in his mask.

'Is there any need for me to explain?' he said. 'You know very well why you have been brought here. You ignored my warning and continued your campaign for defrauding the racing public. For that you will have to be punished!' The emotionless, almost inhuman voice was more impressive than any outburst would have been. It was so impersonal and detached that it carried conviction.

'What do you intend to do with me?' asked Bleck.

'That you will learn at the right time,' answered the Jockey. 'At present you will remain here.'

'Do you suppose,' said the baronet, 'that I shan't be missed? Do you imagine for a moment that you can get away with a thing like this? The entire police force will be scouring the country for me!'

'If they can find you they are welcome,' said the man in black. 'I am quite aware that you will be missed. In fact I took the precaution to send a letter to the Brighton stewards notifying them of your abduction. I have no doubt the evening papers are full of your disappearance.'

'And you think you can get away with it?' said Bleck hoarsely.

'I *have* got away with it,' was the cool reply. 'You need have no illusions that you will be found. This place is secluded and few people know of its existence. I only found it by accident. It used to be a lunatic asylum. This room is one of several others in which the more dangerous of the patients were confined.'

'And you propose to keep me here indefinitely?' Bleck's face was red with fury, and his voice shook so that he could scarcely articulate the words.

The Jockey shook his head.

'Not indefinitely,' he answered. 'Only until such time as I have completed my arrangements for your punishment.'

'You're mad!' snapped his prisoner. 'You're crazy to think that you can get away with a thing like this!'

'That we shall see,' said the other. 'In the meantime, if I may offer a word of advice, I would suggest that you accept the situation calmly. During the period of waiting you will suffer no greater inconvenience than you would in a prison cell. Food will be brought to you at intervals and, if it is any satisfaction to you, there will be others in a similar position to your own.'

'Others? What do you mean?' demanded the baronet.

'Surely you did not imagine,' said the Jockey, 'that I went to the trouble and expense of acquiring a large building like this for your sole benefit? There are many others who have used racing as an illegal means of enriching themselves. One by one those others will be brought here, as you have been, to await the judgment that lies in store for them.'

'I suppose you realise the risk you're running?' said Bleck. 'You understand what awaits you if you're caught — '

'I have taken everything into consideration!' retorted the Jockey.

'And you intend to go through with

this insane scheme?' continued the baronet. 'D'you think the police are fools? D'you imagine that you can set yourself against them for ever?'

'No!' interrupted the high thin voice. 'Not for ever, but long enough to carry out my purpose. When I have accomplished that the Jockey will appear no more. That suitable, but perhaps slightly melodramatic pseudonym will be discarded together with the habiliments which go with it.'

The room was darkening as the light faded from the sky and the tall, thin figure, curiously indistinct in the shadows, looked so unreal that Sir Trevor Bleck wondered for a moment whether this was not some unpleasant dream from which he would shortly awake to find himself in his own bed.

'Who are you?' he asked huskily.

'I am many things,' answered the Jockey. 'To you and others like you I am Nemesis; I am the conscience which you have been born without. To some I bring hope, to others despair. To myself I am both a dream and a reality.'

'What is your object for this ridiculous masquerade?' sneered Bleck. 'What do you hope to gain by this nonsense?'

'I hope to achieve what it is beyond the law to do,' said the Jockey. 'I hope to punish all those who, by their foulness, have corrupted a thing that should be clean and wholesome, who have turned a sport into a money-making swindle, who have brought men to ruin and death.'

'And incidentally put a little money in your own pocket, I suppose!' said Bleck. 'All this highfalutin talk doesn't hoodwink me! Why don't you admit, once for all, that you're out to make as much as you can, like all crooks!'

'Because it would not be the truth,' said the Jockey. 'I am out to make nothing!'

'Then why,' said the baronet, 'go to all this trouble? If you want to punish people connected with the Turf who have possibly, now and again, gone outside the strict rules of racing, why not report them to the proper quarter? Why indulge in all this mummery, all this sensational novel stuff?'

'Because the punishment they would

receive from the proper quarter,' said the Jockey, 'would not be adequate. In the majority of cases, even if sufficient evidence could be produced, the result would only be a warning-off notice. These people are beyond the reach of the ordinary laws of the country and the disgrace attaching to a sentence by the Jockey Club would trouble them very little.'

'What is your idea of adequate punishment?' asked Bleck.

'It depends,' answered the figure, 'on the offence. My punishment will be adjusted to meet the gravity of the individual offence.'

Sir Trevor Bleck uttered a short laugh.

'In that case I ought to get off pretty lightly,' he remarked.

'You think so?' said the Jockey, and there was something in his tone that brought ice to the heart of the listening man. 'Search your memory!'

'I don't know what you mean!' said the baronet. 'I have done nothing serious — nothing terrible.'

'Is not murder serious?' broke in the Jockey. 'Is not the killing of a fellow creature terrible? Or have you forgotten?'

There was silence from the man on the bed.

'Two years ago,' went on the figure in black in that eerie whispering voice, 'a young stable-lad was found on the Downs near Luke Walsh's training stables. His neck was broken and the horse he had been riding was grazing near where he lay . . .'

'It was an accident.' Bleck's voice was hoarse and scarcely audible. 'It was an accident, the boy was thrown . . .'

'It was no accident!' said the Jockey. 'Tom Lemay was killed because he knew of a contemplated swindle on your part and was honest enough to have threatened to make it public. When the time comes for your judgment remember Lemay, for that will be taken into account when your punishment is meted out.'

The tall figure turned, and crossing to the door went out, locking it behind him. Sir Trevor Bleck, grey-faced, lay staring fearfully at the patch of indigo which marked the window. The Jockey had raised a ghost which mouthed at him horribly from the shadows of the little room; a ghost that he had hoped would remain for ever buried in that tiny grave where the unfortunate Tom Lemay had been laid.

28

Who was Norman Wharton?

The usually taciturn Mr. Pilchard was in high spirits and with reason, for during the last few weeks the *Sphere* had not only captured one scoop but three! The Jockey interview, the sensational killing of Joe Wills, and now the disappearance of Sir Trevor Bleck.

'You're doing fine, Templeton,' he said. 'Carry on the good work. Find out the identity of this Jockey fellow and you'll be the greatest reporter in the Street.'

'I'm that already,' said Dick immodestly, and left the news editor to interview the chief sub.

Mr. Budd was not so happy when he heard about the latest Jockey sensation. He came out of the assistant-commissioner's office a gloomy and depressed man, for his interview with Colonel Blair had been both protracted and unproductive.

'This man's got to be found!' had been the key-note of the commissioner's conversation. 'It doesn't matter whether he's a scoundrel or an honest man, he's got to be found! He's a baronet, and unless we do something all sorts of unpleasant questions will be asked in the House, and you know what that means. You've not only got to find Bleck but you've got to find the Jockey and stop him before he commits any further outrages. You've been working on this case now for over a month and you've got no results worth speaking about. It's bad, Superintendent, and you know it's bad.' He went on and on in the same strain, and Mr. Budd listened in silence. Argument was futile, and in any case Blair was right. Nobody realised better than he what a small amount he had to show for his labours.

He went slowly back to his own office, a frown on his big face and his lips pursed in a silent whistle. Leek raised his eyes from a black notebook in which he was laboriously figuring as the stout man came in.

'I've got a system — ' he began brightly.

'A disorderly system!' grunted Mr. Budd nodding. 'I've often wondered what was the matter with you. What are you takin' for it?'

A pained look crossed the lean sergeant's melancholy face.

'I don't mean that kind of system,' he explained. 'I'm talking about racing.'

Mr. Budd made a gesture of impatience.

'Can't you talk about anythin' else?' he demanded. 'Get this racin' bug out o' your head and turn your attention to a little honest work for a change.'

'There's nothing dishonest about racing,' said the aggrieved Leek, 'and if I can make a little money on the 'side' there's no 'arm, is there?'

'On whose side?' grunted the superintendent. 'You be content with your salary and don't go chasin' ifits!'

'There's something a bit exciting in a bit of money for nothing,' said Leek.

'Well, you get that every time you draw your pay envelope!' retorted Mr. Budd, collecting his hat. 'I'm goin' out, and if anyone wants me I'll be back just before midday.'

He jammed his hat on his head and left the office, and with a sigh of relief Sergeant Leek returned to the intricate calculations in the black notebook . . .

★   ★   ★

Lord Mortlake took the card from the salver which the footman held out and read it with a slight frown on his genial, good-humoured face.

'What does this fellow want, Thomas?' he asked.

'I don't know, my lord,' answered the footman. 'He asked if he could speak to you privately on an urgent matter.'

'H'm!' His lordship twisted the thin pasteboard between finger and thumb. 'Oh, well, show him in. I suppose I'd better see him.'

The footman withdrew and presently returned, ushering into the big, comfortably furnished library the portly Mr. Budd.

'Come in, Superintendent,' said Mortlake. 'What is this urgent matter you wish to see me about?'

The stout man eyed him sleepily.

'I'm inquirin' into this business of the Jockey and the disappearance of Sir Trevor Bleck, m'lord,' he murmured, 'and I'd like to ask you one or two questions, if you don't mind.'

Mortlake raised his eyebrows.

'What in the world do you imagine I know about the Jockey or this man Bleck?' he demanded.

'I don't think you know anythin' directly,' said Mr. Budd, 'but I believe indirectly you may be able to help us.'

'I can't imagine how,' said Mortlake. 'Sit down, Superintendent, and tell me what you want to know.'

Mr. Budd carefully settled himself in a huge leather chair and laid his hat on the floor at his side.

'Well,' he said, 'I daresay you'll think what I'm goin' to ask you is irrelevant, but I should like you to give me all the information you can concerning Mr. Norman Wharton — the late Norman Wharton.'

A cloud passed over the genial face of

the man before him. Since Norman Wharton's tragic death, over a year previously, Lord Mortlake had done his utmost to wipe from his mind his connection with that unhappy affair. Although, strictly speaking, he was not to blame in any way, he felt, to a certain degree, responsible for what had happened, and any reference to Wharton made him feel uncomfortable.

'What exactly do you want to know?' he inquired a little stiffly.

Mr. Budd sensed his reluctance and hastened to apologise.

'I'm very sorry, m'lord,' he said, 'to have to bother you, but we hold a theory at the Yard' — nobody held it except Mr. Budd himself so he was not being strictly truthful — 'that in some way the Jockey is connected with Mr. Wharton.'

'Connected with Wharton?' said Mortlake sharply. 'Nonsense!'

'Maybe it's nonsense, m'lord.' The stout man was completely unruffled. 'We find that a lot of these things are nonsense, but we have to inquire into 'em just the same. I believe you knew Mr.

Wharton very well.'

'Very well indeed,' admitted Mortlake. 'I went to school with his father.'

'That's just what I want to ask you about,' said Mr. Budd. 'You're talkin' about Colonel Henry Wharton, I suppose?'

'Of course,' said his lordship. 'Who else should I be talking about?'

'Well, Colonel Wharton wasn't Mr. Wharton's father,' said the superintendent.

Mortlake stared at him, his mouth agape.

'Wasn't his father?' he echoed. 'Don't be ridiculous, of course he was!'

Mr. Budd shook his head.

'He wasn't, m'lord,' he answered. 'We've made very strict inquiries into that, and Colonel Wharton never had a son, he had no children at all.'

'But, but — ' Mortlake stammered incoherently.

'I daresay that's rather a shock to you,' went on the stout man, 'but it's true, all the same.'

'Then — then' — gasped the astounded

Mortlake — 'who was Norman Wharton?'

'That's just what I'm tryin' to discover, m'lord,' said Mr. Budd. 'Who *was* Norman Wharton?'

'I was always under the impression he was Wharton's son!' exclaimed Mortlake. 'Even now I can't believe he wasn't. Are you sure of your facts, Superintendent?'

'Quite sure!' declared Mr. Budd. 'We've gone into the matter very carefully, m'lord. Colonel Wharton married a Miss Board and there was no issue.'

'It's incredible!' Lord Mortlake rose from his chair and began to pace up and down the long room. 'Incredible! I never doubted for one moment that Norman Wharton was their son.'

'Neither did anyone else, apparently,' murmured the stout man. 'But he wasn't. And what I'm interested to discover is if he wasn't Colonel Wharton's son, who was he?'

Mortlake shook his head helplessly.

'I'm afraid I can't help you, Superintendent,' he said. 'I always believed he was Wharton's son. Why, I knew him when he was a kid, I used to play with him. Dammit, there must be some mistake!'

'There is,' said Mr. Budd, 'and the mistake, if you'll excuse me saying so, m'lord, is on your side. This child that you played with may have been adopted by Colonel Wharton and passed off as his son to everybody, but he wasn't the same flesh and blood.'

'You mean that Wharton adopted him as a baby?' said Mortlake, and the superintendent nodded.

'That's how I've worked it out, sir,' he said, 'and I don't see any other explanation. I was hopin' that you, bein' such friends with the late Colonel Wharton, might be able to tell me whose baby it was he adopted.'

'I'd no idea he'd adopted any baby,' said Mortlake. 'You have astounded me!'

A slow smile crossed Mr. Budd's heavy face.

'I've astounded many people in my time, m'lord,' he said. 'P'raps you can suggest someone who can help me?'

His lordship pursed his lips.

'Wharton's solicitors might know,' he

318

suggested after a pause. 'I should think it's very likely they *would* know.'

'Who were his solicitors?' asked Mr. Budd.

'Stenson and Shepherd, of Lincoln's Inn,' replied Mortlake.

'I'll go and see them,' said Mr. Budd. 'There's nothin' you can remember, m'lord, that might help us trace the identity of this child who was supposed to be Colonel Wharton's son?'

Mortlake shook his head.

'I'm afraid there isn't,' he answered candidly. 'If I could think of anything I should be only too pleased to tell you. It's the most extraordinary and amazing thing! Not only I but everyone who was acquainted with him was under the impression that Norman Wharton was his son.'

'It's surprisin',' said Mr. Budd, struggling with difficulty to his feet, 'how little people really know about the private affairs of their friends and acquaintances. It's one of the things we're always comin' up against.' He picked up his hat. 'Well, it's very good of you to have seen me,

319

m'lord, and I'm sorry to have had to bother you.'

'No bother at all,' said Mortlake, 'and I shall be glad if you will let me know what discoveries you make, if any, at the solicitors'.'

He accompanied Mr. Budd to the door, and when that sleepy-eyed and disappointed man had gone he returned with a frown to his interrupted newspaper. But the stately columns of *The Times* held no further interest for him. Until the soft gong summoned him to lunch he sat staring into the fireless grate, his mind completely occupied with the revelation of his recent interview.

Mr. Budd, emerging into Berkeley Square, stood for some seconds on the pavement torn between laziness and the soulless official who would question his expense account if he took a taxi. His habitual antipathy to any form of exertion won, and he hailed a passing cab, giving the address of the solicitors in Lincoln's Inn that Mortlake had mentioned.

He had no difficulty in securing an interview with Mr. Shepherd, but the information he succeeded in acquiring was nil. The solicitor listened to what he had to say with an expressionless face.

'I can give you no information, Superintendent,' he said, when Mr. Budd put his question, 'because I do not possess any. I had no idea that the late Mr. Norman Wharton was not Colonel Henry Wharton's son. If he was not, and I have always been led to believe he was, then who was he?'

The stout superintendent would have been only too pleased if it had lain in his power to answer that question. It was a question which he was most anxious to clear up; a question, the answer to which he firmly believed would do much towards clearing up that other and equally unanswerable question — the identity of the Jockey. But that mysterious individual and Norman Wharton had one thing in common, their origin was shrouded in mystery, and no amount of inquiry and probing seemed capable of penetrating the veil of secrecy which covered them both.

29

Mr. Crabthorne Makes an Appointment

Three days had elapsed since the disappearance of Sir Trevor Bleck, and in spite of the fact that the police force of the whole country was looking for him not a trace of him had been found.

The inquiry into the running of Beauty Queen, which the veiled accusation contained in the 'Jockey' letter had brought about, resulted in the 'warning off' of Luke Walsh. The veterinary surgeon's examination of the horse's saliva and perspiration had resulted in the definite discovery that a drug had been administered. The trainer had volubly denied all knowledge of it, but his denials had not been accepted by the stewards.

On the fourth day of the search for Bleck a fresh sensation sent up the circulation of the newspapers and brought uneasiness to the hearts of many men whose livelihood was garnered from the turf.

Michael Linnet, the well-known jockey, disappeared on his way back from Sandown, and on the following morning, by post, the stewards of the Sandown Meeting received one of the familiar 'Jockey' letters. It was printed in the *Sphere* and caused considerable comment:

> *'I have taken Linnet because he is not fit to hold a licence. He is a crooked rider and for some years has been making money at the expense of the public and his employers. He will receive in due course adequate punishment for his offence.*
>
> *'The Jockey.'*

The general public read the letter and the two-column account that went with it and discussed the matter volubly, expressing for the most part sympathy with the Jockey's aims if not wholehearted approval of his methods.

'It's time somethin' was done,' remarked

a burly labourer over his midday beer, and putting into words the views of the majority, 'and this feller's doin' it. Now p'raps the small punter 'ull have a fair run for his bob!'

The people chiefly concerned reacted in various ways consistent with their characters. Mr. Budd developed an attack of irritability coupled with a predilection for sarcasm which tried the patience of the long-suffering Sergeant Leek, and reduced that melancholy man to a state of gloomy pessimism, which only had the effect of incensing the stout superintendent to further scathing remarks.

Lord Mortlake and his fellow stewards of the Jockey Club refused to discuss the matter at all in public, although in their inmost thoughts it worried them not a little, and one of them a great deal.

Pamela Westmore, in the course of an accidental meeting with Dick Templeton, openly confessed that she was on the side of the Jockey, and Benjamin Cowan, still smarting under the treatment administered by the girl, stormed at the inadequacy of the police to deal with what he called 'this new menace to civilisation' and spent his time scowling in his office, alternating between fits of rage and fear.

Mr. Marius Crabthorne sat in the confined space of his little sitting-room in the small flat at the back of Tottenham Court Road on the morning following the publication of the letter and awaited the arrival of Lew Sleator in a complacent mood. With any luck he would shortly have in his hands evidence that would confirm his suspicion as to the identity of the Jockey, for to-day was Sunday, and on the preceding night Mr. Sleator should have carried out the burglary which the inquiry agent had suggested.

It was half past eleven when the shrill summons of the clockwork bell attached to the front door warned Mr. Crabthorne of the arrival of his expected visitor. He went out into the dark little lobby and admitted the slim man.

'Well,' he said as he closed the door and escorted his visitor into the sitting-room, 'did you do it?'

Sleator nodded.

'Yes,' he answered, 'and it was as easy as opening a tin of sardines.'

'Did you find what I expected?' asked the inquiry agent quickly.

The little man nodded his bald head.

'I found more than you expected,' he answered. 'My word, it's a pretty big thing you're on!'

Mr. Crabthorne rubbed his hands in pleasurable anticipation.

'What did you find?' he inquired.

'Enough to prove,' said the burglar, 'that this feller's the Jockey all right!'

The inquiry agent's small eyes sparkled.

'Sit down and tell me all about it,' he invited, waving his hand towards an armchair and producing from a sideboard cupboard a bottle and glasses.

Mr. Sleator complied, passing a delicate hand over his smooth-shaven, powdered chin.

'I've never had an easier job,' he began. 'I went down on Friday and 'felt' the house, and it didn't take me long to see that it was a walkover. None of the servants slept on the premises, and there was only the feller himself to bother about. I got into the place on the Saturday morning on the pretext that I was from the telephone company. There were no burglar alarms and the fastenings of the windows were childish. At one o'clock last night I did the job.' He paused and gulped the drink which Mr. Crabthorne had poured out.

'And you found — ' prompted the inquiry agent.

'I found a lot of things,' said Mr. Sleator, eyeing him queerly. 'The safe was an old-fashioned one that you could have opened with a toothpick. There was no money in it' — he made a wry grimace — 'but there were plenty of other things. In a box at the bottom was the Jockey's outfit, or rather part of it, a freshly made black silk shirt and black cap. A spare set I should think, for they didn't look as if they'd ever been worn.'

'Excellent,' said Mr. Crabthorne delightedly. 'I think we've got him, Lew.'

'Oh, you've got him all right,' agreed the burglar, 'and you've got somebody else too.'

The inquiry agent looked at him quickly.

'What do you mean?' he asked.

'I found this in the safe among the other papers,' said Mr. Sleator slowly, and produced from his breast pocket an envelope which he passed across to the other.

Crabthorne took it and eyed it frowningly.

'What's this?' he grunted.

'Look at it and see!' retorted Lew Sleator, finishing his drink. 'It'll give you an eye-opener.'

Mr. Crabthorne slipped a finger and thumb under the flap — it had been sealed, but Lew Sleator's curiosity was evidently accountable for its being broken — and withdrew the contents, a single sheet of typewritten paper.

The inquiry agent's eyes read the first few lines and his lips pursed into a silent whistle. Eagerly he finished perusing the document and noted the sprawling signature.

'What do you think of it?' asked Mr. Sleator.

'What do I think of it!' The fat, oily face of the inquiry agent was expressive of his amazement. 'This wants consideration, Lew. No wonder Cowan was so anxious to find this feller, knowing he had that in his possession. I wonder he's been able to get any sleep.'

'Perhaps he hasn't,' said the thin burglar sardonically. 'And I shouldn't think, now that's come into our possession, he'll ever get any again. If we work him properly we're in for easy money for the rest of our lives.'

Mr. Crabthorne frowned, and the look he gave his visitor was not entirely friendly.

'What are you getting at?' he muttered. 'You're not in this, you've done your part and when I've paid you your thousand, or to be exact nine 'undred and fifty, since you've already had fifty, our relationship is at an end.'

'I think not,' said Mr. Sleator smoothly. 'Don't you flatter yourself, Crabthorne. I'm in this, and I'm stayin' in, on a fifty-fifty basis!'

'Fifty-fifty of what?' demanded the inquiry agent.

'Fifty-fifty of what you get out of Cowan!' retorted Sleator. 'And if you play your cards well it should be a pretty comfortable little sum. Any man 'ud be willing to pay his last penny sooner than have that document sent to the right quarter. It's a confession of murder, and he ought to be willing to pay a lot to anyone who'll keep it dark.'

Mr. Crabthorne was silent. The same idea had instantly occurred to him when he had read that confession which the Jockey, on the night he had visited Benjamin Cowan, had forced that terrified man to sign. But he was not at all pleased at the prospect of having to split with Lew Sleator. However, at the moment he could see no other alternative. The little burglar was in possession of the facts, and unless they came to an agreement would undoubtedly use them to his own advantage. In the circumstances he decided to make the best of a bad job.

'All right,' he grunted ungraciously. 'We'll talk about that presently. Did you bring away the 'Jockey' stuff?'

Sleator shook his head.

'No, I left it,' he answered. 'I thought it was better. You told me in the beginning you wanted this job to look like an ordinary burglary, and no respectable burglar would bother to take a collection of black silk.'

Mr. Crabthorne looked dubious.

'A pity,' he remarked. 'We've got no proof that this feller is the Jockey.'

'We don't need any,' answered Sleator quickly. 'We know he is ourselves, and that's all that matters.' He pulled out a cigarette case and lit a cigarette, trickling smoke luxuriously through his nostrils. 'This is a good thing,' he said. 'One of the best things I've struck. With the income we can get from these two people we ought to be on velvet for the rest of our lives.'

'It was my idea,' murmured Crabthorne. 'I think we ought to make it seventy-thirty.'

Mr. Sleator ignored the suggestion as beneath his notice.

'We've got two strings to pull,' he continued. 'Cowan and this Jockey feller, and there's unlimited money on the end of both of 'em.'

'Are you suggesting,' said the inquiry agent, 'that we put the 'black' on the pair of them?'

'Of course,' said Sleator, looking at him as though such a question was needless. 'Isn't it obvious? We've got 'em both in the hollow of our hands. If we squeal on Cowan he'll swing, and if we squeal on the Jockey he'll go to prison. We can ask what we like — and get it!'

Crabthorne nodded slowly. In spite of the unpleasantness of having to split with his companion he was more than pleased at the result of the scheme. He had never expected that Cowan would be delivered into his hands in this way. It amazed him that the bookmaker should have put his signature to such a dangerous document, but it was understandable now why he had been so anxious to discover the identity of the Jockey. This had rather puzzled Mr. Crabthorne since his interview with Cowan, but now the anxiety of the bookmaker was explained. Before his eyes rose visions of easy money rolling regularly into his banking account, and the prospect was very much to his liking.

'You'd better leave this to me,' he said, tapping the document on his fat knee. 'I'll handle this business.'

Mr. Sleator made no demur. He was, in fact, quite prepared for the inquiry agent to deal with the subtle task of extracting money from these men, provided he received his due share. He said as much, at the same time putting forward the suggestion which he thought was necessary to safeguard his own interests.

'We'll have a little agreement in writin' between us in case of accidents,' he said, and stuck to this point, in spite of Mr. Crabthorne's arguments to the contrary.

The agreement was drawn up in duplicate, after much discussion, and signed, and with one copy of this in his breast pocket Mr. Sleator took his departure, leaving Marius Crabthorne to formulate his plans.

He spent the greater part of the day on this, and towards the evening put through a telephone call to Benjamin Cowan's flat. The bookmaker was at home, and came to the instrument when the name of the caller was given him.

'Hullo, Crabthorne!' he grunted crossly, for he was not in the best of tempers. 'What do you want?'

'I want to see you,' said the inquiry agent curtly, and Cowan noticed that his usual unctuous politeness was absent. 'Come round to my flat this evening.'

'Is it very urgent?' asked the book-maker.

'Very!' replied Crabthorne curtly. 'I have some news which I think will interest you.'

'You've made a discovery concerning the Jockey?' asked Cowan eagerly.

'I'll tell you the news when I see you,' said the inquiry agent, and rang off.

He put through another call, the result of which filled him with an immense satisfaction, and settled down compla-cently to await the coming of Benjamin Cowan. The time he had spent over the Jockey business looked like paying a very profitable dividend.

It was lucky for Marius Crabthorne's peace of mind that he had no knowledge of the future. Had he been able to see what was to happen during the next twenty-four hours he would have rushed panic-stricken from his cosy flat to hide himself from the fate which his schemes for easy money were to bring upon him.

30

The Figure in Black

Benjamin Cowan climbed the stairs to Mr. Crabthorne's dingy flat as the clock in an adjacent church struck nine. A taxi had set him down at the corner of Tottenham Court Road and he covered the rest of the distance on foot, having no wish that there should exist a record, however slight, of his visit to the inquiry agent. For some unaccountable reason Mr. Crabthorne's telephone message had filled him with a sense of unease; a curious foreboding of impending trouble. Why it should have had this effect the bookmaker would have found difficulty in explaining. He had been expecting such a message for some time; had indeed been impatiently awaiting it ever since he had commissioned the man to discover the identity of the Jockey. But there had been something in Crabthorne's tone, a subtle difference in his usual deferential voice that was both peculiar and puzzling. There had been a hint of imperiousness — a demand rather than a request — in the way he had made the appointment that Mr. Cowan resented.

He told himself as he paused on the dark landing that he was probably imagining things. If Crabthorne had made a discovery, his natural elation over his success was most likely the cause of that slight difference in his demeanour towards his employer.

He pressed the bell and waited. The door was opened by Crabthorne himself, a stout figure clad in a gaudy dressing-gown.

'Oh, it's you at last,' greeted the inquiry agent. 'Come in, Cowan.'

Benjamin Cowan stepped across the threshold, a scowl on his heavy face.

'I've got a handle to my name, Crabthorne,' he grunted crossly. 'Use it will you?'

The other shrugged his broad shoulders without speaking, and the action infuriated the bookmaker. The tremendous streak of

vanity in his character demanded defer-
ence from those whom he regarded as
beneath him.

'Just remember who you're talking to!'
he snarled, as he followed Crabthorne
into the sitting-room.

'Who am I talking to?' demanded the
inquiry agent unpleasantly. 'Ever since
I've had any dealings with you, Cowan,
you've treated me like dirt. Now you're
getting some of your own medicine and
you don't like it.'

The bookmaker glared at him, almost
speechless with rage.

'You — you oily swine!' he said thickly.
'How dare you speak to me like that? Do
you realise that a word from me would
send you to prison — '

'Sit down!' snapped Mr. Crabthorne.
'And shut up! I'm going to do the talking
this evening for a change, Cowan, see? A
word from you would send me to prison,
eh? I wonder where a word from me
would send *you?*'

'You're either mad or drunk!' began
Cowan angrily, but the inquiry agent
interrupted him.

'I'm neither!' he declared. 'Forget the slanging match, Cowan, and sit down. I asked you to come here to talk over a matter of business.'

'Well then, keep a civil tongue in your head!' snarled the bookmaker dropping into a chair. 'What's come over you?'

Mr. Crabthorne took up his position in front of the empty grate and regarded his visitor calmly.

'Nothing's come over me at all,' he answered smoothly 'It's not I who's got to remain civil in future, Cowan, it's you.'

Cowan eyed him through narrowed eyes. What had happened to change this usually subservient and unctuous man before him into a dictatorial bully? He had not been drinking — that was not the reason for the metamorphosis. What then?

'What did you want to see me about?' he growled.

'Just a matter of business,' replied Crabthorne. 'A certain document has come into my possession which, if it reached the proper quarter, might cause you a lot of trouble — a *lot* of trouble,' he added slowly.

A sudden fear seized Cowan's heart. What was the man talking about? Could he possibly be referring to — to — No, it was absurd, ridiculous! That confession which he had been forced to sign was in the possession of the Jockey. It couldn't possibly have come into Crabthorne's hands . . .

'What do you mean?' he asked.

'Got a bad memory, haven't you?' said the inquiry agent, helping himself to a cigar from the box on the mantelpiece and piercing the end with his nail. 'Forgotten all about Simon Corbett. Forgotten Ted Green, too! Forgotten how they died!'

The bookmaker felt the blood drain away from his face.

'I haven't forgotten,' he muttered. 'I know how they died. They were murdered by the Jockey.'

'Of course they were,' said Mr. Crabthorne. 'That's why you signed a confession stating that you were responsible for killing them.'

Cowan's face was leaden-grey.

'I don't know what you're talking

about!' he breathed thickly. 'I signed no confession. You're crazy!'

The fat face of the inquiry agent creased into a smile that was not good to look upon.

'Maybe the police 'ull think I'm crazy,' he said significantly. 'Maybe they won't. It's no good bluffing, Cowan. I've got that confession, and unless you make it worth my while I'm sending it to Scotland Yard.'

Cowan saw that he was telling the truth; knew that in some unaccountable way that fatal document, the existence of which had caused him to lie wakeful and uneasy through many a long night, had come into his keeping.

'How did you get it?' he asked huskily, his throat dry and the palms of his hands damp.

'It doesn't matter how I got it!' retorted Crabthorne. 'I have got it, and that's sufficient. It isn't here,' he added hastily, as he saw an expression come into the other's eyes. 'It's in safe keeping. The question is how much are you going to pay me to keep quiet about it?'

'Blackmail, eh?' whispered Cowan.

'Call it that if you like!' snapped the inquiry agent. 'I prefer to call it a business proposition.'

The bookmaker licked his dry lips.

'What do you want for that document?' he asked, and the other's reply astonished him.

'Nothing!' said Mr. Crathorne briefly.

'Nothing?' Cowan's tone was incredulous.

'Nothing,' said Crabthorne, 'because I'm not selling. You don't suppose I'm going to part with a certain income, do you? Not me! The arrangement I'm willing to make with you is this: On the first of every month you pay me a thousand pounds. So long as the money reaches me regularly that confession of yours might never have been written. But miss a payment and it goes straight to police headquarters!'

'It's absurd! Ridiculous!' said Cowan, the colour coming back to his face in his anger at this exhorbitant demand. 'How do you suppose I'm going to find a thousand a month to give you?'

'I don't care how you find it,' said the inquiry agent. 'That doesn't interest me, so long as you do find it. After all, twelve thousand a year is not a great deal to pay — for your life.'

'It's impossible for me to find anything like that amount!' said Cowan. 'My financial position at the moment is by no means as good as people think. Besides, what safeguard have I? Suppose I agree to this outrageous proposition how am I to know that the document is safe? Supposing it got into other hands? Supposing anything happened to you — '

'You've got to take the risk of that,' broke in Crabthorne pleasantly.

'Why not fix a reasonable lump sum? I am prepared to pay anything within limits . . . '

The inquiry agent shook his head.

'Nothing doing,' he declared. 'I'm not the only one in this, Cowan. I've talked the matter over with my — my partner, and we agree that a thousand pounds a month is the only thing we are prepared to accept.'

'You must give me time to think it over,' muttered the bookmaker. 'Even if I agreed I should have considerable difficulty in raising the money and — '

'I'll give you till twelve o'clock to-morrow morning,' said Mr. Crabthorne generously, 'and not a minute longer. You'll agree, Cowan, and you can find the money if you want to. It's no good trying to pull that stuff on me about being hard-up.'

The bookmaker was silent. The man before him had the whip-hand and he knew it. At any cost that confession must never become public. At the best it would lead to unpleasant inquiries, and at the worst — he shuddered. Before his eyes rose a picture of the condemned cell and the death-house.

'You won't consider a compromise?' he suggested unsteadily. 'Think how much better off you would be with a lump sum. Supposing for the sake of argument that anything happened to me, your income would cease. You couldn't blackmail a dead man!'

This aspect had not struck Mr. Crabthorne before and he frowned.

'No, that's true,' he admitted grudgingly. 'There's something in what you say, Cowan.'

The bookmaker pressed his advantage eagerly.

'I'll give you twelve thousand pounds in cash,' he said, 'the day after to-morrow, in return for that document.'

'Not enough,' said the inquiry agent. 'I'll take a lump sum but it'll have to be thirty thousand.'

'You might as well say thirty million!' retorted Cowan. 'Twelve thousand I could manage, but thirty thousand is impossible!'

'I'll take it in three instalments,' said Crabthorne. 'Twelve thousand the day after to-morrow, ten thousand in a month, and eight thousand the month after that. And when you hand over the eight thousand you shall have the document.'

Cowan argued and almost entreated, but the other was adamant.

'You're sure the thing is in a safe place?' he said, and Mr. Crabthorne smiled confidently.

'Don't you worry about that,' he replied reassuringly. 'It's safe enough!' Almost unconsciously his eyes strayed to the communicating door that led to his bedroom.

So the confession was on the premises, thought Cowan. He rose to his feet.

'I suppose I shall have to agree to your terms,' he said. 'But you must give me a couple of days to find the first instalment.'

'I'm agreeable to that,' said Crabthorne. 'Better say twelve o'clock on Wednesday morning.'

The bookmaker inclined his head.

'Very well,' he said. 'In the meanwhile I have your assurance that you will keep the document safely?'

'Does one destroy the goose that lays the golden eggs?' said Mr. Crabthorne jovially. 'Is it sensible for a man to blow up the mine that pays him his dividends? You can rest assured that that confession will be my most treasured possession until such time as you have completed your payment.'

He escorted his visitor to the door, and

when Cowan had gone returned to the sitting-room at peace with the world. It had been easier than he had expected. He had anticipated a greater amount of resistance; possibly even an attempt at physical violence. He had not got quite what he wanted, but thirty thousand pounds was a nice round sum, sufficient to supply him with most of the luxuries which his mean little soul craved. It was true he would have to divide this with Sleator, which was an unpleasant thought, but even fifteen thousand was more than he had ever had in his life before. There were places abroad where a man with fifteen thousand pounds could enjoy life to the full, and there was more than that. He still had the other string to pull.

He wondered, as he smoked his cigar and drank his whisky and soda, whether the Jockey would prove as amenable as had Benjamin Cowan. Perhaps it would be better in his case, too, to suggest a lump sum. After all there was something certain and solid in that. No unforeseen contingencies could arrive later to denude him of the spoils.

Altogether he was rather glad that he had listened to the bookmaker's suggestion. It was sensible. Cowan was not a young man, and if anything happened to him the income would cease. Whereas the thirty thousand pounds, once paid over, was his for good — or fifty per cent of it.

He frowned. Perhaps something could be done there. Perhaps his brain would suggest a way by which Sleator could be got rid of for a lesser amount. He thought this over until he found himself yawning, and then, rising to his feet, stretched himself and retired to his bedroom with the satisfactory feeling that the day had not been an unprofitable one.

He undressed slowly and got into bed, switched out the light, and was almost instantly asleep . . .

In the dark and narrow street outside a policeman passed slowly on his beat, soft-footed and alert for unfastened doors and open windows. He paced majestically to the end, and turning the corner vanished from view. The street became empty except for a forlorn cat who appeared from a nearby area and prowled softly in the gutter. And then from the opposite direction to that taken by the constable came the figure of a man walking rapidly and noiselessly.

The cat, disturbed in its nocturnal amusements, shot across the street and disappeared into a patch of shadow. At the main door of the building in which Mr. Crabthorne lay sleeping the black figure of the newcomer paused, looking quickly up and down the deserted length of the pavement. There was a street lamp farther down the road, but its light fell short of the doorway at which he had stopped, throwing it into deep shadow.

Into this murky gloom the man stepped, remained for a moment dimly visible, and then appeared to melt away as the heavy door swung noiselessly open and closed behind him. In the darkness of the vestibule he stood for a second listening, but all around him there was silence. Cautiously he advanced to the foot of the stairs and with infinite care began to ascend them. Outside the entrance to Mr. Crabthorne's flat he paused again. From the pocket of the long coat he was wearing he took a silken object which he adjusted to his face and head in place of the cap he was wearing.

There was scarcely an audible sound, nothing that would arouse the lightest sleeper. The faintest possible click, a scarcely discernable creak, and the door was open. The man whose face was now concealed behind the black silk mask stepped across the threshold. The heavy breathing of the sleeper within came distinctly to his ears as he softly shut the door.

His gloved hand dipped into his pocket and came out holding an automatic pistol, to the barrel of which had been screwed a cylinder of dull blue metal.

He went over to the open door of the sitting-room and entered, moving with the swiftness and silence of the cat he had disturbed in the street below. The sound of the breathing was louder here, for the communicating door to the bedroom was ajar. The figure in black tiptoed towards it, pushed it farther open, and slid into the room beyond . . .

Mr. Crabthorne, noisily sleeping and dreaming of the delights of perpetual sunshine in some foreign town, knew nothing of the black-clad doom that stood motionless beside his bed.

The man in black stooped, felt with a gloved hand, and touched the sleeper's face. With a husky cry Mr. Crabthorne woke and started up in alarm. Two yellow spears of flame stabbed the darkness, but he only saw one of them, for the first bullet tore through his heart, blotting out in one instant of excruciating agony sight and sound and hearing . . .

31

Mr. Budd Makes a Discovery

That Sunday which heralded the extinction of Mr. Marius Crabthorne was also notable in other ways, for it formed a period in the lives of those more or less intimately connected with the Jockey that they were long afterwards to remember.

Mr. Budd spent the greater part of that day in the garden of his small house at Streatham, lovingly tending the roses which provided him with an all-absorbing hobby. It was not until the evening of that memorable day that he reluctantly tore himself away from his pleasant task and boarded a bus for Scotland Yard.

Getting down at the corner of Whitehall he was moving ponderously towards the arched entrance when a girl passed him, walking rapidly and obviously in a hurry. It was Pamela Westmore.

He wondered as he continued on his way, what had brought her up from Ditchling on this Sunday evening and where she was going to in such haste. But his curiosity was only ephemeral, and by the time he reached his office the incident had passed from his mind. Later he was to remember it and try and find a place in the puzzle he was laboriously piecing together.

His office was empty, for Sergeant Leek was off duty, a fact for which the stout superintendent was extremely thankful. His irritability had not diminished, and he felt that the lugubrious face of the melancholy sergeant would not tend to brighten his gloomy outlook. For Mr. Budd admitted that he was up against it. Never had he tackled such a thankless task as that which had been entrusted to him — the finding of the Jockey. Never had he been engaged in such a case which was so complicated or so devoid of anything solid in which he could get his teeth.

He had come up that evening in the hope of finding results from the various inquiries which he had set on foot. The mystery surrounding the birth of Norman Wharton was the source of his principal worry. He believed — although he had nothing more to go on than a personal conviction — that in this was to be found the main reason for the Jockey having come into existence.

He sat down at his desk, lit one of his atrocious cigars, and smoked for a moment or two in order to recover from the exertion of climbing the stairs. When he was breathing normally again he stretched out a fat hand to the bell. To the messenger who answered the summons he issued an order and sat back to await the arrival of the man he had sent for. He came almost immediately, a thin-faced, quiet-looking individual, greeting the stout superintendent with a respectful 'Good evening, sir.'

'Good evening, Sergeant,' murmured Mr. Budd, who had arranged for Sergeant Boyd to deliver his report at that hour. 'Sit down.'

The sergeant seated himself on a chair in front of the desk.

'Now,' continued the big man, 'what's your news?'

'Not a great deal I'm afraid, sir,' said Boyd, producing a black-covered notebook and consulting it. 'I've made close inquiries into the past of Colonel Wharton, but I can trace up nothing concerning this supposed son. All I have been able to do is to unearth the fact that Colonel Wharton had a brother, which is apparently not generally known.'

Mr. Budd's sleepy eyes opened a fraction.

'Oh, he had a brother, eh?' he grunted. 'H'm! Is the brother alive?'

The sergeant shook his neat head.

'No, sir,' he answered. 'The brother died in a French prison twenty years ago, when he was serving a sentence for forgery.'

'Oh!' The stout man's lips formed the exclamation to the accompaniment of a faint whistle. 'Serving a sentence for forgery, was he? What was his name?'

'His name was Norman Wharton,' replied Boyd. 'From what I can discover he was something of a black sheep. He got into trouble at Oxford and apparently was continuously in trouble until he died in the prison. His family had practically disowned him. He seems to have lived most of his life abroad, and to have married a French actress, who died a year after the wedding.'

'Any children?' inquired Mr. Budd.

'That I have been unable to discover, sir,' said the sergeant.

There was a silence while the stout man leaned back in his chair and blew a succession of smoke rings towards the ceiling.

'There was a child, Boyd,' he remarked at last. 'There was a child. I'll bet any money there was! And that child was Norman Wharton.'

The sergeant nodded in agreement.

'The same thought occurred to me, sir,' he said.

'How soon after the wife died was this fellow arrested?' asked Mr. Budd sleepily.

Sergeant Boyd glanced at his notebook.

'Two weeks,' he answered.

The big man nodded.

'That's it,' he said. 'This brother of

356

Colonel Wharton married this woman and they had a child, Norman Wharton. She died and the brother was arrested for forgery. Colonel Wharton adopts the baby and passes it off as his own. It's as clear as daylight.' He frowned. 'But it doesn't get us much further. I suppose there's no doubt that this fellow, I'll call him Norman Wharton, Senior, died in the prison?'

'No doubt at all, sir,' declared the sergeant.

'H'm!' remarked the stout superintendent. 'Well, we've got a little further, but not much. If this father of Norman Wharton, Junior, was still alive I'd begin thinkin' things. I'd begin thinkin' that possibly he was at the bottom of this Jockey business, but he can't be if he's dead.' He took the cigar from between his lips and eyed it thoughtfully. 'You've done very well, Sergeant,' he said. 'I'll have a word to say in the right quarter. Don't let up on this, see what else you can find out. I want to know everything it's possible to discover about these Whartons.'

His words were a dismissal. Sergeant

Boyd rose, closing his book and returning it to his pocket.

'Very well, sir,' he said, and left the office.

For some time after he had gone the big man sat motionless, his eyes completely closed and lost in thought. Then once more he stretched out his hand and pressed the bell.

'Is Sergeant Bailey in?' he inquired of the messenger who came after a short delay.

'I think so, sir,' said the man.

'Send him in to me,' said Mr. Budd.

The thick-set, jovial-faced man who presently entered the office was in direct contrast to Sergeant Boyd.

'Sit down, Bailey,' said Mr. Budd, and when the other had complied: 'What have you got to tell me about Cowan?'

'I've checked up on him, sir,' replied Bailey, 'and there's no proof that he was in London at the time Wills was killed.'

'I thought there wouldn't be,' murmured Mr. Budd with satisfaction. 'Anythin' else?'

'His record's a pretty bad one,'

continued Bailey; 'he's never done anything actually against the law but he's sailed pretty close to the wind. In his early days he ran a shooting gallery in Whitechapel — '

'Eh? What's that?' Mr. Budd sat up quickly. 'Say that again,' he said.

'He ran a shooting gallery in Whitechapel, sir,' repeated the sergeant in astonishment.

'Oh, he did, did he!' The stout man gently rubbed his many chins. 'That's interestin', very interestin'! Now, a man who ran a shootin' gallery would naturally be a good shot, wouldn't he?'

'It's quite likely,' smiled the sergeant.

'I should say it's very likely,' affirmed Mr. Budd. 'And the man who killed Wills was a good shot, an excellent shot. Very interestin'. Did you find out where Cowan was on the night Corbett was killed?'

The sergeant shook his head.

'No, sir,' he answered. 'So far as I can discover he was in bed and asleep.'

'In bed and asleep, eh?' said Mr. Budd. 'Well, bein' a respectable man an' a bachelor, he couldn't prove it. I'll bet I know where he was! I'll bet he wasn't very far away from that trainin' stable at Ditchling.'

'You think Cowan was responsible for the killing of Corbett and the other man?' inquired the sergeant.

'You'd be surprised what I think!' said Mr. Budd. 'I think such a lot of things that I don't know where to leave off thinkin' and start doin'.' He sighed. 'Nothin's come in about Bleck or the other feller, Linnet, I suppose?' he said, and he wasn't so much addressing the sergeant as speaking his thoughts aloud. 'They've just vanished like a burst soap bubble, and the police of the whole country can't find them. This Jockey man's a clever feller, and he's all the cleverer because I'm certain he doesn't work with a gang. He works on his own, and that's why we're goin' to find it so difficult to pull him in. There's nobody to squeal, nobody to supply information.'

The sergeant listened but offered no comment. He knew Mr. Budd sufficiently well to know that comment was not expected. The big man had a habit of rambling on. It helped, he had explained once to Leek, to clarify his thoughts, and nobody knew better than he how badly they needed clarifying. He felt that among the chaotic jumble which filled his brain he possessed all the necessary pieces to make a clear and coherent picture if only he could drop them into the right places.

He dismissed the sergeant and sat on, smoking cigar after cigar until the office became filled with a blue and acrid fog. It was late when he made up his mind to go home, and rose laboriously to his feet. His evening had not been wasted. He had learned two facts which he was certain were of the utmost importance. That incident in Cowan's past life which concerned the shooting gallery at Whitechapel and the brother of Colonel Wharton who had died in a French prison . . .

Walking slowly up Whitehall, for he had decided to seek a secluded restaurant and eat a modest supper before returning to his little house at Streatham, he ran into Dick Templeton.

'Hello!' he said, stopping and surveying

the reporter. 'What are you doin' in London? I thought you'd taken up a permanent residence in the country.'

Dick grinned.

'I thought I'd pop up to see the sights,' he remarked. 'It was getting a little dull at the village inn. Where are you off to on this lovely summer evening?'

Mr. Budd explained carefully, and Dick offered to accompany him as far as Soho, which was his objective.

'I saw that gal Westmore earlier this evenin',' said the stout man as they walked along and Dick looked at him quickly.

'Miss Westmore? In London?' he asked.

'In Whitehall,' said Mr. Budd carefully, 'which I suppose is the same thing.'

'I wonder what she was doing up here?' muttered the reporter. 'I didn't know she'd left Downlands.'

'Does she usually notify you of her movements?' murmured Mr. Budd, and there was something in his tone that caused Dick to redden.

'No, of course not,' he said a little grumpily.

'Maybe she thought it was a bit dull too,' said the stout man, and then suddenly: 'Talk of angels, there she is!'

They had paused at the corner of Trafalgar Square, and following the direction of his companion's eyes Dick saw the girl standing on the opposite side of the road, outside the Post Office. She looked as though she were waiting for someone, for she was glancing quickly this way and that. His supposition proved correct, for even as he looked a man came quickly round the corner, stopped, and spoke to the girl. They moved off together and were lost among the crowd of people in the Strand.

'Did you see that?' murmured Mr. Budd. 'It's extraordinary!'

'What's extraordinary about it?' demanded Dick, a little irritably, for the meeting had curiously annoyed him. 'Surely Miss Westmore is entitled to meet a friend if she wants to?'

'Of course she is,' said the stout superintendent, 'but it depends to a great extent on the friend.'

'What do you mean?' asked Dick. 'Do

you know who that man was?'

'I know him very well,' murmured Mr. Budd. 'So do you, I think.'

There had been something familiar about the short, rather shabbily-dressed individual, but the reporter couldn't place him.

'Who was it?' he asked.

'Glossop,' answered Mr. Budd. 'The late Mr. Corbett's manservant. Not the sort of person you'd imagine that a girl like Miss Westmore would choose as a companion for the evenin', is it now?'

32

The Story of the Fancy-Dress Ball

Dick stared at Mr. Budd, his brain working rapidly.

'I'll see you in the morning,' he said, coming to a sudden decision, and before the astonished superintendent had a chance of making a reply he had left him standing on the edge of the pavement and was making his way quickly through the crowd in the direction taken by the girl and her companion.

There were no signs of them, but he concluded that they couldn't have got very far. Mr. Budd's information concerning the identity of the man whom Pamela had come to meet had filled the reporter with curiosity. For what reason had this appointment been made? Glossop, as the stout superintendent had said, was not the type of man with whom Pamela would elect to spend an evening.

There was something behind that meeting, and Dick was determined if possible to find out what it was. It might have a considerable bearing on the Jockey. The reporter was convinced that Pamela Westmore knew a great deal more about that mysterious individual than she said.

He forced his way along the thronged pavement, keeping a sharp look-out for the people he was following. Presently he caught a glimpse of the girl's hat, and increased his pace. At that moment a man who was coming towards him brushed against him, stopped, and seized him by the arm.

'Hello, Templeton!' said a voice. 'It's a long time since I've seen you!'

Dick, who had been forced to stop, jerked his arm free.

'I'm in a hurry, Vivian,' he muttered. 'See you some other time.'

But Leonard Vivian, who was responsible for the 'Gossip' page in the *Daily Illustrated*, was not to be got rid of so easily.

'What's the hurry?' he demanded. 'If you're making for the office you've got plenty of time before the 'dead line'. Come and have a drink.'

Dick looked anxiously ahead. There was no sign of the girl and her companion, and he sighed resignedly.

'You're a darned nuisance!' he said irritably. 'What did you want to stop me just then for?'

Vivian grinned.

'I crave companionship,' he answered. 'Let her go and come and have a drink.'

'Let who go?' snapped Dick.

'The girl you were so energetically chasing,' retorted Vivian. 'No good denying it, old man! I could tell by the brightness of the eye and the eager look that you were hot on the scent of some unfortunate female who'd attracted your wayward fancy.'

Dick grunted.

'You always were an idiot, Vivian,' he said offensively, and as the other led the way towards Romano's: 'Why must you turn up when you're not wanted?'

'Habit, old boy,' said Vivian good-humouredly. 'Let us exchange reminiscences over a spot of Haig.'

They passed through the swing doors and found an empty table in the lounge. Dick was annoyed. Vivian's appearance had spoiled his plans. Under the quizzical glance of his companion, however, his annoyance quickly faded. Perhaps, after all, he hadn't missed much. It would have been next to impossible for him to have got near enough to the girl and Glossop to hear what they were talking about, and that was the only thing that would have supplied him with the information he wanted.

'Well, here's fun!' said Vivian, swallowing half the whisky and soda he had ordered. 'How's things? You're on the Jockey business I hear.'

Dick set down his own glass and nodded.

'How's it going?' went on the gossip writer. 'Can we expect a sensational announcement in the *Sphere* at any moment?'

'You cannot!' retorted Dick. 'It isn't going at all. I've never been up against such a tough proposition!'

Vivian clicked his teeth sympathetically.

'I wouldn't have your job for a million!' he declared. 'It may be exciting and all that, but the strain — ' He whistled softly.

'You wouldn't mind if you were a real newspaper man instead of a lounge lizard!' returned Dick crushingly. 'My stars, what a life! Climbing into boiled shirts and attending society functions. Going here, there and everywhere to find copy for anæmic paragraphs. What a hell of a life for a grown man!'

His companion listened, completely unabashed.

'It's not so bad,' he said. 'We get plenty of good food and free drink and we hear all the latest scandal.' He took out a thin cigarette case, helped himself to a cigarette and tapped it thoughtfully on the metal. 'I've just seen something,' he continued, 'that might repay following up.'

'What's that?' asked Dick, unprepared for the answer.

'Just before I met you,' said Vivian, 'I passed Pamela Westmore in company with a fellow who looked like a cross between an ostler and a jockey who'd run

369

to fat. Peculiar looking bloke. I wonder who he was?'

Dick could have satisfied his curiosity, but he had no intention of doing so.

'That girl's always getting in the news,' went on the gossip writer, lighting his cigarette and returning the little gold lighter he had used to his pocket. 'I remember, let me see when was it? Oh, more than a year ago now — I got a bright paragraph about her.'

'What about?' asked the reporter interestedly.

'It was a fancy-dress dance Lord Mortlake gave, on the eve of Derby day,' said Vivian reminiscently. 'Pretty good crush it was, all the leading luminaries of the turf and, of course, a sprinkling of the usual Bright Young Things. That poor fellow Wharton was there. You know, the chap who killed himself over that 'warning off' business.'

Dick nodded.

'This girl we're talking about, Pamela Westmore, was engaged to him at the time,' continued Vivian, 'and she came to the dance dressed as a jockey in

Wharton's racing colours. Darned nice she looked, too.' He took a sip of his drink and set down the glass, while Dick stared at him, controlling his feelings with an effort.

'Is that what supplied you with your paragraph?' he asked carelessly.

Vivian shook his head.

'No,' he answered. 'That happened after supper when everybody was a little bit merry. Lord Mortlake, as you probably know, is the Senior steward of the Jockey Club, and Lady Sybil Tyson, the Earl of Dithering's daughter, for a joke came dressed as the Jockey Club. She had on a dress representing a large bottle of perfume and trimmed with bottles of the actual scent. Rather a clever idea, although she had to stand a good deal of chaff during the evening. After supper some of the young bloods, Wharton included, collared her, pulled off half a dozen of the bottles of scent and drenched Pamela Westmore with it. It was only a stupid rag, but it supplied me with a paragraph — What the deuce is the matter?'

Dick was staring at him with open mouth, his face incredulous.

'Eh? Oh, nothing!' he stammered hastily. 'Just a — a touch of toothache.' He picked up his glass and swallowed the remainder of his whisky so quickly that he almost choked. 'Stupid kind of trick,' he went on rapidly and a little incoherently. 'What did the girl say?'

'She was laughing too much to say anything,' said Vivian. 'It wasn't very bright, I'll admit, but it was one of those things that people like to read about.'

The reporter signalled to the waiter to replenish the glasses. What he had learned had surprised him so much that he found it difficult to think. He remembered the black silk jockey cap found in the hand of little Ted Green and the faint perfume which Mr. Budd had detected clinging to it. He remembered the stout superintendent's conviction that he had noticed the same perfume on Pamela Westmore that morning, and the girl's peculiar behaviour. Was this echo of a stupid joke the explanation? And if it were, what did it lead to?

His mind was confused. There seemed only one sensible conclusion to be drawn from what he had just heard. That the jockey cap which had been clutched in the dead man's hand was the same as that which Pamela Westmore had worn when she had been drenched with perfume at Lord Mortlake's fancy-dress ball, and this suggested the further conclusion that Pamela Westmore was the Jockey.

'It's ridiculous!' he muttered aloud, and Vivian eyed him curiously.

'What the devil's the matter with you?' he asked. 'You're going on in the most extraordinary way!'

Dick reddened.

'I was thinking over what you've just told me,' he said. 'It's a ridiculous thing for grown-up people to do.'

'Some of 'em have done worse,' remarked the gossip writer, 'and anyway, I don't see why it should affect you so strongly.'

The waiter brought the fresh drinks, and the diversion gave the reporter an opportunity to change the subject. He plunged into an anecdote concerning the

News Editor of the *Sphere*, and in the laughter which followed Leonard Vivian forgot his friend's rather curious reception of his little story. It was half-past ten when they parted and Dick walked back to his flat a puzzled and thoughtful man.

His chance meeting with Leonard Vivian had supplied him with an item of information which was of the greatest importance, information that would most assuredly interest Mr. Budd when he learned of it. It was incredible that Pamela Westmore could be the Jockey, and yet that episode of the perfume seemed to admit of no other conclusion. She had gone dressed as a jockey in Norman Wharton's racing colours, a curious coincidence, if nothing more.

By the time he reached his flat he decided that he was *not going* to pass on his discovery to his official friend. If Pamela Westmore *was* the Jockey then not by word or deed would he be responsible for that fact being made public. He was shocked at his decision, but unwavering. His duty to the *Sphere*, his duty to the public at large was not so strong as the urge which welled up within him, to protect the girl from her own foolishness at all costs. It was only in that moment that he realised the truth, and the discovery was the second surprise he had received that evening. No matter if Pamela Westmore *was* the Jockey, no matter even if she was a murderess, he loved her!

33

The Finger-Prints

Mr. Budd was awakened on the following morning by the bony hand of his housekeeper shaking him by the shoulder. Still a little dazed with sleep he blinked up at the gaunt woman resentfully.

'What's the matter?' he growled.

'You're wanted on the telephone!' she snapped curtly. 'You'd better get up.'

The stout superintendent, who lived in daily terror of this thin-faced, forbidding Scots woman who ran his small house and himself so efficiently, uttered no protest, but when she had left the room rose reluctantly, pulled on a dressing-gown and thrust his feet into slippers.

The telephone was in a little room which he used as a study, and it was the assistant-commissioner's voice that reached him over the wire as he picked up the receiver.

'The Jockey's been busy during the night,' announced Colonel Blair. 'Get up to the Yard as soon as you can.'

Mr. Budd glanced at the clock on the small writing table: it was barely seven.

'I'll report at eight, sir,' he said, and put the telephone back on its rack.

After a diffident suggestion to his disapproving housekeeper that he would like his breakfast immediately, he retired upstairs to complete his toilet, his big face one large frown.

What had the Jockey been up to during the night? he wondered, as he shaved and had his bath. What was the latest exploit of this mysterious individual which had necessitated that early call and brought the assistant-commissioner to Scotland Yard two hours before he usually made an appearance?

He was still frowning when he left the house to catch a bus to the Embankment.

Colonel Blair, a tired and rather harassed man, received him in his office immediately on his arrival.

'It's murder this time,' he said. 'A man called Crabthorne was discovered during the early hours of this morning shot dead in his bed. Pinned to the coverlet was a letter signed by this Jockey fellow. Here's the dead man's address and the report from the divisional inspector. You'd better get round there at once, and for goodness' sake see if you can't get hold of something that'll lead to this man's arrest. I understand that notice has been given to the Home Secretary that several questions are to be asked in the House regarding what the police are doing.'

'I'll do my best, sir,' said Mr. Budd, and went along to his own office to read through the information that had been given him concerning this fresh crime.

It was meagre and there was nothing very illuminating. The murder had been discovered by a patrolling policeman. Trying the outer door of the block of flats in which Crabthorne lived he had discovered that it was open. Further investigations had awakened one of the tenants, who in turn had made the discovery that the door of Crabthorne's flat was also open. They had entered and found the owner lying dead on the bed,

378

two bullet wounds in his chest and the sheets smothered in blood. He was in his pyjamas, and from his appearance had been awakened from sleep by the person who had killed him. A note in printed characters and signed 'The Jockey' had been found pinned to the blood-stained coverlet. The constable had notified his station by telephone, and the divisional inspector, accompanied by a doctor, had arrived on the scene within ten minutes of the discovery. The doctor's report was that both bullets had passed through the heart, and that the man had been dead for approximately three to four hours. The body had been found at half-past five, so death had taken place somewhere in the region between one and two o'clock. The finding of the 'Jockey' letter had caused the night man at the Yard to get into communication immediately with the assistant-commissioner.

Mr. Budd read the official report, sat for a moment or two in thoughtful silence, and then set off for the address at which Crabthorne had been killed. He had no difficulty in finding the place. A knot of curious sightseers were gathered on the pavement outside the unprepossessing building, and in the vestibule he discovered a constable, who informed him that the divisional inspector was upstairs.

Mr. Budd found the man, introduced himself, and listened to a recapitulation of the report he had already read, looking sleepily meanwhile round the shabbily-furnished sitting-room.

'The poor devil must have died immediately,' said the divisional inspector. 'Both bullets were fired at close range, and it's surprising to me that nobody in the building heard the reports.'

'There are such things as silencers,' grunted the stout superintendent. 'Let's go and have a look at this feller.'

The inspector led him into the inner room and he stared down at all that remained of Mr. Marius Crabthorne, who looked no less repulsive in death than he had done in life. The lips were curled back from his yellow teeth in a grin of terror and there was fear in the staring eyes.

'He knew what was comin' to him,'

said the inspector, 'but he hadn't time to prevent it, poor fellow.'

Mr. Budd made no comment. He was stooping over the square of paper attached to the bedclothes. In roughly printed characters he read:

'This man died because he
was dangerous.'

The familiar 'Jockey' signature was appended.

Straightening up, the stout man felt in his pockets and drew on a pair of cotton gloves.

'This hasn't been touched at all, I suppose?' he inquired, without turning his head.

'No, sir, nothing's been touched,' said the divisional inspector.

Carefully the big man unpinned the note and slipped it into an envelope which he took from his pocket. When this had been done and he had put it away he turned to the inspector.

'Any idea how the killer got in?' he asked.

'So far as I can make out, by the door,' answered the man. 'It's pretty certain he escaped that way, and left both doors open behind him.'

Mr. Budd nodded slowly, pinching at his lips.

'This feller hadn't too good a reputation,' he murmured. 'I knew one or two things about him. He's been 'inside' once for puttin' the 'black' on a feller. It looks to me as if he may have been up to his old tricks again. I suppose you've made a search of the rooms?'

The inspector nodded.

'Yes, sir,' he answered. 'There was nothing.'

'H'm!' said Mr. Budd. 'Well, you'd better get on to the Yard and tell 'em to send along the photographers and finger-print experts and then we'll see about gettin' this chap to the mortuary. Nobody in the 'ouse heard anythin', I suppose?'

'Nobody heard anything!' declared the local inspector. 'I've questioned everyone.'

He went away to telephone the Yard and Mr. Budd, left to himself, began a leisurely and methodical inspection of the bedroom, but the inspector had been right, there was nothing of importance to be found. He was not disappointed, for he had expected nothing.

The divisional inspector returned and they chatted until the police car arrived with the photographers and other experts. Mr. Budd left them to deal with the purely routine aspects of a murder case, and made his way back to the Yard.

Leek had arrived and was waiting, a gloomy and melancholy figure, in the office.

'Good morning,' he greeted his superior dismally. 'I 'ear there's been a murder.'

'You're always full of news,' grunted Mr. Budd, as he slid into the chair behind his desk. 'You'll be tellin' me next that Queen Anne's dead!'

He took the envelope containing the Jockey's note from his pocket, laid it on the desk in front of him, lit one of his cigars and glowered through the smoke.

'Yes, there's been a murder,' he went on, after a long pause, 'and I'm a bit puzzled.' He plunged his hand into his pocket, found his cotton gloves, and put them on. Opening the envelope he withdrew the sheet of paper he had taken from Mr. Crabthorne's coverlet and spread it out gingerly. 'Take a look at that!' he said.

Leek stooped over the desk and stared with lack-lustre eyes.

'It seems plain enough, don't it?' he remarked.

'Does it?' said the stout man. 'I wonder.'

He leaned back in his chair and stared at the ceiling, and the sergeant refrained from breaking in on his thoughts. Presently he jerked forward, took an envelope from the rack on his desk, carefully enclosed the 'Jockey' letter and held it out to Leek.

'Take that along to the F. P. department,' he said, 'and ask 'em to test it. Tell 'em I'd like a report as soon as possible.'

'D'you expect to find any prints?' asked Leek, as he moved slowly towards the door.

'No!' snapped Mr. Budd witheringly.

'Somethin' 'ull strike you one of these days,' said Mr. Budd darkly, 'and it'll strike you so hard you won't wake up until it's time to draw your pension.'

'What d'you expect me to say?' mumbled Leek.

'I've given up expectin' you to say anythin' sensible,' grunted the stout superintendent, 'but at least you can refrain from bein' obvious. Queer!' He sniffed disparagingly. 'Of course it's queer! The whole thing's queer. It's the queerest case I've ever been on, and I've dealt with a few queer things in my time. What I'm tryin' to make up my mind about is whether this Jockey feller is a murderer or whether he isn't. And I've got an idea he isn't.'

'Then who killed these people?' asked the sergeant.

'That's the question,' said Mr. Budd thoughtfully. 'Who killed 'em? I'm pretty certain in me own mind that Cowan killed Wills, and if he killed Wills there's no reason why he shouldn't have killed Corbett. The trouble is I can't prove it, any more than I can prove he had anythin' to do with this fresh crime, though I *do* know he was mixed up with Crabthorne.'

'I don't see what motive 'e 'ad for killing the feller,' said Leek, striving desperately to be intelligent.

'No more do I,' grunted the big man. 'But then that equally applies to the Jockey. What did he want to kill 'im for?'

The sergeant stared steadily at the shabby ceiling, his face contorted into an almost painful expression of concentration. But the only inspiration he received was apparently negative, for after some time he shook his head helplessly.

'Well,' said Mr. Budd yawning wearily, 'I suppose it'll all work out in the wash. It's one of those things you can't force.'

There was a tap at the door and Leek opened it, to admit an official from the finger-print department.

'We've tested this note,' said the man, coming over to the desk, 'and found two fairly clear prints. On the front of the top left-hand corner, as you can see, there's the print of a forefinger, and in the back a thumb print.' He pointed them out to the interested Mr. Budd.

That gentleman nodded heavily.

'The peculiar thing about it,' continued the man, 'is that these prints are identical with the ones we found on that letter in the Corbett case.'

Mr. Budd looked at him sharply.

'Oh, they are, are they?' he murmured. 'You're sure about that?'

The finger-print expert nodded.

'Oh, yes, there's no mistake,' he answered. 'They were both made by the same person.'

The stout man pulled open a drawer in his desk, produced an envelope and extracted from it a torn scrap of paper. On it was a fairly clear thumb-print, brought out with graphite.

'Take a look at that,' he said. 'Is that the same?'

The finger-print man compared them and nodded.

'Yes,' he said. 'This was made by the same person who made the others.'

'I thought so,' remarked Mr. Budd, and there was a note of satisfaction in his voice.

'D'you know whose print this is?' asked the expert, indicating the thumb mark, and Mr. Budd nodded several times slowly.

'Yes,' he answered. 'I know whose it is, and I went to a lot of trouble to get it. That print was made by Benjamin Cowan!'

34

The Passing of Lew Sleator

Mr. Lew Sleator sat huddled up in a shabby armchair in his equally shabby sitting-room, biting at his nails. His sallow face was even more sallow, and a nerve at the corner of his thin-lipped mouth twitched spasmodically.

Mr Sleator was afraid, and, with what he believed, good and sufficient reason. Although no account had yet appeared in the newspapers concerning the murder of Crabthorne, the news had reached him by means of that extraordinary and elusive method of communication which is known as the 'grape vine', and by which all sorts of out-of-the-way information is spread with great rapidity among the denizens of the ever-shifting strata of society which is loosely labelled 'the underworld'. And the news had put Mr. Sleator into a state of panic.

He knew very well why Crabthorne had died. He had died because he had poked his stubby fingers into business which didn't concern him, and since Mr. Sleator was also closely connected with that business he was scared.

He remembered a certain document which, in his cleverness, he had insisted should be drawn up in duplicate and signed by both himself and Crabthorne. A document which set out briefly the terms of the partnership into which he had entered with the inquiry agent. A copy of that agreement reposed in his breast pocket, the other copy Crabthorne had kept, and what caused Mr. Sleator so much fear and perturbation was the fact that his name and address appeared plainly on both. If the man who had killed Crabthorne had found that paper he would realise that his secret had not died with the inquiry agent, that Mr. Sleator was also a party to it, and if he had killed once he would kill again.

Ever since he had heard of the murder the little burglar had remained locked in his room, a prey to acute terror, fearful of every step that passed his door, and scared to leave the comparative safety of his lodgings.

It had never occurred to him, when he had triumphantly shared his knowledge with Crabthorne, that there was any danger. Never for a moment had he imagined that the Jockey would safeguard himself by murder. For that it was the Jockey whose hand had sent Crabthorne swiftly into eternal darkness, he had no doubt, and he knew who the Jockey was.

Over and over again throughout that dreadful day he had considered the advisability of placing his knowledge at the disposal of the police. Once the man was safely under lock and key he would be able to breathe freely again — the danger that hung over him would be removed. But he could not make up his mind to take the necessary steps. It was not far from his lodgings to Scotland Yard, but in his imagination he saw death in every inch of the way. And yet, if he could only overcome his fear, it was the safest course he could take.

He was not a squealer by nature, but he

was prepared to do anything to save his own skin. Life was a very precious thing to Mr. Sleator, and he had no intention, if he could avoid it, of going the way which Marius Crabthorne had gone.

He sat on, trying to screw up his courage, while the light slowly faded from the sky and the darkness of the summer night shrouded the little Soho street in which he lived. It would be so simple to slide out unobserved, board a 'bus at Cambridge Circus, and be set down at his objective. He would be safe enough on a 'bus, but there was that distance to cover between the house in which he lived and the 'bus stop. That was where the danger lurked. The very thought of emerging from the safety of his room sent a cold shiver down his spine.

The street was dark and gloomy, and there were many doorways in which a man might wait concealed. Even now, somewhere in the gloom of the street, he pictured the Jockey waiting, watching, and his courage oozed away like liquor from a cracked bottle.

He licked his dry lips, staring at the

fireless grate, while the shadows in the room deepened. If he had had money he would have cleared out, but with the exception of a few pence he was penniless. The fifty pounds which Crabthorne had advanced had already been spent, and the nine hundred and fifty which he had been expecting to receive that day would now never be paid.

He got up presently and carefully drew the dingy curtains over the window and put on the light. The glow from the shaded electric bulb was comforting. It showed up every corner of the barely furnished little room and reassured him.

For some time he paced up and down, longing for the drink that would soothe his shattered nerves, but he had no money with which to purchase such a solace.

He must throw off this clinging terror, this dreadful fear which turned his blood to water. Safety lay in that big building on the Thames Embankment, if he could only reach it. Safety, not only for a day or a night, but safety for ever. There were men who would welcome him there, be only too glad to receive the information he had to offer.

He glanced at the cheap little clock that ticked noisily on the mantelpiece. Half-past eight! By nine, if he acted at once, he would be free of this grinning phantom that stood at his elbow. It required such a small effort. Just a moment or two of courage and then no more fear.

He picked up his hat, squared his shoulders, and going to the door gripped the handle. But with his fingers on the knob came the thought of the shadowy street and those narrow, darkened door-ways which he would have to pass before he reached the safety of the 'bus. His fingers slid from the grimy brass and he stood, hesitant. While he remained where he was the danger was remote, but once past that door anything might happen.

The perspiration broke out on his forehead and he wiped it away with the back of his hand. And yet something must be done. He could not face the coming night with that fear still hanging over him. If only he had the means to supply himself with a little Dutch courage . . .

He searched his pockets in the vain hope that he had overlooked some forgotten store of money, but he found nothing beyond a sixpence and a few odd coppers.

There was nothing for it, he must take the plunge. Perhaps after all there was no danger, no watcher in the darkened street waiting for his appearance. Perhaps the Jockey, having killed Crabthorne, would be too scared to attempt another murder so soon after. He argued this way, trying to convince himself. But in his inmost heart he knew that the premise was false. The Jockey, if he was going to act at all, would act at once. And he was bound to act, he couldn't afford to wait.

Mr. Sleator braced himself. With a trembling hand he turned the key in the lock and opened the door. The passage-way outside was dark and silent. His landlady had told him that she was going to the pictures that evening and the rest of the tenants seldom came in until late. He had the house to himself, and the knowledge was not reassuring.

He listened, but there was no sound.

Switching out the light he made his way to the head of the narrow staircase. There was no light in the hall. Pausing, he looked down into utter darkness. A sudden desperate desire took possession of him, an almost overpowering longing to run back to his room and lock himself in, but he mastered it. Slowly and stealthily he began to descend the stairs.

There was no reason why he should try to move without making a noise, but he was afraid of the slightest sound, afraid of his own footsteps. He reached the hall and again he stopped. The outer door was shut, and forcing his unwilling hand to perform the action he twisted the catch and pulled it open.

Somebody passed, walking swiftly along the street outside as he did so, and he jerked the door to again in a momentary panic.

The footsteps faded and realising how stupidly he was behaving he pulled the door wider in a sudden accession of boldness and stepped out into the street. The door swung shut behind him, and controlling a fervent desire to run, he set off briskly up the narrow pavement.

One or two cars were parked at the edge of the sidewalk and he passed these with scarcely a glance. All his attention was focused on the narrow doors and alleys that flanked his way. It would have been luckier for him had he given more attention to the cars, for as he went quickly by a closed coupé, a man in the dark interior, who had been watching, slipped out, and coming up rapidly behind him pressed something hard into his side as he gripped his arm.

With a terrified gasp Mr. Sleator stopped.

'I want you,' said a husky voice, 'and you'd better come quietly. If you make a sound I'll put three bullets through your heart!'

The little burglar gazed wildly about him. The street was deserted. It crossed his mind to raise an alarm, and the man who had accosted him must have sensed something of the sort for he muttered harshly:

'If you scream it'll be the last thing you do!'

'What — what do you want with me?'

breathed Sleator, with an effort. His terror was so great that it had almost robbed him of the power of speech.

'Information!' snapped the man curtly, and dragged him unwillingly towards the car. 'Get in!' he ordered, and as Mr. Sleator obeyed he caught sight of the ugly-looking weapon the other held, a pistol, with a queer, bulbous-shaped thing attached to the muzzle.

The man whose heavy face, dimly visible beneath the brim of his soft hat, was unknown to him, got in beside him. The engine started with a touch and the coupé moved forward.

'Where are you taking me?' muttered Lew Sleator, his face wet with perspiration.

'To a place where we can talk without fear of interruption!' snapped the other. 'Shut up and keep quiet!'

He made a menacing gesture with the pistol, and the little burglar relapsed into silence.

The car negotiated several side turnings and came out into the busy, brightly lit Charing Cross Road. Mr. Sleator, dazed with fear, noted that they were heading towards Westminster. The man beside him drove with one hand, the other gripped round the butt of the automatic which rested on his knee. They crossed the bridge, came into Westminster Bridge Road, and continued towards Kennington; past the Oval into Stockwell, and presently out on the North Side of Clapham Common. Turning into a street that bisected the great stretch of common land they stopped, half-way along its deserted length.

'Now!' said the unknown. 'At the request of Marius Crabthorne you discovered information concerning the Jockey. Tell me what you discovered.'

'Who — who are you?' quavered Mr. Sleator.

'Never mind who I am!' broke in the other impatiently. 'Answer my question. What did you learn about the Jockey?'

'I — I learnt nothing,' declared the little burglar.

'Don't lie!' snapped the man beside him. 'It won't help you. Tell me what you know!'

Hesitantly, his teeth chattering and his throat dry, Mr. Sleator complied . . .

Five minutes later the coupé came speeding out of the deserted road and headed back the way it had come. But now there was only one occupant, the man who gripped the wheel and stared ahead with a set face. Behind him, on the edge of the empty and desolate road, lay something that had once been a living, breathing man, but was now a limp, twisted heap with a fear-distorted face and terror-filled eyes that stared sightlessly at the night sky!

35

The Photograph

The body of Lew Sleator was found by a horrified local tradesman who was taking a short cut home from a visit to friends. He notified the police, and when they arrived on the scene they discovered that the man had been shot at close quarters. The identity of the victim was revealed by the contents of the pockets, but the document which the little burglar had exchanged with Mr. Crabthorne was not found. So that although the murder was reported to Scotland Yard, and incidentally came to the ears of Mr. Budd, it was not until much later that he associated it with the Jockey.

Since his discovery that Cowan's finger-prints were on two of the letters, the stout superintendent had been a very busy man. All day and late into the night he sat in his office issuing instructions, consulting reports, and generally utilising all his energy to try and fit together the facts in his possession and make a coherent story.

An unobtrusive, quietly dressed man was put on to tail the bookmaker wherever he went, and another, equally quiet and unobtrusive, took his place when his hours of duty came to an end. Sergeant Boyd, who was handling the Wharton inquiry, crossed over to France, and making his way to Toulouse spent a considerable time interviewing the prison authorities.

There was still no trace of Sir Trevor Bleck or the jockey, Linnet. The reports that came in from all over the country were negative, but in spite of this and the assistant-commissioner's insistence that the baronet had to be found, Mr. Budd was not worrying very much. He concluded, rightly, that if the other side of the business could be cleared up and the identity of the Jockey revealed the discovery of Bleck and Linnet would come automatically.

During the two days that followed the

murder of Sleator the stout man succeeded in acquiring a great deal of information, the most important of which was the fact that Corbett had called on Cowan on the morning of his death. Sergeant Bailey had discovered this during a tactful interview with the bookmaker's secretary. He also learnt that Wills had interviewed Cowan on more than one occasion, and Mr. Budd, putting two and two together when he heard of this, came within measurable distance of guessing the truth. Coupled with the large sums of money which Corbett had from time to time paid into his bank and which seemed to have come from nowhere, it seemed fairly safe to conclude that these two men had been blackmailing Cowan, and if this was the case it supplied a motive for their deaths. Neither was it difficult to form a theory concerning the reason for this blackmail. They had all three been connected with the Wharton conspiracy, and, since without doubt Benjamin Cowan had been the leading spirit in this, it was fairly safe to conclude that the other two had used their knowledge in order to extract money to ensure their silence.

The more Mr. Budd thought about it the more convinced he became that Cowan was responsible for the killing of Corbett and the little jockey. His difficulty was to prove it, for this was by no means as easy as it might appear. The police are very chary of instituting a prosecution, particularly in a case of murder, unless the prospect of a conviction is practically certain, and the stout man knew that the evidence in his possession was far from sufficient to satisfy the Public Prosecutor. And so he worked patiently, collecting stray bits of evidence to add to the structure he was erecting against the man he suspected.

He was sitting in his office glancing through a number of reports when there came a tap on the door and it opened quietly to admit the thin-faced Sergeant Boyd.

'I've just returned, sir,' announced the sergeant unnecessarily, 'and I think I've got all the information you wanted.'

'Good!' murmured Mr. Budd, and no

one, judging from the bored expression on his face, would have imagined that he was the least bit interested. 'Sit down and tell me all about it.'

The sergeant sat down, producing from his pocket his black notebook and a square envelope.

'I interviewed the present Governor of the prison at Toulouse,' he said, 'and went into the facts concerning the death of Wharton. He could tell me very little for he was a new man and had only held the governorship for three years. The retired Governor, however, still lived in the town, and from him I was able to get a detailed account of the business.' He paused, moistened his lips, and turned over a page of his notebook. 'Wharton apparently died in a fire which started in the prison infirmary. He was an orderly at the time, and in company with four other men was burned to death.'

Mr. Budd, who had been listening with his eyes completely closed, partly opened them.

'Burned to death,' he repeated. 'Is that absolutely certain?'

'There seems to be no doubt of it, sir,' replied Boyd. 'I interviewed several of the police officials who remember the occurrence, and they state that the entire wing of the prison was gutted.'

'Were the bodies found?' murmured the superintendent.

Boyd shook his head.

'No, I went into that, sir,' he answered. 'A number of charred remains were found, but the fire had been so fierce that there was nothing sufficient to supply a means of identification.'

'Then there's no proof,' said Mr. Budd slowly, 'that this fellow Wharton was killed. Now we're gettin' at somethin'. I'm beginnin' to see daylight now.'

'There's also no proof that he wasn't, sir,' put in the sergeant quietly. 'The authorities at Toulouse are certainly under the impression that he died. I suggested that he might have escaped, but they laughed at me.'

'Maybe they did,' said the stout superintendent. 'But all the same I'm not convinced that he *did* die. In fact I'm pretty sure that he's still livin', and that he's walkin' about wearin' a black silk jacket and a silk cap. It fits — I don't mean the cap — I mean the fact that he's alive. Because if he's alive and if he's the Jockey he's Norman Wharton's father, and Norman Wharton's father would have more cause for a grudge against the people responsible for drivin' his son to his death than anyone else.' He looked at the envelope that the sergeant had laid on the table. 'What have you got there?' he asked.

'Well, sir,' said Boyd, 'being a little doubtful, the same as you are, concerning whether this man had died or not, I thought I'd better get hold of a photograph of him if possible. They hadn't got one at the prison, but they told me there was one at police headquarters in Paris, so I went there and succeeded in getting hold of this.' He picked up the envelope, opened it and withdrew a photograph which he held out.

Mr. Budd leaned forward wearily and took it with a podgy hand. It was a sharp police photograph of a youngish-looking, mild-faced man, and the stout superintendent eyed it, his forehead wrinkling.

There was something familiar about those features, something that reminded him of someone whom he had recently seen, but who for the moment he couldn't place.

'He was charged in his own name?' he asked.

Boyd nodded.

'Yes, Norman Wharton,' he answered.

'Norman Wharton,' murmured Mr. Budd musingly.

Suddenly his brows cleared and a look of incredulous surprise slowly came over his big face . . .

Dick Templeton met him half an hour later as he was passing out through the arch into Whitehall, and the reporter was surprised at the almost jaunty appearance of this usually sleepy-eyed and weary-looking man.

'What's happened to you?' he demanded. 'You look as if you've just won the first prize in the Calcutta Sweep.'

'I've done better than that!' said Mr. Budd complacently.

'I've found the Jockey!'

36

Cowan Sees the Red Light

Mr. Benjamin Cowan paced restlessly up and down his comfortable study, pausing every now and again to shoot a quick, uneasy glance through the window into the dim street below. The watcher was still there lounging on the opposite side of the road, apparently immersed in an evening newspaper which he was reading in the light of the street lamp.

The bookmaker had aged visibly during the last week. His heavy, flabby face was lined and grey, and there were unhealthy sacs beneath his eyes. Worry and sleeplessness had contributed their share, but the main reason was the fear which never left him. The time had come, as he well knew, to make a decision, for the terror which inspired him was no longer that of the Jockey but of the law. His secretary had reported the arrival of the pleasant-faced man who had questioned her concerning Simon Corbett and Joe Wills, and Mr. Cowan had realised that in spite of all his endeavours the police were suspicious. The quiet man who lounged by the railings in the street below had been on his heels all day. He knew that in an hour or so he would be relieved by another who would watch vigilantly throughout the night. And the knowledge frightened him, for he was not certain how much they knew. To safeguard himself he had steeped his hands in blood, and he was under no illusion concerning the ultimate penalty if he was found out. To cover up one crime he had been forced to commit another, until his guilt had grown like a snowball rolling down a hillside.

How much was suspicion, and how much was knowledge? He had no means of telling. That the police must still lack certain evidence was obvious from the fact that he was still at large. At the present moment they were only keeping him under observation. Had they been certain, a warrant for his arrest would have been issued before now. How long would it be before they *were* certain? It was impossible to tell, but the best thing he could do was to make a getaway while he still had the chance. It would not be difficult. He had prepared for such an emergency. Moored off Gravesend was a small but comfortable yacht, manned by a captain and crew who asked no questions, and for the past week it had been ready for instant departure. There were places where the law of extradition did not apply, where a man could live in comfort on the money which lay stacked in the concealed safe so near to him. And yet, although reason told him that this was his sanest course, vanity urged him against it. He hated the thought of relinquishing his position, of giving up all he had worked and schemed and striven for. Hated the knowledge that men who had been his intimates would talk about him behind his back as a criminal who had had to flee the country. Particularly was he reluctant to give up all chance of marriage with Pamela Westmore. That, probably more than anything, was the reason for his hesitation.

He paused by the big desk and lit a cigar and then began once more his steady pacing of the room. Better to give up everything than his life. Better to be talked about than pointed at in the dock at the Central Criminal Court. Better to give up all thought of Pamela Westmore than to be taken from the condemned cell at eight o'clock and hanged by the neck until he was dead.

He shuddered as in a rapid succession of vivid pictures he saw what would follow his arrest.

No. Better go now while he still had the chance. Go before a warrant was issued. It would be easy to elude the watcher, and once he reached the ship he would be safe.

A thought struck him and he stopped suddenly, his eyes gleaming. There was no need to give up everything. There was no reason why he should go — alone.

The idea which had come so insidiously into his mind brought a faint flush to the unhealthy grey of his cheeks. After all, if he was caught it would make very little difference. If he wasn't caught —

He began to pace up and down again, his mind working swiftly. The girl should go with him. It would not be difficult to get hold of her, and a drug would keep her quiet until she was safely on board. Once the boat had put out to sea she could do as she liked. The captain and the crew were foreigners, he would have no trouble from them, and a marriage at sea was legal.

His eyes brightened with excitement. What a revenge to take for the injury he had suffered at her hands! What a sop to his vanity it would be to wipe the contemptuous look from her eyes and replace it with one of supplication. It was worth any risk, and the risk was not so very big after all. Abduction was a minor crime compared with those he had already committed.

He sat down abruptly and began to work on the scheme, wondering why it had not occurred to him before. The question was: How to get hold of the girl?

He sat pondering over this for some

time, evolving and rejecting scheme after scheme. And then at the end of an hour he saw a way, a way that was so simple that he was surprised it had not suggested itself immediately.

Pulling open a drawer of his desk he searched for some blank paper and finding some began laboriously to write a letter. The waste-paper basket was filled with discarded efforts before he succeeded in producing what he wanted to his satisfaction. He read it through, nodding approvingly. Folding the sheet he slipped it into an envelope, licked it down, and addressed it in the sloping, disguised handwriting which he had adopted. That ought to achieve the result he wanted.

He stamped it and slipped it into his pocket. There was still time to catch the post, and now that he had made up his mind there was a lot to attend to.

Carefully he collected the soiled sheets from the waste basket and carrying them over to the empty fireplace put a match to them. The paper blazed up and he watched it until it was consumed, and then taking the poker reduced the ashes to powdery dust. Going over to the wall beside the fireplace he slid back one of the panels, revealing the polished door of a safe. Swiftly he spun the dial and pulling open the heavy door took from the interior numerous documents and three thick wads of notes.

Carrying these over to the desk he counted them. There was approximately forty thousand pounds, a respectable sum with which to start life anew in a foreign country. The documents he read through, placing one or two aside and destroying the others the same way as he had destroyed the paper from the waste basket.

It was half-past ten when he left his flat, and descending in the automatic lift, passed through the vestibule and made his way along to the pillar-box at the end of the street. The watcher was still in evidence, but ignoring him the book-maker posted his letter and returned. That was done! Pamela would receive it in the morning and he had little doubt her curiosity would ensure her keeping the appointment.

He came back to his study and poured himself out a drink. So far so good! There was little else to be done. Iris would have to look after herself. He had no intention of disclosing to the girl his plans, and her future worried him not at all. That he was leaving her penniless and unprovided for caused him no pangs of conscience. He was interested in only one thing — himself. What happened to his daughter was of little importance, and he did not even waste a second in speculating on what she would do.

There was one thing he would have liked to have attended to before he left the country, to get back at the man who had caused him so much worry and anxiety. His face hardened and his eyes narrowed. But for the Jockey he would not have found himself in this position, in the position of a suspected criminal fleeing from justice. It would be good to get his own back on the man who so far had had it all his own way. And he knew him! He had wrung the identity of the Jockey out of Sleator before sending the bullet that had killed him crashing through his heart.

He debated for some time how it could be done, and reluctantly decided that it was too risky. He would have all his time occupied with the girl without dividing his attention. Better leave him to the police. They must have found the note which he had forged and left on the coverlet after the killing of Crabthorne, and it was unlikely they would suspect him of that. He was unaware of the finger-print he had left, for it had never occurred to him that although he had worn gloves when he had written the note, the paper he had used already bore the imprint of his thumb and finger.

Far into the night he sat on, smoking and going over in his mind the things he had to do. It was late when he rose to his feet, locked the money away in the safe, and went to his bedroom . . .

The weary watcher in the street below saw the light go out and sighed. He had many hours of vigil before him, and he envied the man whom at that moment he pictured retiring to a comfortable bed.

He would have envied him less had he known that this was the last night's untroubled sleep Benjamin Cowan was ever destined to have.

37

The Jockey

Pamela Westmore received the letter by the second post and puzzled over the illiterate scrawl:

> 'Dear Miss,
>   'I can tell you a lot about Mr. Cowan and the late Mr. Wharton wot you've been wantin to no for a long time miss I will be at the cros roads outside the vilage at elevin oclok ternight and wil tel you all I no if you wil be there dont tel anybody about this or I may get into truble partiklerly from Mr. Cowan if he should no I am taking a risk so dont fale to be there.'

There was no signature, and the girl speculated without result on the identity of the sender. Most probably it was from someone in Benjamin Cowan's employ, a servant perhaps. That's what it suggested. The spelling was shocking and the handwriting careful and laborious. Its purport, however, filled her with curiosity. Was she to learn at last what she had been trying for so long to discover — definite proof that there had been a conspiracy against poor Norman Wharton?

She had always believed that there had, and that he had been innocent of the charge which had been brought against him, and which had resulted in his death. She had hoped to find proof of her belief from Corbett, and with that end in view had attempted to cultivate the man's acquaintance against the wishes of her father. She had gone over to the training stable for the purpose of seeing Corbett on that never-to-be-forgotten morning when she had discovered the dead body of the little tout lying under the hedge. Even now the memory of the shock it had given her when she had learned of the trainer's murder was sufficient to make her heart jump. There had been a time when she thought success was going to crown her efforts, for Corbett had more than once appeared willing to divulge what he knew. He had even hinted that for a consideration he might be able to augment what was publicly known about the Wharton business. Had she been able to supply the consideration she was convinced he would have spoken, but she had not. And then death had come to silence the man for ever, and she had felt that all chance of learning the truth was gone.

It was only subsequently it had occurred to her that possibly Glossop might have overheard something. When the idea came to her, however, the stables were closed up and the man had gone. She had succeeded in tracing him, however, and had made an appointment to meet him, which he had kept, unfortunately without any tangible result. He was able to tell her that on several occasions prior to the inquiry held by the Jockey Club stewards into the running of King's Holiday, Benjamin Cowan had been down at Ditchling interviewing Corbett, but was unable to say what it was they had talked about.

Her heart beat a little faster as she read the letter for the third time. Was it possible that at last she was to learn the truth? Anyway, she would keep the appointment, and hoped that it would bring better results than her previous efforts in the same direction. It was not that she had felt anything akin to love for Norman Wharton, but she had held him in very high regard, and the affection between them had been very deep. His tragic death had affected her in much the same way as the death of a brother would have done, for they had played together as children and she could not remember the time when Norman had not been a never-failing companion. They had more or less drifted into the engagement. She had grown up to accept the idea of Norman as a husband, and it was not until she had met. Dick Templeton that she had realised exactly what her feelings towards the dead man had been.

She went about her household duties that day so preoccupied that Westmore remarked upon the fact more than once anxiously.

'What the deuce *is* the matter with you, Pamela?' he inquired at dinner, when he had twice put a question to her and received no reply. 'Aren't you well?'

'Yes, I'm all right,' she answered, pulling herself together with a start. 'I'm sorry. I was thinking about something else.'

The colonel grunted.

'Must have been deuced interesting,' he said.

It was on the tip of her tongue to tell him, but she thought better of it. If her father knew what she was contemplating he would forbid her to go. He had done his utmost to dissuade her in the case of Corbett, for it was his conviction that she could do no good and might easily place herself in an unpleasant position. If he was aware that she was going to meet an unknown person at the lonely crossroads on the outskirts of the village at a late hour that night he would either insist on accompanying her, or definitely stop her from keeping the appointment.

With an effort she detached her mind from the subject that was interesting her above all else and forced herself to enter into an intelligent conversation. But the evening seemed to drag more than any she had ever experienced, and it was with an inward sigh of relief that at last she was legitimately able to make an excuse and retire to her room.

Except when they had people staying with them the Westmores went to bed early. Long sojourn in the country had inculcated in them habits of retiring early and rising early, and it was nothing unusual for Pamela to be in bed by ten o'clock.

Reaching her room she hastily changed her semi-evening frock for a coat and skirt, put on a pair of brogues in place of her high-heeled shoes, and lighting a cigarette sat down on the edge of her bed to wait until it was time to go and meet her unknown correspondent.

She calculated it would take her half an hour to reach the crossroads, which meant that she would have to leave the house by half-past ten. Glancing at her watch she saw that she had a quarter of an hour to fill in. It would not be difficult to slip down the stairs and out by the big door without anyone being the wiser. With the exception of Cressit the rest of the servants would be in bed and the dignified butler would, as likely as not, be in his pantry until he came out to make his final rounds of the house and lock up.

She had already arranged for her return. There were two keys to the back door and one of these reposed in the pocket of her jacket, and there were no bolts.

She finished her cigarette and, with a second glance at her watch, rose to her feet. Opening the door softly she crept out into the passage and down the stairs. The light was still burning in the hall, and a glance at the massive fastenings of the front door told her that Cressit had not yet locked up for the night. She crossed the polished floor cautiously, pulled back the catch, opened the door, and slipping out, closed it noiselessly behind her.

It was a dark night but windless, and there was a feel of rain in the air. She made her way quickly down the drive, walking, while she was near the house, on the grass border to deaden any faint sound her footsteps might make. The drive gates opened on to a private road and she passed through, quickening her pace when she was free of the approach to the house.

She turned her back on the village as she came out on to the main thoroughfare and walked rapidly towards her destination. There was not a soul about, the road stretched before her dark and deserted, and presently she arrived at the triangle of grass which marked the intersection of a secondary thoroughfare and the place mentioned in the letter. There was nobody within sight.

She paused under the grey-white arms of a signpost and looked about her. No one.

For the first time it crossed her mind that the letter might be a hoax, although she could think of nobody who would be likely to perpetrate such a stupid joke. And then, almost as the thought came to her, out of the shadows into which the road faded appeared two dim lights. They approached rapidly, the headlights of a car with the dimmers on . . .

Pamela frowned. Surely the person who had written that letter was unlikely to possess a car? More probably it had nothing to do with her appointment at all, but was just someone driving through Ditchling on the way to Lewes. She had no wish to be seen, however, hanging about, and she drew back in the shadow of the signpost as the car came level. To her surprise it stopped and a husky, uneducated voice called her name.

She hesitated for a moment and then crossed quickly over to the side of the motionless machine. The dim figure of a man was sitting at the wheel.

'You Miss Westmore?' he grunted huskily.

'Yes,' she answered. 'Did you write me that letter?'

'Yes,' he replied. 'I'm Mr. Cowan's chauffeur. Get in, will you, Miss? We can 'ave a talk.'

He leaned sideways — the cloth cap he was wearing prevented her seeing his face — and jerked open the door. Quite unsuspectingly she squeezed herself into the seat beside him, and at the same moment felt a sharp pain shoot through her right arm.

'Got you!' cried the familiar voice of Benjamin Cowan triumphantly, and even as she recognised it and opened her lips to utter the cry of alarm that rose in her throat her senses swam and she slumped limply back in the padded seat . . .

Cowan, a grin of delight on his face, thrust an arm in front of her and slammed the door. His foot pressed the clutch and he shifted the gear lever out of neutral. The car moved forward, gathered speed, and shot off into the darkness of the night. It had been as simple as he had anticipated.

He laughed exultantly. He had beaten them all, the Jockey, the police. Before another night came he would be putting out to sea, heading for the Moroccan coast, and he was not going empty-handed. He glanced at the figure of the unconscious girl at his side, and slowing the car brought it to a halt. It was unwise to continue with the girl where she was. A hold-up, an inquisitive policeman, and his plans might be wrecked. He opened the door and got out, came round to the other side, opened that door, and leaning in, picked up Pamela. It would be safer to conceal her in the back of the car, and this he proceeded to do. He had armed himself with rugs and cushions, and he made her as comfortable as possible on the floor, covering her with a rug, so that, to a casual glance, the back of the car would appear empty.

When he had done this he picked up the hypodermic syringe from where it had fallen after he had used it, replacing it in its case and once more took his seat behind the wheel.

He had a long journey before him across country, for he had planned to reach Gravesend before dawn where the motor launch from the yacht would be waiting to pick him up.

The rain began to fall as he passed through Tonbridge, and it seemed to him that even the weather was on his side. He wondered as he drove on how long it would be before his flight was discovered. The watchful detective had not seen him go, for he had left his flat as he had done on previous occasions by way of the fire-escape, leaving the light in his study still burning so that to the watcher it would appear as though he was still there.

He drove on through dark and sleeping villages and silent towns, the rain lashing the windscreen and pattering on the roof.

His instructions to the captain of the boat had been explicit, embodied in a letter and posted with a batch of other correspondence from Paddocks. Nothing could go wrong, and his thick lips pursed and he whistled a tune as he found himself nearing the end of his journey.

He drove down to the place where he had arranged for the launch to pick him up and brought the car to a standstill. It was a desolate spot, a waste of mud flats, and getting out he picked his way towards the water. There was no sign of the launch he expected and he clicked his teeth impatiently. A glance at his watch showed him that he was half an hour too soon.

The rain was coming down in torrents, and having no wish to be soaked to the skin he returned after a few minutes to the car. It occurred to him that the girl might possibly be recovering from the effects of the drug he had administered and that in any case it would be advisable to give her a second shot since he wanted no trouble until she was safely landed aboard the yacht. He took out the syringe, fitted it together, and filled it from a little bottle which he extracted from an inner pocket. Opening the door he leaned into the dark interior of the car and pulled aside the rug. And then he started back with a choking cry that was almost a sob, for a dark figure rose up where he had expected to find an unconscious girl.

Something cold and hard was pressed against his forehead and a high-pitched, whispering voice said:

'I've been waiting for you, Cowan. Know any prayers? If you do you'd better say them quickly for to-night you are face to face with death!'

Benjamin Cowan saw the black peaked cap, the silk-covered face, and knew that his end was at hand.

38

The Judgment Room

Pamela came slowly out of a sea of blackness to the accompaniment of a curious and inexplicable sensation. Her head felt light and far beyond its normal size and her body seemed to be floating in some intangible substance which was in a constant state of vibration. She felt too languid to attempt to analyse the cause, but was content to receive the impression without bothering about the reason for it.

It was rather pleasant than otherwise — a sort of semi-wakefulness in which nothing mattered very much. The sense of motion too, was very comforting, and a delicious languor enveloped her. She could see nothing, and was only conscious of that gentle movement, and then the blackness came again . . .

When she opened her eyes for the second time she was in a softly-lighted room, and in the instant of raising the lids she remembered, and with memory came fear.

She sat up quickly, and the sudden movement made her head swim, but the dizziness was only momentary. She was on a cushion-covered couch in a small apartment with scarcely any other furniture. The dim light came from an electric bulb in the ceiling, about which had been tied a handkerchief to dull its brightness. The place was completely strange to her. She had never seen this small room before.

She was feeling a little dull and heavy, but otherwise experienced no unpleasant after-effects from the drug which she guessed had been administered to her.

Where was Cowan? The thought of him terrified her. For what reason had he brought her to this place?

She was still a little dazed, and her brain refused to function with its normal rapidity. Cautiously she swung her legs off the couch, sat on the edge for a moment or two, and essayed to rise to her feet. She found it difficult. Her knees felt weak and shaky and at her first attempt she had to clutch the curved side of the couch to prevent herself falling. After a while, however, strength came back to her. She went over to the curtain-less window and peered out, but all she could see was a mass of trees dimly visible in the grey light of early morning. She guessed that she was somewhere in the heart of the country, but that was as far as her knowledge took her.

Leaving the window she crossed to the door, expecting to find it locked, but to her surprise it was nothing of the sort, for when she turned the handle it opened easily beneath her hand.

She came out into a dark corridor and as she stood listening she heard the faint sound of voices. They seemed to come from somewhere below, and as her eyes grew accustomed to the gloom she made out the head of a staircase emerging into a broad landing at which the corridor ended.

Slowly and carefully, for she was still a little weak and shaky, she tiptoed along the passage and paused again, supporting herself by the banister. A broad staircase led downwards, a staircase devoid of carpet, as had been the passage which she had just left. She peered over, but she could see little of what lay beneath, for the stairs lost themselves in deep shadow. The voices, however, were a little louder.

Step by step she began to descend, her heart beating painfully, and presently she reached a big, square vestibule, totally devoid of furniture and carpetless like the stairs. The sound she had heard came from a partly-closed door on the right, and as she recognised the high-pitched voice her fear left her — the Jockey.

He was speaking slowly and evenly and now she could distinguish the words.

' . . . You were to be the last, but Fate has ordained that you shall be the first, carrying out the old adage.'

'What do you intend to do with me?' The slurred, thick tones were those of Benjamin Cowan, and the listening girl shivered.

'You have taken five lives!' replied the Jockey. 'For that you must suffer the penalty which civilisation has imposed.'

'You would not murder me?' said Cowan, and there was fear in his voice.

'It would not be murder,' was the answer. 'It would be justice. As you have killed, so in your turn will you die, and the time has nearly come. You would, but for my presence to-night, have escaped the law, and in doing so perpetrated an even worse crime than those of which you are already guilty. But for my intervention you would have done this.'

Pamela crept closer until she was able to peer into the room through the crack of the half-closed door. It was a large apartment and as she saw its furnishings she gasped. Once, during the racing at Newmarket, her father had taken her into the stewards' room behind the stands. The room in which Norman Wharton, on that fatal summer morning, had heard judgment passed on him and gone forth a broken man to solve his problem with a bullet. And this room was an exact replica. Behind the desk at one end stood the black figure of the Jockey, a silken mask covering his face, one hand resting lightly near the butt of an automatic pistol. Cowering in a chair before him was Benjamin Cowan. He still wore his heavy overcoat and his face was the colour of death.

'You know me,' said the Jockey. 'You learned my secret from Lew Sleator before you killed him. You know who I am, but you have yet to learn *what* I am.'

'What do you mean?' muttered the man in the chair.

'I am a ghost,' went on the high whispering voice. 'I have no legal existence, for I died twenty-eight years ago.'

Cowan shrank back, his eyes staring.

'My God, what are you saying?' he whispered hoarsely, and the perspiration broke out clammily on his forehead. 'You're crazy . . .'

'I am as sane as you are,' said the Jockey, and he no longer spoke in the affected voice which he had adopted. 'What I have said is nothing more than the truth. Officially I died twenty-eight years ago in the prison at Toulouse. There was a fire in the infirmary at a time when I was acting as orderly. During the general excitement I saw my chance and I took it. I escaped . . . '

'Who — who are you?' Cowan spoke the words with difficulty, his eyes still fixed in a fearful stare on the figure before him.

'I am the father of the man you hounded to death!' said the Jockey sternly. 'The father of the man who preferred to die sooner than face the disgrace which your evil schemes had brought upon him. I am Norman Wharton!'

Pamela watched and listened breathlessly. The revelation which had just been made was no news to her. Ever since that night, three weeks before the death of Corbett, when in the moonlit grounds of Downlands she had listened to this man's story, she had known. But the effect on Cowan was extraordinary. His big, flabby figure seemed to shrink until the heavy coat looked as though it had been made for a larger man.

'Wharton's father!' he muttered huskily. 'So that's why — '

'That is why,' said the Jockey. 'That is why I adopted the rôle. That is why I have

440

lent myself to this rather theatrical mummery. I knew Norman was not guilty of the charge which you and your associates, Corbett and Wills, hatched up against him. It was my intention to seek revenge against all of you. In the cause of Corbett and Wills you saved me the trouble. It is nearly dawn; before the sun rises, Cowan, you will have passed over the borderland to join those you have sent there before you.'

His words broke the last remaining vestige of courage that the bookmaker possessed.

'No, no!' he shrieked, a mouthing, obscene, terror-crazed thing. 'No, no! Anything but that! I will give you all the money I have in the world. I will give you anything! Only give me a chance. Let me live! You can't kill me. You don't want murder on your soul! Will my death bring these others to life? If I die will it restore Norman Wharton . . . ?'

'You are not fit to live!' broke in the Jockey contemptuously. 'Nothing you can say will alter my decision. I have watched you for days, for weeks, for months, looking forward to this moment. I have played with you as a cat might play with a bird, knowing that when the time was ripe I would crush you out of existence. I could have done so long ago, but I preferred to give you the torture of suspense. You have suffered many uneasy moments, many sleepless nights, and now you will suffer no more. The end has come for you, Cowan, and it is very near.'

The bookmaker was breathing heavily, stertorously.

'Have a little pity,' he croaked. 'What I did I was forced to do. Can't you see that . . . ?'

'It is useless,' said the Jockey. 'Why don't you accept your punishment like a man?' His gloved hand closed on the butt of the automatic, and the action sent Cowan into a frenzy. He flung himself on his knees in front of the desk, sobbing and babbling incoherently.

Pamela saw the pistol raised and in her fear forgot discretion.

'Oh, stop!' she gasped, pushing open the door, and the Jockey, startled, turned towards her.

442

'Miss Westmore — ' he began, and broke off, for Cowan, seeing the chance that the interruption offered him, took it.

With an upward and forward leap he hurled his heavy form towards the man behind the desk, and gripping the pistol wrenched it from his hand.

'You'll kill me, will you?' he screamed exultantly. 'If you do you'll do it from hell!'

His finger tightened on the trigger and two deafening reports echoed through the room. The black-clad figure of the Jockey staggered, uttered a little choked cry, and fell forward across the desk.

'You've got yours!' snarled Cowan, and swung towards the girl. 'Out of my way!' he cried. 'Or I'll serve you the same! It'll take a clever person to stop me now!'

'I always thought I was pretty clever,' remarked a slow, ponderous voice. 'Put that gun down, Cowan, you've done enough damage.'

Pamela gave a gasp as she turned quickly to the door. In the dark opening stood Mr. Budd, a pistol in one podgy hand, and his usually placid face hard and stern. Only one momentary glimpse of him she caught and then, as the room suddenly became filled with men, she slid to the floor . . .

39

The Revelation

Somebody murmuring incoherently . . . the soft pressure of lips . . .

'You mustn't call me darling and you mustn't kiss me,' murmured Pamela, and opening her eyes looked up into the anxious face of Dick Templeton.

'Better now?' he asked, and she nodded.

She was back again on the couch in the room in which she had first recovered consciousness.

'Did I faint?' she said.

'Yes,' he answered. 'Keep still and you'll be all right.'

'Somebody kissed me,' she said.

'I thought the shock would bring you round,' he said calmly. 'Sure you're feeling all right?'

'Yes. What happened?' she asked.

'Don't worry about what happened,' he

replied. 'Just keep still.'

'But I want to know,' she protested, and then, as he didn't answer: 'Is — is the Jockey dead?'

He nodded slowly.

'Yes,' he said.

'Oh!' She felt the tears gather in her eyes. 'I — I'm sorry.'

'You knew him, didn't you?' said Dick gently, and again she nodded.

'Yes, I knew him,' she answered. 'At least I knew he was Norman's father. I — I didn't know who he was otherwise.'

'How did you know?' said the reporter.

'He — he came to me, one evening at Downlands,' answered Pamela, 'about a month before — before Mr. Corbett was murdered. He told me everything then. He told me that although Norman had always been supposed to be the son of Colonel Wharton he was, in reality, his son. He told me that during his youth he had been rather wild and that he had been in prison, in a French prison at Toulouse for forgery. That while he was in prison his wife had died in giving birth to a son, and that his brother, Henry

Wharton, adopted the son on hearing of his supposed death. He told me that he had escaped during a fire and had come to England, making himself known to his brother. That they had agreed between them that for the boy's sake the fact that he was still alive should be kept a secret. Norman never knew who his real father was.'

'Why did he tell you all this?' asked Dick.

'Because he wanted me to help him prove to the world that Norman had been innocent of the charge which — which Benjamin Cowan had brought against him. He — he not only wanted to do this but he wanted also to prevent a similar thing happening to anyone else, to clean up racing, as he put it. He told me his idea that the Jockey should represent a symbolical figure of Justice.'

'I see,' said Dick. 'And — and you gave him the clothes you had worn at Lord Mortlake's fancy dress ball.'

Her eyes went wide with surprise.

'How did you know that?' she said. 'Yes, I did. I'd kept them in a drawer in my bedroom with some other things ever since and I gave them to him then.'

'And except that he was Norman Wharton's father you never knew who he was?' he inquired.

She shook her head.

'No,' she answered. 'At that first interview I never saw his face, he kept a muffler he was wearing over his mouth and chin.'

'Was that the only time you saw him?' asked the reporter, and she hesitated.

'No. I — I saw him once again before to-night,' she answered, but said nothing of the reason for that second meeting with the Jockey when he had come in the dead of the night and interviewed her at her bedside, bringing with him the money which had enabled her to rid herself of Cowan's hold. 'Who was he?'

'I don't know,' said Dick. 'I was too anxious about you to wait and see.'

'What — what has happened to Cowan?' she asked after a slight pause.

'He's under arrest,' said a weary voice, and looking round hastily they saw that Mr. Budd had come noiselessly into the room. 'He's under arrest and eventually he'll come up for trial and be hanged. Nothing's more certain than that! How are you feelin', Miss Westmore?'

'I'm all right now,' she answered. 'How did you manage to get here?'

'We've got Sergeant Leek to thank for that,' answered Dick, and the stout superintendent nodded.

'Yes,' he answered. 'For the first time since I've known him that feller's done somethin' useful. I put him on to shadow the Jockey and he was followin' him when he was shadowin' Cowan. You've got Leek to thank, in a way, for savin' you from a very unpleasant experience and he pinched a car to do it.' He yawned. 'He was followin' the Jockey,' he continued, 'and when he'd seen him safely back here he telephoned the Yard. He acted with more sense than I'd given him credit for, because it 'ud have been foolish for him to try and do anythin' on his own. We turned out the Flyin' Squad and came down at once with Mr. Templeton here, who was in my office at the time the message came through.'

'What is this place?' asked Pamela.

'A disused asylum,' answered Mr. Budd. 'Just outside Sevenoaks.'

'And — and was the Jockey following Mr. Cowan?' asked Pamela.

The big man nodded.

'Yes, luckily for you,' he answered. 'Leek saw him take you from Cowan's car while Cowan was down at the waterfront lookin' for his boat.'

'I'm sorry he's — dead,' she whispered.

'I'm sorry too,' said Mr. Budd. 'But I think it was the best thing that could happen. He'd have had to stand a trial and — well — ' He shrugged his broad shoulders. 'We found Bleck and the jockey, Linnet, upstairs,' he said, changing the subject. 'They've had a pretty bad time, but not more than they deserve. They've had nothin' but bread and water since they've been here.'

A speculative look came into his eyes and he stared thoughtfully at the wall.

'I wonder what he was goin' to do with 'em,' he murmured. 'Well, we shall never know now. If you like, Miss Westmore, I'll get one of the 'Squad' cars to take you home.'

She looked at Dick.

'Can I go with her?' asked the reporter, and the fat man nodded.

'I don't see why not,' he answered. 'You're no use here. You knew he was Norman Wharton, didn't you?' he asked abruptly, looking at the girl.

'Yes,' she answered.

'I thought so,' sighed Mr. Budd. 'I'm afraid later on I shall have to come and get a statement from you.'

'Who was he, otherwise?' asked Dick.

The stout superintendent looked at him queerly.

'I'll bet you'd never guess,' he answered. 'Will you be ready in five minutes, Miss?'

'I'm ready now,' said Pamela.

'No, five minutes 'ull do,' said Mr. Budd. 'I want a word with Mr. Templeton.'

He took the reporter by the arm and led him out into the corridor.

'I pretty well know everythin' now,' he said. 'Except how that silk cap got into Ted Green's hand, and I've got to guess that. My guess is that the Jockey lost it on the night Corbett was killed while he was makin' his way through the garden, and Green picked it up.'

'Is that what you wanted me for?' asked Dick, and the other shook his head.

'No, I wanted to show you somethin'.'

He led the way down the stairs, across the hall, and into the room in which the Jockey had died. Releasing his hold of the reporter's arm he took him over to the motionless figure, still clad in its black silk jacket and silk cap, and gently drew aside the mask.

'Meet the Jockey,' he said softly, and Dick stared incredulously into the dead, peaceful face of Mr. Pyecroft . . .

THE END

GRIM DEATH
MURDER IN MANUSCRIPT
THE GLASS ARROW
THE THIRD KEY
THE ROYAL FLUSH MURDERS
THE SQUEALER
MR. WHIPPLE EXPLAINS
THE SEVEN CLUES
THE CHAINED MAN
THE HOUSE OF THE GOAT
THE FOOTBALL POOL MURDERS
THE HAND OF FEAR
SORCERER'S HOUSE
THE HANGMAN
THE CON MAN
MISTER BIG

We do hope that you have enjoyed reading this large print book.

Did you know that all of our titles are available for purchase?

We publish a wide range of high quality large print books including:
**Romances, Mysteries, Classics
General Fiction
Non Fiction and Westerns**

Special interest titles available in large print are:
**The Little Oxford Dictionary
Music Book, Song Book
Hymn Book, Service Book**

Also available from us courtesy of Oxford University Press:
**Young Readers' Dictionary
(large print edition)
Young Readers' Thesaurus
(large print edition)**

For further information or a free brochure, please contact us at:
**Ulverscroft Large Print Books Ltd.,
The Green, Bradgate Road, Anstey,
Leicester, LE7 7FU, England.
Tel:** (00 44) **0116 236 4325
Fax:** (00 44) **0116 234 0205**

TWELVE HOURS TO DESTINY

Manning K. Robertson

At the height of the Cold War one of the most trusted and important British agents in Hong Kong, Chao Lin, suddenly vanishes, and in London Steve Carradine is put on the case. Now hints are filtering through to Hong Kong of a new weapon with which the Chinese hope to dominate the world, and Chao Lin is the only man outside of China to possess this vital information. Carradine's assignment is simple: Find Chao Lin, discover the nature of this secret weapon, and bring both out of China!